STRANGERS
in
COMPANY

Fawcett Crest Books
by Jane Aiken Hodge:

WATCH THE WALL, MY DARLING

THE WINDING STAIR

GREEK WEDDING

MARRY IN HASTE

SAVANNAH PURCHASE

STRANGERS IN COMPANY

SHADOW OF A LADY

ONE WAY TO VENICE

RUNAWAY BRIDE

REBEL HEIRESS
and

ONLY A NOVEL—The Double Life of Jane Austen

ARE THERE FAWCETT PAPERBACKS
YOU WANT BUT CANNOT FIND IN YOUR LOCAL STORES?

You can get any title in print in Fawcett Crest, Fawcett
Premier, or Fawcett Gold Medal editions. Simply send title and
retail price, plus 50¢ for book postage and handling for the first
book and 25¢ for each additional book, to:

MAIL ORDER DEPARTMENT,
FAWCETT PUBLICATIONS,
P.O. Box 1014
GREENWICH, CONN. 06830

There is no charge for postage and handling on orders for
five books or more.

Books are available at discounts in quantity lots for industrial
or sales-promotional use. For details write FAWCETT WORLD
LIBRARY, CIRCULATION MANAGER, FAWCETT BLDG.,
GREENWICH, CONN. 06830

STRANGERS
in
COMPANY

A NOVEL BY

Jane Aiken Hodge

A FAWCETT CREST BOOK

Fawcett Publications, Inc., Greenwich, Connecticut

STRANGERS IN COMPANY

THIS BOOK CONTAINS THE COMPLETE TEXT OF THE
ORIGINAL HARDCOVER EDITION.

A Fawcett Crest Book reprinted by arrangement with Coward,
McCann & Geoghegan, Inc.

Copyright © 1973 by Jane Aiken Hodge.

All rights reserved, including the right to reproduce this book or
portions thereof in any form.

Library of Congress Catalog Card Number: 72-87582

This book is not based on actual people or events, and in no way
is to be interpreted as a representation of any real person or any
real occurrence. All the characters and events in the book are
wholly fictional and imaginary.

Printed in the United States of America

STRANGERS
in
COMPANY

Chapter 1

THE GIRL was looking the other way, gloomily, almost sullenly across the crowded departure lounge. Satisfied, Marian Frenche dug with quick stealth in her huge over-the-shoulder bag. Passport, tickets, traveller's cheques —Ah, there it was, the small silver pillbox Mark had given her—dear God, nineteen years ago. Another quick sideways glance. The girl—must think of her as Stella— Stella Marten was still looking listlessly away towards the departure indicator that showed obstinately blank so far as their flight was concerned.

Marian's hands trembled a little as she unscrewed the tiny egg-shaped container. Tranquillisers, Dr. Brown had said; entirely harmless. He had smiled that vast, not altogether reassuring smile of his.

"Can't have you getting delusions now, Mrs. Frenche. You've done so well."

"Thank you." For a moment, they had looked silently back together over the eighteen years since Mark had left her, since the twins had been born. Done well? Poor fool, she had sometimes even thought so herself.

It was difficult, but not impossible, to swallow the tiny pill without water. Replacing the box in her bag, she felt it coming over her again, the horrible, unidentifiable feeling—no, call it certainty—that someone was watching her. Delusions? Dr. Brown had talked of long strain, of sudden shock and of a handful of phobias, settling finally, with obvious relief, for agoraphobia, because she always had this feeling of being watched when she was out of doors. She was afraid of open spaces, he had told her kindly, had urged a holiday, a change. . . .

Open spaces. Could the departure lounge of Gatwick Airport, grossly overcrowded at ten o'clock on a Saturday night, be so described? Would Dr. Brown, if he had been here, have told her comfortably that she was suffering from claustrophobia, too? Because here it was, stronger than ever, the certainty that somewhere, in this restless crowd of people, eyes were fixed on her, and in no friendly spirit. Absurd? Of course it was absurd. That was what had sent her to the doctor rather than to the police, and he had given her the explanation that, in her heart, she had expected. It was natural enough, after all, that the double shock, emotional and financial, should have left its mark. But she had managed to keep going, somehow, until the twins had actually left to join their father in America. That was like her, Dr. Brown had said. He used praise she thought wryly, where other doctors might use tonics.

It had been when she got back from his office that she had found the card on the doormat. "Need a Job?" it had read. "Or a Guardian Angel? We provide both." The "we" called themselves "Jobs Unlimited" and operated from a highly respectable Sloane Square address. On an impulse, she had gone straight to the telephone and called their number. And—here she was, three weeks later—a magnificently overpaid guardian angel. And grossly neglecting her charge, she reminded herself, forcing a smile as she leaned forward.

"How about a cup of coffee? Or a Coke perhaps?" She had met Stella Marten only once, briefly, at the office of Jobs Unlimited and under the benevolent eye of Miss

Oakland, the friendly, grey-haired dragon who presided there.

"I'd rather have a whiskey." The girl shook unkempt, perhaps dirty black curls out of her eyes. Her tone was a a challenge.

"Of course. Stupid of me." Marian's brain was whirling like a computer, putting together the various bits of information she had been given about her charge. She was, after all, nearly twenty-one, three years older than the twins. And the one thing, at least, that Miss Oakland had not mentioned was a problem over alcohol. There had been practically everything else: trouble with her adoptive parents; an unlucky affair; and, finally, a state of "complete nervous exhaustion" which their prospective bus tour in Greece was supposed to cure. It had seemed, at the time, an odd enough prescription, and so had the rider that Stella was to be left alone as little as possible. But then, talk about the blind leading the blind. . . . "I must say," Marian went on almost immediately, "it's not a bad idea." She picked up her heavy bag.

"I'll get it." Stella was on her feet already. "Ice? Soda?"

"Straight, thanks. But, let me. . . ." Marian produced her purse.

"Nonsense, I'm loaded. They were so glad to be rid of me—even for two weeks—that they kept giving me more money." She turned away towards the crowded bar with the angry grace Marian had noticed in all her movements. "They," of course, were Stella's adoptive parents, the Martens, to whom she never referred by name. Miss Oakland had not explained what the trouble was between them. "Better not," she had said. "The less you know, I think, the easier you will find it."

Marian devoutly hoped she was right. But at least it was restful to find herself being waited on like this. Had she let the twins take her services too much for granted? But she was not to think about the twins. It had been Dr. Brown's last bit of advice, when he gave his blessing to this extraordinary project, and she recognised it as just as sound as his other, earlier warning that she should say nothing at Jobs Unlimited about her own nervous state.

"No one's going to employ you if they think you're suffering from delusions. And work's the best cure for them, take my word for it."

She had taken his advice, and he had been delighted with the result. "A bus tour of Greece! It's what I'd have liked to prescribe for you." They both knew how impossible such a prescription would have been. If Mark's cheques had really stopped coming, she must work or starve.

National Assistance. . . . Her mouth was suddenly dry. It had begun again. She could feel the imagined eyes upon her, inimical, probing as an X ray, and as damaging. "Think of something else." All of Dr. Brown's advice was good, if one could only follow it. She made herself concentrate on the crowd around the bar and saw that Stella had made good progress through it. And not with her elbows either, as one might have expected from that sullen face. Men seemed simply to give way before the small, determined figure. She was at the bar now, and instantly being attended to by one of the men who would have taken five minutes to notice Marian. It had always infuriated the twins when she let herself be pushed out of her place in one of life's inevitable queues.

Don't think about the twins. Stella was coming back now, a glass in each hand, her patchwork suede bag hanging precariously from one elbow. "I got you a double." Her tone was brusque as ever. "You look as though you could do with it." Her own glass was large, and pale, and fizzy. "I like it with ginger ale." She sat down with a cat's precise grace, then picked up her glass. "Here's to us," she said. "And Mercury Tours."

"Yes." The whisky burned and comforted. Life was ordinary again. "I've been looking for labels, but I haven't seen any."

"No." Stella glanced down at the scarlet labels on their own hand luggage. "But it's early yet."

"Yes." They had met, by arrangement, quite absurdly early, and it had taken some blandishment on both their parts to talk their way through into the departure lounge.

"It's like being in limbo," said Stella surprisingly, as an

inhuman voice announced Flight Number Something for Majorca, now boarding at Gate Eleven.

"Departures arranged for hell or heaven," said Marian.

"Heaven, of course, from Gate Eleven." Suddenly, amazingly, the tension that had stretched between them slackened; they caught each other's eyes and smiled. And, smiling, Stella was beautiful. "Mercury Classical Tours," she said. "Aren't we just going to be educated?"

"I'd never heard of them," Marian admitted. Nor had she had time to investigate them. "I suppose"—she looked doubtfully round for other red labels—"they're all right."

"Oh, I think so. 'They' always pick the best—or at least the most expensive. And it's the cheapest ones that don't get off the ground."

"Yes." The departure lounge was even more crowded now. Children ran about and screamed. Exhausted parents sat on the floor, backs to the wall, and ignored them. A group of returning Germans, with enormous rucksacks, shouldered their way past. One of them tripped, swore unintelligibly and glanced down with quick suspicion at Stella. But she was looking, suddenly, quite different, about sixteen, the drink in her glass obviously non-alcoholic.

"Stella—" Marian began, but Stella was on her feet.

"There are some of ours," she said. "Look!" She made a face. "Just what I thought. Escaped schoolmistresses, every one of them." She sat down as abruptly as she had risen. "Just exactly the people I least want to see. I told them. . . ."

There had been trouble at school, too. "Well, let's stay here," said Marian pacifically. "No need to get involved till the last minute."

"No need to get involved at all."

"Not if you don't want to." Miss Oakland had warned her about this, but just the same Marian suppressed a sigh as she looked at the eager, cheerful group of young women, conspicuously red-labelled, who seemed so busy talking that they had not even bothered to try and find seats in the crowded lounge. Most of them looked hardly older than Stella herself. It seemed a pity, thought Marian, but there it was. "She probably won't want to talk to anyone," Miss Oakland had warned her. "You'll need to keep with her all the time. I think you'll find you earn the high pay."

But at least they were to have single rooms, procured, no doubt at enormous expense, by the Martens. Stella, it appeared. had flatly refused to share. And that was all right with Marian. "Just keep her cheerful all day," Miss Oakland had said. "No need to worry at night. The one thing she hasn't done is attempt suicide."

Looking at her charge now, Marian could believe that. It might be a sulky face, but it was far from being a weak one. The dark eyes under heavily marked brows, the firm set of the lips in repose, even the high, strongly shadowed cheekbones all suggested a basic strength. Impossible not to wonder about the real parents, who had let their child go for adoption at a few days old. But, "Don't," Miss Oakland had warned. "It's part of the problem, naturally, but no one talks about it."

Perhaps better if they did? But that was none of Marian's business. She had taken on this job, at an astronomical wage, and it was the least she could do to follow instructions. And two weeks was such a short time. Time. . . . She looked at her watch.

"Yes, it's overdue." Stella had noticed the gesture. Doubtless she, too, had been busy summing up her companion for the next two weeks. "That's the worst of charter flights." And then, "Good lord!" Marian had already noticed a delightful and surprising mildness about language. Impossible not to remember the twins, with their obvious need to shock. Well, perhaps it was easier for adoptive parents. . . .

Excuses again. And Stella was saying something. "Can't be the courier, surely?"

Following the direction of the firmly pointed finger, Marian saw at once what Stella meant. It was a very young man indeed who was wearing the red label of Mercury Tours in his buttonhole. "He hardly looks out of the egg," said Stella scornfully, and then, with her rather harsh little laugh, "Oh, look, the schoolmarms have spotted him!"

Marian had just time to decide that the extremely blond young man was probably, in fact, rather older than his pink complexion made him look, when he was surrounded by the eager crowd of young women. Surprisingly, Stella was on her feet again. "I might as well go and see what he's got to say."

"But if you don't want to get involved?" Marian had a strong feeling that she ought to go herself, but the whisky, or the tranquilliser, or both, had loosened her defences against the accumulated exhaustion of the last few weeks. She was not sure she was capable of getting up. The double had been a mistake, she thought muzzily, but a well-meant one.

And, "Don't worry, I shan't." Stella hitched the bright patchwork bag up over her shoulder. "Back in a moment."

Left blessedly alone, Marian allowed herself the luxury of closing her eyes for a moment. Instantly, she was lost in a whirling dizziness, a mad kaleidoscope of the last weeks. The letter from Mark. . . . No cheque. . . . The twins. . . . Don't think about the twins. Miss Oakland: "You'll find you earn the high pay."

But was she? With an immense effort, she opened her eyes, to find Stella bending over her. "You look flaked out, you poor thing." A note of real sympathy in her voice. "And it's bad news, of course. There's an hour's delay. 'Operational difficulties.' We'll be lucky if it's only that. Here." She bent, with her swift efficiency of movement, and pushed her small overnight bag towards Marian. "Put your feet on that. Try and get some sleep. You're all in."

"Yes. I'm sorry." Talk about the blind leading the blind. She made a great effort. "What's the courier like?"

"Useless," said Stella Marten succinctly. Her laugh was harsher than usual, and somewhere, deep down, Marian registered a tiny half-conscious alarm signal. "It's his first tour," Stella went on. "The regular man hasn't turned up. I never did find out why. This one took over at an hour's notice. The schoolmarms are 'ever so sorry for him.'" She picked her scarlet cotton raincoat off the back of her chair and draped it carefully over Marian's legs. "Try and get some sleep, Mrs. Frenche. You're going to need it. God knows when we'll get to Athens. Don't worry. I'll wake you when the flight's finally called. If it ever is."

Once again, her tone sent that unexpected alarm tingling way down in Marian's consciousness. But she was too tired to pay attention. "I wish you'd call me Marian," she said, and slept.

Someone was shaking her. Viola? Sebastian? No. Reality flooded back as she sat up and ran shaky fingers through her short, brindled hair.

"Lord, you were dead to the world." Stella was smiling down at her. "I hate to wake you, but our flight's actually been called. They're all milling through Gate Twelve and I reckon by the time you're ready to move, the worst will be over. But how do you feel?"

"Much better, thanks." It was true. The short, deep sleep had done her more good than nights of endless half-sleep, half-wakeful tossing. "But I must look like hell.'"

"You don't, you know. Did anyone ever tell you you look like Lady Olivier?" She laughed. "Joan Plowright, I mean, not Vivien Leigh. I don't quite see you as Scarlett O'Hara." She yawned. "Come on, you look fine, and anyway, who's going to notice at this godawful hour of the night? We're nearly two hours late now. You've been out cold the whole time."

Marian laughed as she picked up her small zip-topped case. "A fine chaperone I make. Just as well Miss Oakland's not here to see. Thanks for watching over me."

"No trouble." An odd expression in that so far unreadable face? Hard to tell. . . . And no time to be thinking about it, while they gathered together their possessions. As it was, they were the last through Gate Twelve and walked along the endless echoing Gatwick corridor well behind the rest of the party.

"They've been fraternising like mad." Stella cast a darkling look forward. "Of course there are lots of other tours using this plane, but our labels are so ghastly unmistakable."

Marian yawned uncontrollably. "What time is it?"

"Two in the morning. We'll just about get to Athens for breakfast. How I hate night flights." The sentences came out jerkily, and Marian remembered that curious, unidentifiable feeling of something wrong that she had had before she fell asleep. Oh, well, night was the time for imagining things.

The last to board the plane, they were greeted with unceremonious briskness by an exhausted-looking stewardess.

"Back there. The two empty seats." She turned away to put a coat in the luggage rack and remove a heavy-looking case. "On the floor, please."

"Sounds like the end of a long, horrible day." Stella, leading the way, had found the two vacant seats in one of the inevitable rows of three. The one by the window was already occupied by the blond young courier, who was on his feet at once, offering to change seats. But, "No thanks." Stella sat down firmly in the middle seat of the row. "There's nothing to see anyway," she pointed out, rising again to throw her red raincoat and Marian's brown one expertly up into the rack, while he made ineffective attempts at helping her, hamstrung by the fact that he was cramped under the overhang.

"There." She turned her back on him to tuck her small bag and Marian's under the seats in front. "Something to put our feet on. I bet no one's ever asked a woman to design a plane. Have you flown the Atlantic?"

"No." The knife turned in the wound. "I saw my children off, the other day. Of course, I didn't get near the plane."

"Just as bad as this one." To Marian's relief, Stella showed not the slightest interest in the fact of her children. "Nowhere to put your feet, and the minute you get almost settled, the seat in front falls back on you with a crash." She fastened her seat belt with a quick, irritable movement of the hands, then turned the other way as the courier asked her the same question for the third time.

"Did you get through in the end?" he had been asking.

"Through? Oh—on the telephone you mean. No, my friend must have been out." She turned from him dismissively. "I thought I might as well say good-bye," she explained to Marian.

"Yes." The disastrous affair? She smiled wryly to herself, remembering how grateful she had been for Stella's watching over her while she slept. The courier's question implied, surely, a considerable number of attempts to make the call. Oh, well, poor Stella. . . .

Fatigue was coming over her again, wave on wave of it, in the synthetic air of the plane. She fastened her seat belt, leaned back and closed her eyes.

"My name's Cairnthorpe." The young courier was trying again with Stella. "I'm your courier, heaven help me."

"On a Mercury classical tour? Shouldn't you be invoking Zeus?"

"Oh, well." He was delighted to have got a real answer out of her. "Strictly speaking, that's the guide's job. We pick him up in Athens on Monday. Tomorrow, I mean." He looked at his watch as if it would tell him the day of the week. "Mind you," he went on. "The delay was lucky for me. I wouldn't have made it otherwise. And what a chance!"

"Why?" Stella sounded so profoundly uninterested that Marian suddenly realised this was the question she had wanted to ask.

"Oh, didn't you know?" He was young enough to assume that everyone must be interested in his affairs. "I only took over at the eleventh hour. Literally. The other man was knocked down by a car," he explained and then added a perfunctory "poor fellow."

"Killed?" asked Stella.

"Oh, I do hope not. That would make me feel bad, wouldn't it? They didn't know, when they telephoned me. Just that he was badly hurt, and could I take over? Well —it was a rush, but of course I could. It's the chance I've been waiting for. I've been on standby for these tours ever since I came down—left the university," he explained kindly, and Marian, on the far side, was aware of the ripple of irritation that ran through Stella. "I teach, you know." He was well away now. "Classics, of course. But it doesn't run to Greek holidays. I've not been there since I was up—at Oxford," he explained again.

"I've heard of it." Stella closed the conversation.

After that, it was just the usual, exhausting night flight, with bright-voiced, weary hostesses doling out duty-free goods and cut-price drinks across the furious, semi-recumbent bodies of the passengers who wanted, more than anything, to sleep. There were, at some point, plastic sandwiches and coffee in plastic mugs. Marian, rousing enough to refuse them, heard Stella do the same and heard the courier—Cairngorm was it?—accept his enthusiastically. "Missed my dinner," he tried to explain to Stella, who ignored him, sleeping ostentatiously.

Behind them, the group of teachers they had seen at Gatwick were celebrating their reunion by a long, elaborate, whispered conversation about what had happened to whom since they last met. Listening, because she could not help it, Marian decided that they had been at Teachers' Training College together; that this was an annual occasion; that they were very nice girls. . . . Thinking this, at last, she slept. . . .

Stella was shaking her again. At least, this time, recognised at once as Stella. "Athens, Mrs. F. Rise and shine."

"Oh, God," said Marian. "Did you sleep at all?"

"Not much!" She gestured sideways with her head. "Should I wake him, do you think?" Beyond her, Mr. Cairnthorpe slept like a child.

The NO SMOKING and FASTEN SEAT BELTS signs were on. "Yes, I should think so. He's to take charge of us, I suppose."

"So do I." Stella met her smile for smile, but her face was grey, as if, Marian thought, she had not slept at all, but had spent all the hours of the flight brooding about the young man who had not been at home. She dug Mr. Cairnthorpe ruthlessly in the ribs. "We're here."

"Oh . . . thanks." Struggling up from sleep, he looked younger than ever, and Marian's heart sank. Certainly Stella, so far, seemed normal enough, but suppose the "nervous exhaustion" were to manifest itself in some drastic way, what use in the world would this very young man be? None, she told herself, and once again Miss Oakland's voice echoed in her head. "You'll earn your high pay."

The plane touched, bounced just a little, then touched again and was bumpily earthborne. "Not a large airport," said Stella, unfastening her seat belt.

A hostess swooped. "Please keep your seat belts fastened, and remain seated until the plane is stationary."

"Oh—" Stella bit off the next word, but Marian could feel the rage seething in her as she refastened the belt. Trouble at school. . . . Trouble with authority? So what would happen when authority was represented by poor Mr. Cairnthorpe?

But, surprisingly, Stella was laughing. "Don't look so anxious! At least I didn't *say* it."

"My imagination's boggling just the same."

"Poor Mrs. F." Stella delved in her bag, produced a comb and began a rather slapdash attack on her shaggy hair. "Do you wish you were safe in bed in England?"

"I certainly wish I was in bed." The plane had stopped at last, and Marian turned resolutely from the thought of the cold little house, the twins' bedrooms so empty, so unnaturally tidy. "I don't much care where."

"They've opened the doors," said Mr. Cairnthorpe hopefully.

"Have they?" Stella got out her compact. "Oh, God! My face!" She delved unsuccessfully in her bag for a while, her right shoulder hunched against her restless neighbour, finally produced a pair of tweezers and fastidiously removed one straggling hair from one eyebrow. "That's better." The compact again, for a long, considering look.

Marian had had enough. "Well, I'm on my way." She stood up, dropped Stella's red coat in her lap, picked up her own brown one and small bag and inserted herself neatly in a gap in the queue. The twins, she thought, would have been amazed. And, equally amazing, Stella had got all her paraphernalia stowed away and was following close behind.

"Cruelty to children?" Her voice was at once mocking and, Marian thought, apologetic.

"Something like that." Cairnthorpe, she saw, was pushing his way towards the other exit. So much for any hope of him as an ally. But at least, she thought, he had the gumption to resent being baited.

Outside, the dark, warm air smelled of pines. Stella drew a deep breath. "Retsina," she said. "Delicious."

"You've been here before?" Marian was surprised. Nothing Miss Oakland had said had suggested this.

"Lord, yes. On a cruise. With them. Ghastly, but I loved it. That's why I held out for this, don't you see? It takes you to all the places you don't get to on a cruise."

"Yes." It made sense. And yet— "It's funny," she said. "I could have sworn Miss Oakland said. . . ."

"Oh, Miss Oakland! Why should she know? All she had to do was hire you, after all. Someone like you," she amended.

Marian laughed. "My lucky day. Look! It's almost dawn." The faintest suggestion of light in the sky emphasised the dark loom of mountains.

"Yes. We shan't see the Acropolis floodlit after all. Have you ever been to Greece, Mrs. Frenche?"

"No. Never." She had wanted to come for their honeymoon, but Mark had had an engagement at the last moment, too good a one to be missed, as all Mark's engagements were, and Marian had found herself simply tagging along, allowed a slightly dubious recognition by Mark's fan club. It should have warned her, she thought now, looking back on the whole disaster of that time. Too late, of course. Anyway, she had been blinded by the glamour of it all, by the illusory Mark she adored, and who said, when he had a moment to spare, that he adored her, too. "You're my star," he would say, with one of those butterfly kisses of his, and she was his slave.

But they had reached the lighted terminal building, and the smell of pines was lost in the smell of airport. Following the crowd, they found the formalities blessedly swift. "One good thing about traveling at night." said Stella, as they emerged on the other side of the controls.

"They're all too tired to search you for drugs." And then, aware of Marian's swift, anxious glance. "Oh, *really*, Mrs. Frenche, you must know I don't." And, with a look Marian would learn to know all too well, "Anyway, what about you? Have you got the prescription for yours?"

"Oh—" Marian was dumbstruck. The situation was slipping hopelessly out of her control, and she could feel only sympathy for Mr. Cairnthorpe when they came on him, standing helplessly among a red-labelled crowd in the lobby. Other tours seemed to be marching resolutely away in all directions. Only Cairnthorpe, quite evidently, had not the slightest idea what to do.

"Someone is to meet us here," he was explaining it, obviously, for the second time, to a large, anxious lady in a floppy hat, presumably acquired in a moment of madness on a previous holiday. Hovering behind her was the only young man of the party, unmistakably her son, though features sullen in her plump face were surprisingly handsome in his young one, even shadowed as it was with lack of sleep and an incipient beard.

"Fancy!" Stella had noticed him, too, but not, by the sound of it, with approval.

"Ladies and gentlemen." Cairnthorpe managed to raise his voice above the growing hubbub of anxious questions. "We're sure to be met. Let's all keep together, please, and wait here."

They murmured a little, tiredly, but stood around him, exhausted, quiescent. "Insufficiently briefed," said a brisk Civil Service, female voice behind Marian, and wondering if Mr. Cairnthorpe had heard, she found herself thinking about their fellow tourists. She looked at the tired faces, extra-pale in the garish light of the lobby. Mostly women, of course. A few middle-aged men here and there, most of them very much occupied with wives. A honeymoon couple, and, "poor things" she was thinking, when an unmistakably American voice spoke up from the far side of the group.

"It looks to me as if everyone else has gone outside." Marian could not see the speaker, but he sounded as tired as she felt. "Shouldn't we?"

"Well?" Cairnthorpe hesitated and was lost. The party moved of its own volition towards the doors and he could only follow, muttering something unintelligible, but Marian was afraid, with the word "Americans" in it.

It was good to be out in cool, retsinated air again and better still to see a row of buses lined up with their backs to the airport steps. It was perceptibly lighter now, and Marian could see the immaculate golden coiffure of the uniformed girl who came briskly forward to meet them. "There you are at last. . . . I was beginning to wonder. . . . Oh!" She had picked out Cairnthorpe from the crowd.

"I'm a stand-in, I'm afraid." Not for the first time, Marian felt sorry for him as he launched into the now familiar explanation. But beside her, Stella twitched with impatience and muttered something under her breath.

Chapter 2

FULL DAWN broke as the coach hauled its exhausted load of passengers towards the city. There was a sudden, excited babble: "There. There it is." One clear voice: "It's just like the postcards." Marian had missed seeing the Acropolis. She closed her eyes again, beyond caring, then opened them as the microphone at the front of the coach rasped into life. The blonde Greek girl who had taken charge of them was standing up, swaying gracefully to the movement of the coach. She spoke clearly, in her accented, fluent English. There was a small change of plan. . . . Mercury Tours was so sorry, but the hotel advertised was not yet open. . . . They were going to a better one, the Alexander, in Alexander Avenue. . . . Very quiet, very select, very restful.

"Which means several miles from the city centre." A voice Marian had heard before, the one that had found Cairnthorpe "insufficiently briefed."

"I knew it was a mistake to come on the first tour of the season." This was the woman across the aisle from Marian, a conspicuous figure in scarlet and black. Beyond her, a harassed-looking husband muttered something soothing.

Up front, the golden girl took no notice. "Mercury Tours will, naturally, compensate you for any inconvenience," she went on. "The hotel porter will arrange taxis for anyone wishing to visit the centre of town, and Mercury Tours will be happy to repay the small expense involved. Coming back, of course, you will be in the Hotel Hermes as arranged." She replaced the microphone in its bracket and sat down, turning her back on a rising tide of weary grumbles. In the seat behind her, Mr. Cairnthorpe was fast asleep.

"Oh, well." Marian was resigned now to being awake. "I don't see that it makes much difference. I know I'm going to sleep all morning, and we've got Sounion this afternoon." Her tone sounded disconcertingly like the one she had used when breaking bad news to the twins. It was odd to be so sure that the silent girl beside her was seething inwardly.

"Muddle!" was all she said, hunching a shoulder to stare out the window at suburban buildings, strange and ugly in pitiless morning light. The streets were waking up now. A black-clad woman emptied a bucket of water across the pavement; girls in blue uniforms loitered towards an uncompromising modern building that must be a school. A small boy waved vigorously from a window.

Across the aisle of the bus, the woman in scarlet and black settled an unfortunate hat more firmly over her ears. "Alexander Avenue?" she asked. "Where in heaven's name's that?"

"It's not too bad." Her husband had produced a map. 'See!"

"But it's miles," she wailed. "Way over beyond Lykabetos. I told you we shouldn't have booked for the first tour."

"And I told you it was the only time I could get away." It was obviously not the first time he had said it.

"It's a bit much." She leaned across the aisle to address Marian. "You've not been here before? Well, the Hermes Hotel's right in the centre of everything, by Omonia

Square. There's a shop there—I meant to go in this morning and get some espadrilles. For the ruins, you know. It's as much as your life's worth to try to do them in heels." She looked down for a moment from her old-fashioned stilettos to Marian's neat, light walking shoes. "You've been sensible, I can see." It was more criticism than praise. "I don't know what in the world I'm going to do. I must have my sleep." She turned on her husband. "What am I going to do, George?"

"I told you to bring the old ones." His voice was weary as he refolded the map. "Sunday morning it would likely be closed anyway."

"Oh, nothing closes here." She sounded uncertain for the first time. "Look!" She leaned forwards. "There's that temple. The one we never got to see." It was his fault.

"The Temple of Zeus." He unfolded the map again. "We're going the other side of it. See. Along King Constantine Street."

"I wonder they don't change the name, now they've thrown him out."

"I rather think that was a different king," he said mildly, but she took no notice.

"Looks like we're going to be clear over at the wrong end of Alexander Avenue." She had seized the map. "See!" She turned her back on her husband to pass the map across to Marian. "Miles from anywhere." And then, momentarily distracted, she peered past Marian and Stella. "Look! There's the modern stadium. Isn't it splendid?" And, an obvious connection, "I suppose I'll just have to wear my heels till I can find some espadrilles."

"Would you like to see?" Marian offered to pass the map to Stella, who shrugged it away with daunting rudeness. "At least we're nearly there." She unfolded the map and handed it back, reminding herself unhappily that she was not supposed to involve Stella with other people. It looked as if this were going to be a more difficult task than she had understood.

"Our name's Hilton," said the black and scarlet woman, confirming this. "Like the hotels, but not so rich." She had said it many times before. "What I always say"—

she was cheering up as they neared their journey's end
—"is that on these tours you've just got to introduce yourselves, or you never get to know a soul."

"No. I mean, yes. I'm Marian Frenche, and this is
Miss Marten."

"I thought she wasn't your daughter," said Mrs. Hilton
at Stella's back.

The bus swerved formidably across the traffic and turned
left. Alexander Avenue. Marian was relieved to see that
street names were given in both Roman and Greek lettering. "I wish I could read Greek," she said as the bus
began to slow down.

"You won't need to, love," said Mrs. Hilton comfortably. "It's all in English, too."

The Hotel Alexander, it turned out, was not actually
on Alexander Avenue, but tucked away on a side street
that led up towards the tree-covered hill that was identified,
without enthusiasm, as Lykabetos by Mrs. Hilton. "No
chance of a view of the Acropolis from here." She got
up as the bus stopped and began to push her way forward
down the aisle. Following, her husband had one quick
apologetic glance for Marian. He was a small, neat man,
half a head shorter than his buxom wife, with a face that
should have been roundly cheerful, but was scored with
deep lines of anxiety. Following in his wife's ruthless wake,
he cast more glances of apology to right and left.

Feeling sorry for him, Marian turned to see her own
companion staring at her with frank dislike. "Honestly!"
She reached into her bag, produced cigarettes and a lighter
and lit up with one of her quick, cross gestures. Then,
belatedly, "Sorry! Have one?"

It was a challenge and must be accepted. "Thanks. But
I think I'll wait till we get out of here."

"You'll wait some time." Some sort of blockage had
developed up at the front of the bus, and the aisle was
crowded with waiting figures, frozen in curious, awkward
positions, cluttered with small baggage. "God," said Stella,
"what in the world made me think I'd like a bus tour?"

Since Marian had been thinking very much the same
thing, she did not try to answer, but sat staring out past

Stella at the Alexander Hotel. It looked promising, she thought, from what she could see; clean and new-painted in the morning light. There were window boxes along its front, filled with gay, unidentifiable flowers. "It looks nice," she ventured pacifically.

"Nice!" Stella's anger overflowed suddenly. "And this is a nice bus, and what a lot of nice people we are, this nice morning."

Marian managed a laugh. "You're quite right. It's a terrible word. I used it in an essay once, and my tutor made me read *Northanger Abbey* before I wrote another one."

"Oh, God, Jane Austen," said Stella.

People were moving down the aisle again. Stella stubbed out her cigarette as ruthlessly as she had lit it, and Marian wondered whether, in fact, she disliked them as much as she herself did. "Let's get out of here," said Stella. "I'm getting claustrophobia."

And that, Marian thought, meekly rising to get their coats and hand baggage from the rack, was all they needed. She turned without a word and found herself blocking the way of a tall middle-aged man, whose bushy black eyebrows contrasted strangely with short-cut silver hair, under the kind of Panama hat favoured by American tourists. "I'm so sorry." She moved back a little, but he waved her on.

"Ladies first." His was the American voice of the airport. "Frankly"—his smile eased the deep lines of a tanned face— "I don't think hurrying's going to get us anywhere. We've lost that splendid girl, did you notice? She went off like a bat out of hell when the bus stopped. Well, we're late, of course. But poor Mr. Cairnthorpe. . . ."

"Useless," said Stella.

The scene in the lobby of the Alexander confirmed her words. It might be late for the Greek girl, but it was very early for the hotel, and an aged night porter was on duty at the desk. He spoke no English, and Cairnthorpe, it appeared, no Greek. A total impasse had developed, with Cairnthorpe trying various pronunciations of the magic words "Mercury Tours," none of them successfully.

Around him, the other members of the party sagged in anxious exhaustion. The few seats had been appropriated by the first comers; the others were rapidly filling the small lobby to overflowing.

"Hell and damnation," said the American. What on earth was someone like him doing on a tour like this? Now Marian watched with awed amusement as he contrived to make his way, courteous but firm, forward through the depressed crowd. Arrived at the desk, he spoke loud and surprisingly bullying, in German. "The manager. Send for him at once."

The night porter looked at him with intense dislike but lifted the telephone on the desk and spoke rapidly in Greek. "She comes." He ignored Cairnthorpe and spoke, now in German, to the American, still with dislike, then detached himself from the whole affair by producing an enormous pair of dark-rimmed glasses and poring over the hotel ledger.

"Thanks," said Cairnthorpe, a little breathlessly. "Stupid of me; I never thought of German."

"They don't like it," said the American. "But it works."

It did. A door at the back of the lobby had opened to reveal an enormous black-clad lady of some age, who came through the crowd like a frigate to confront Cairnthorpe by the desk. "But you are a day early." She reached over the desk, produced a file, opened it and handed him a piece of paper. "See. Here it says April fifth. And today it is the fourth."

"Oh, my God," said Cairnthorpe.

"We were given the wrong date." She shrugged, her motherly smile for Cairnthorpe alone. "But what matter? Since it is our first booking, all is ready. I, Anastasia, am always ready. So: welcome, ladies and gentlemen." She moved with heavy grace round to the back of the desk, said something in quick Greek to the night porter and turned a page of the huge ledger. "Names and passports, please. We will pretend that it is already tomorrow."

What followed was, inevitably, more muddle. She could not pronounce the English names: Cairnthorpe, quite naturally, could not connect names with faces; it took a very long time to get the rooms allocated. Marian waiting passively in a corner, where at least she had found a pillar to lean against, found herself wondering if, by chance, the blonde Greek girl had known what was going to happen and had made good her escape before it began.

"If they'd only keep quiet." Beside her, Stella was still, perceptibly, simmering with rage. And, of course, she was quite right. The tired chorus of grumbles made it difficult for people to hear their names when they were called. Now, at the third try, the name "Eeltong" was heard and recognised.

"And about time, too." Mrs. Hilton bustled forward to accept the key. "And what about our baggage, eh?"

"It comes." If Mrs. Hilton was buxom, Anastasia was statuesque. "You will go to your room, please, and await it." It was an order, not a request, and Mrs. Hilton went, her husband meekly, sadly following.

"She'll eat him alive when they're alone." Stella abandoned her pose of weary detachment. "Poor man." She looked round the emptying lobby. "Will our turn never come?"

"I have a nasty feeling," said Marian, "that singles come last."

She was right. The proprietress dealt first with all the doubles, then turned to the singles, starting with the woman whose voice had suggested the Civil Service. She was a Mrs. Duncan, and Marian found herself wondering, absurdly, if some dreadful fate had befallen her husband.

" 'Wake Duncan with your knocking.' " quoted Stella, *sotto voce,* as she disappeared.

"You took the thought out of my mouth!" Marian felt oddly reassured by this evidence of common ground.

"It's unlucky to quote *Macbeth,*" said Stella, gloomy again, and, damn, thought Marian, she doesn't want to share her thoughts with me. And why should she?

Anastasia was having trouble with the next name, and as Cairnthorpe bent forward to try and read it, upside down across the desk, the tall American came forward. "Me, I expect. Thor Edvardson." He took his key, smiled apologetically at Marian, said something about the luck of the alphabet and disappeared with long strides towards the stairs.

"Mr. and Mrs. Esmond," said Cairnthorpe, and the large woman in the floppy hat moved forward, her son dutifully following.

"Adjoining rooms, I asked for." Mrs. Esmond had one of those English voices that would be heard though the Tower of Babel fell.

"Did you?" said Anastasia blandly, handing one key to her and the other, despite her still outstretched hand, to her son.

"Oh, come *on*, Mother." His pleasant voice held what sounded like an old despair, and Marian thought he was more surprised than anyone when she shrugged large, angry shoulders and turned, defeated, towards the lift.

"You'd better bring the bags, Charles." She would have the last word. "No use waiting for those boys."

"Mrs. Frenche." Marian was distracted by the sound, at last, of her own name. Moving obediently forward to collect her key, she realised what the American— Mr. Edvardson—had meant about the alphabet. "Shall I wait for you?" She turned back to Stella.

"No, thanks." It was politely final. "Are you break-fasting? Nor am I. See you at lunch then."

Marian turned away, with an uncomfortable sense of being dismissed, as Anastasia called the names of Miss Gear and Miss Grange, two oddly similar, horse-faced, middle-aged ladies, who appeared to be travelling to-gether, but with single rooms. They followed her up the stairs, talking loudly and cheerfully about their plans for the morning. Sleep, it appeared, had no part in them; they were discussing whether it was to be the museum or the flea market.

Marian found her own door, had a moment of despair when the key refused to turn, tried it the other way and discovered that the door had been unlocked all the time. She found herself at last in a cool, twilit room. Sanctuary. What an odd thing to think. She put down coat and bag and moved like a somnambulist to throw back the shutters, then stood there breathing deeply, entranced with what she saw. Her room was at the back of the hotel and looked straight over tiled roofs to the tree-covered side of the hill called Lykabetos. Washing flapped on a line, brilliant white in the morning sunshine that flooded everything. Plants burgeoned out of petrol tins on roofs, a thin tabby cat washed itself busily on a wall. Somewhere nearby, a cock crowed, in odd counterpoint to the muted roar of traffic from Alexander Avenue. She stood for a moment, drinking it in, then moved back, filled with a strange, unfamiliar sensation of peace and safety, to strip off her clothes, rinse face and hands in cold water, pull the seersucker nightgown out of her small bag, and plunge, oceans-down, into sleep.

She woke as suddenly as she had slept and lay for a moment wondering where on earth she was. Midday sunshine, flooding the room, brought it all back, and she looked quickly at her watch. Twenty to one. She was out of bed on the instant, pulling the shutters to with a last delighted glance at the view, somnolent now for the Mediterranean siesta, even the cat—or its twin—fast asleep not far from where she had seen it before. But mad dogs and English tourists—she pulled a cotton dress out of her large case—go out to Sounion.

Fatigue still dragged at her. The face she dealt with briefly looked aeons more than thirty-five. Even her hair, which could usually be relied on to curl crisply round her face, hung limp and sad from the synthetic air of the plane. Combing it irritably, she reminded herself of Stella and stopped for a moment to smile, with an effort, at the reflection in the glass. "Your smile makes you beautiful." Who had said that to her? One of those half-remembered young men who had taken her out after Mark left. The one, she rather thought, who used to call her the Snow Queen. Well, it was true, something in her had frozen when Mark left her. Or—before he left her? But that was the past; forget it. She made herself smile again and almost thought, this time, that the young man might have had something. Ridiculous. She turned away from the glass and picked up her bag. High time to stop this maundering and go down to meet Stella for lunch.

Ten to one. The hotel lobby was crowded all over again with the members of their party, becoming almost distinguishable now that fatigue was merely a blurring at the edges of thought, not a tide submerging it. Not all of them, of course, but enough to make the room seem uncomfortably crowded. What were they *doing?* Marian saw Mrs. Hilton moving in her direction and took instant, instinctive counteraction. It took her across the lobby to a cool loom of darkness and then, blessedly, to a little bar that opened on to a terrace at the back of the hotel. The American—Edvardson—was peacefully reading the *International Herald Tribune* in one corner, and Stella was sitting limply in the other, gazing out at the view. Both of them had milky white drinks and little saucers of olives and white cheese beside them, and Stella raised her drink in salutation when she saw Marian.

"Come and have your first ouzo," she said.

"Shall I like it?" Marian sat down beside her.

"If you don't, you'll die of thirst. I'll get you one— They're short-staffed of course." Stella threw it back over her shoulder as she disappeared through a door beyond the little bar.

Returning a few minutes later with another glass and saucer, Stella threw a caustic glance in the direction of the lobby. "Did you see them queueing?"

"Queueing?"

"Of course. For lunch. The British abroad. There'll be a stampede when the doors open. We all have to eat together," she explained. "I have the most dismal feeling we are going to have to share tables."

"Oh, dear." Marian glanced quickly across at Mr. Edvardson, but he seemed to be absorbed in his paper. She sniffed her glass dubiously. "Aniseed?"

"More or less. Come on, Mrs. F. It's the national drink, after all."

"Ouch!" Marian drank, coughed, laughed and felt a fine rosy warmth flood through her. "Much better than whisky," she said. "I should have been a Greek." She picked up an olive and found herself nibbling it ravenously. "I'm famished," she discovered.

"Yes, so'm I, but let's for goodness sake let the rest of them get settled before we go in. I won't queue for anyone or anything."

"It's only just one"—Marian sipped at the reviving drink—"and I'm certainly not going to hurry with my first ouzo. Who's that over the bar?" The photograph hung obviously in the place of honour.

"Colonel Papadopoulos, of course."

"Oh, dear, the colonels," said Marian.

"Does your conscience prick you for coming?" Stella's tone was sardonic. Would you go to Franco's Spain?" she asked. "Or Caetano's Portugal? Or South Africa, for the matter of that."

"I know." But Marian was surprised that Stella did.

Mr. Edvardson folded his paper and got up. "At least one can get the newspapers here." He paused beside them. "And—excuse me for butting in, Mrs. Frenche— but I don't know that I'd talk about it too much in public, if I were you."

"Oh—thanks." Marian could not decide whether to be irritated or grateful, but Stella's reaction was predictable.

"Interfering old so-and-so." She had at least waited until he had disappeared in the direction of the now-empty lobby.

"Hardly old," said Marian. "And kindly meant."

"Hell's paved with them. Shall we eat?"

The dining room was crowded with their party. "It looks as if we fill the hotel." Marian looked round for an empty table.

"Just as well, or we'd never have got in. Honestly, talk about inefficiency. . . ."

"But not poor Mr. Cairnthorpe's fault." Marian's heart sank as she spotted the only empty places. They were at a table over by a wide-open window and already occupied by Cairnthorpe. Edvardson was just joining him. All too obviously, Cairnthorpe had got in early and been avoided, doubtless from a variety of reasons, by his tour members. Now she and Stella were for it.

"There." She pointed.

"Oh, God," said Stella.

"Can't be helped."

"No."

"My lucky day." Cairnthorpe rose with an attempt at gallantry, to greet them and pull out Marian's chair for her. And then, to Stella, "Did you get your letter, Miss Marten?"

"No!"

"I'm sorry. I went over to the Hotel Hermes to ask about mail, but the place is overrun with interior decorators. Nobody knew a thing."

Characteristic." Mercifully, Stella did not specify whether she meant Greece in general or the tour in particular. "Don't we get a menu?" She made one of her abrupt transitions and confirmed Marian in an instinctive decision to say nothing about the missing letter. Presumably from the hero (or villain) of the telephone call and the unlucky affair. If she had expected a letter at the Hermes, it was no wonder Stella had been so enraged by the change of plan.

"No," Cairnthorpe explained patiently, and not for the first time. "We're lucky to get food at all. Madame's been on the go all morning, God bless her."

"A real foul-up," said Edvardson. "Not your fault," kindly, to Cairnthorpe, "but let's hope the dates are right for the rest of the trip."

It was the most delicate of hints, and Cairnthorpe took it without umbrage. "Yes, I thought of that. I got on to the office and had them confirm the other bookings. They're all right, I'm glad to say."

"Thank God for that," said Stella.

"You mean you've had no sleep?" asked Marian.

"I'll catch up tonight." He smiled at her gratefully, and she was aware, for the first time, of a pleasant young man lurking behind the innocuous-seeming English public school exterior. "Ah, food." He turned with another smile to Madame Anastasia, who had appeared behind him, juggling plates. "I've been telling them what miracles you've worked for us, madame."

"You should say *kyria.*" She dealt out the plates expertly.

"Stuffed vine leaves," said Edvardson. "God bless you, *kyria,* and may we have a large bottle of white Demestica."

"At once." She smiled at him with approval. "I'm glad you like my vine leaves. They don't all."

"Crazy." Edvardson was tucking in with a will. "Try them, Mrs. Frenche. If you know anything about food, you'll like them."

"Is that a threat or a promise?" But she took a bite and smiled her pleasure. "Delicious. But what's the rice flavoured with?" She thought about it. "Lemon, of course, and a herb I don't know. Sorrel perhaps?"

"Search me," said Edvardson cheerfully. "I'm the idiot in the art gallery. I just know what I like."

"What is this Demestica?" Facing each other, Stella and Cairnthorpe were eating with silent preoccupation, as if food were everything. If there was to be conversation, Marian thought wryly, she and this odd, interesting American would have to provide it.

"The local wine. Wherever you are. It's like carafe, really; only they bottle it. The labels are always the same, but you can count on the wine to be different. And that"—he finished the last mouthful of his stuffed vine leaves—"is a profound philosophical remark about Greece."

"Do you know, I believe you're right." Stella looked at him with reluctant approval.

"You know Greece, Miss Marten?" Cairnthorpe plunged into the conversation with unlucky eagerness.

"Hardly at all." She was indifferent to the point of rudeness. "One cruise. But I read the papers—sometimes." Cairnthorpe blushed painfully and crumbled bread on his plate.

"I hope you don't mind my ordering for us all." Edvardson filled the uncomfortable silence by addressing Marian. "I thought we could use a glass of wine after that night. And here it comes." He smiled round at Madame Anastasia, who had appeared with a bottle and a flowering handful of glasses. "We are making you work too hard, *kyria*."

"It is nothing." She deposited the glasses, one-handed, on the table, produced a corkscrew from a pocket on her enormous bosom and went expertly to work on the bottle. A sweeping glance surveyed the room as she did so. "It is discouraging to have your tourists on their first day." She spoke now to Cairnthorpe. "They have not yet learned that our wine is good—and cheap." She poured a drop into Edvardson's glass.

"Yes." His smile made it the fullest compliment.

"Inedible," said a loud voice in the middle of the room.

It caused a small, uncomfortable silence, through which broke another voice from the far side of the room. "The museum," it was saying. "Did you know that Mercury is Hermes, and Hermes means death?"

Chapter 3

"NONSENSE." The American's voice was the loudest of many that hurried into an uneasy silence.

"Of course." Cairnthorpe agreed gratefully. "Hermes merely guides the dead to the underworld. They must have been looking at funeral steles."

"How jolly!" Stella was crushing. "Isn't education wonderful?"

After that, not even the bland wine and a savory dish of chicken, followed by the best oranges Marian had ever tasted, could revive the conversation at their table. Stella refused an orange, pushed her chair back suddenly and rose. "I've a filthy headache." She ignored the two men. "I don't think I'll come to Sounion. See you at dinner?" She was gone, threading her way deftly through the crowded room.

"Oh, dear." Marian looked after her doubtfully.

"Don't." Edvardson answered the question she had been asking herself. "We're all tired. She'll be better off on her own."

"Yes. I'm so sorry. . . ."

"No need," he said comfortably. "Let's have some coffee. Will you risk Turkish, Mrs. Frenche, or play safe with the inevitable Nescafé?"

"Oh, I'll try the Turkish." She was wondering whether she, too, could decently withdraw from the Sounion expedition, when Edvardson forestalled her.

"Count me out for this afternoon, by the way," he told Cairnthorpe. "I'm going to hire me a cab and go out to Marathon. It's a place I've always wanted to visit. Besides, I've an idea I might spot a marsh harrier there."

"Oh, yes—quite so." Cairnthorpe looked at once baffled and disappointed, like a hostess confronted by a recalcitrant guest. "You'll be coming?" He turned to Marian.

"Yes, indeed." She could not find it in her heart to do it to him again. "In fact, I'd better be getting ready. What do Miss Marten and I owe you, Mr. Edvardson?" She dealt firmly with his suggestion that the wine and coffee were "on him," paid their modest share of drachmae and left the two men together.

A considerably diminished party assembled outside the hotel at two o'clock, and Marian began to put names to faces. The schoolteachers were all there, cheerfully calling each other Pam, Sue, Meg and so on, and so was the Civil Service Mrs. Duncan, recognisable now by her neat grey bun and air of quiet authority. There was a rather odd honeymoon couple, too, whom Marian had noticed earlier because their name was Adams, and they had been the first to get their keys. A sullen-looking man, he was old enough to be his wife's father, and Marian could only suppose that he had fallen hopelessly for that chocolate-box prettiness of hers. Certainly, there was something paternal as well as devoted about the way he carried the extraordinary collection of cardigan, scarf, camera and even umbrella that she found necessary for this short excursion.

It was not, in fact, so short as Marian had expected, and she found herself wishing passionately that she had not given way to her ridiculous feeling of sympathy for Cairnthorpe. But at least she had a seat on the bus to her-

self, since a good many of the tour's middle-aged, nameless ladies must be sleeping off their journey. Mr. Hilton
was absent, too, but Marian managed to avoid his
wife's hopeful eye, and settled herself to doze for a
good deal of the long, hot drive, waking from time to
time for a breathtaking panorama of cliff and sea, or,
once, a dreary industrial development that could have
been anywhere in the world. At last, a little ripple of
excitement through the bus brought her wide awake to
see white columns on the promontory ahead and know
that it had been worth coming. The sleep had done her
good, and as the bus swept up the last incline, she
divided her attention between the road ahead, the wide
prospect of sea on the right and, nearer, the purple and
gold embroidery of small flowers along the rock-strewn
hillside.

The bus stopped at last, and Marian, waiting for the
first outward rush to be over, saw a dauntingly crowded
hillside and remembered that it was Sunday afternoon.
Naturally Sounion would be a weekend resort for city-
pent Athenians. There were other buses, too, behind and
in front, letting out their polyglot complement of tourists.
Her own was almost empty now, and she rose, stiff and
tired again, to move forward. The rest of the party were
strung out up the hillside, and she fixed her attention on
Cairnthorpe's light-colored jacket as he hurried ahead,
presumably to buy their tickets at the entrance to the site.
It was only after they had all filed through the gate and
started up the hill towards the shining temple that she
realized he was not coming with them.

"We seem to be on our own." Mrs. Hilton, limping
along in her high heels, turned and caught sight of
Marian. "No guide, no instructions, nothing!"

"He had no sleep, poor man." Looking back, Marian
saw that Cairnthorpe had settled himself in the shade of
a rock. "But it's true. How do we know when to go
back to the bus?"

"I asked him." Mrs. Hilton was pleased with herself.
"An hour, he said, and would I tell the others? I ask you!
I'm not doing his job for him."

"We could tell anyone who asks."

"Well, of course!" She turned her ankle and swore. "Look at the kiddies picking the flowers! They oughtn't to be let."

Marian had been thinking very much the same thing, but found herself demurring. "There are so many."

"Kids? Or flowers?"

"Well." She looked around. "Both, in fact. I say." She paused and drew a long breath. "Isn't it splendid!"

"Poseidon." Mrs. Hilton was reading her guidebook. "Is that how you pronounce it? Magnificent temple . . . twelve standing columns. Pericles had it built." She pronounced him to rhyme with icicles. "Ooh, I say, Lord Byron—you know, the wicked one—carved his name on one of the pillars. I must see that."

"I do call that wicked." Marian bent and pretended to retie a shoelace. It was bad enough to see her first Greek temple in these horribly crowded conditions. She drew the line at Mrs. Hilton's company. Luckily, the schoolmistresses, who had come up by a detour, joined her at this point and stopped to ask if she knew when they were due back at the bus. Telling them, she was relieved to see Mrs. Hilton plunge on ahead, buttonhole a postcard seller on the steps of the temple, then climb purposefully up them.

She herself moved to the seaward side of the temple and then climbed up from there to gaze, entranced, through white pillars out across still, blue sea to a distant island. *"Bitte."* The polite voice roused her, and she moved aside to make way for an eager young photographer. It was no use; the temple was too crowded to be enjoyed. She made her way a little sadly down the steps and followed one of the rambling cliffside paths through beds of yellow and purple vetch. Farther from Athens, she thought, it would be better. And at least, even here, there was the blessing of the hot sun. She found a sheltered corner among the rocks and sat down to bask. When she closed her eyes, voices from the temple above blurred into indistinguishable background music; she could almost pretend that she heard the sound of the sea on the rocks below. It would be pleasant to climb down for a closer look. But once again the extraordinary sensation of peace and freedom was stealing over her. Bless you, Poseidon, she thought, and stayed where she was.

Half-sleeping, half-waking, utterly relaxed, she let time ebb by, until the sound of familiar voices roused her. It was the schoolmistresses climbing cheerfully back up from what they described as very nearly sea level. "The flowers are even better down there," said one. "I wish I'd brought my book."

"I know. It's maddening. I don't know why one wants to know their names, but one does." Marian looked at her watch. "Time to be getting back to the bus, I suppose." She followed them slowly, feeling incredibly older as she listened to their lighthearted nonsense. One last look at the temple, and she turned down the hill towards the gates. But where was the bus? Ahead of her, the schoolmistresses were asking each other the same question. They turned to wait for her. "You did say an hour, Mrs. Frenche?"

"Yes." How pleasantly characteristic that they had learned her name already. "At least, that's what Mrs. Hilton told me."

"They *can't* have left us all behind." It was almost a wail, from a girl who looked young enough to be still at school herself.

"No, of course not." Marian made it sound more certain than she felt, horrid visions of getting them all back to Athens dancing in her mind. "Oh, look!" They were out of the gate now, and there was no need to pretend relief as she pointed down to a second car park to their left. "It must have moved down there."

They found Mr. Cairnthorpe trying anxiously to make sure that they were, in fact, the last. Since he had neglected to count them before they separated, this was no easy matter, but finally they were reasonably certain that no one's neighbour from the ride out was missing. Marian closed her eyes as the bus moved out into the road, grateful that Stella was not there with one of her devastating comments.

She had congratulated herself too soon. Mrs. Hilton, who had dozed peacefully enough across the aisle on the way up, now rose and came swaying across to join her. "Room for little me?" It was all too obviously a rhetorical question. "I don't know about you, but I get sick of being on my own. George has gone back to look for those espadrilles," she explained. "The shop was actually shut when he went this morning. It's lucky we can charge the taxis up to Mercury Tours." She giggled. "Funny about it meaning death, wasn't it? You could have heard a pin drop in that dining room."

"It doesn't really." Marian repeated Cairnthorpe's explanation, grateful that they were far enough back in the bus so that there was no chance of his hearing. She had already noticed that sound tended to travel backwards on the bus. You heard mainly the conversation of the couple directly in front of you, and even that spasmodically.

She was more grateful still for this when Mrs. Hilton plunged into a ruthless cross-examination. Was she enjoying herself? Was Miss Marten an old friend? And then, inevitably, "No children of your own, love?"

Once again, the wound opened and bled. "Oh, yes." Marian, who had fended off the previous questions, kept her voice steady. "Twins, in fact. But they're grown up now."

"Grown up!" Amazed. "You don't look nearly old enough!"

"Thank you." Had there really been a time when she had laughed about that mad seventeen-year-old marriage, convinced that the twins would make up for everything?

"You must have married out of the cradle. I don't know what your mum was thinking of. But come on, love, how old are they really?"

"Eighteen. It's grown up these days. After all, they can vote." And make up their own minds to live with their father in America.

"Crazy, I think. But weren't you lucky to have twins

first off? Two for the price of one, I always say. What are they? Girls or boys? Or one of each?"

"One of each." If she kept to monosyllables, perhaps the remorseless probing would stop.

Forlorn hope. "Aren't you worried, leaving them on their own? Or are they safe with their dad?" It was a remarkable compendium of questions rolled into one.

But at least it was capable of as comprehensive an answer. "Yes," said Marian, "that's just where they are." Thank God the name "Frenche" was a fairly common one, and the publicity about Mark and the twins eighteen years old, like the twins themselves. She shut her eyes, hoping to fend off further questions, and the headlines danced in front of her, as they had through many a sleepless night in the past. "All for love! Pop idol abandons twins. 'I must follow my star,' says Mark Frenche." But it was a new star. Marian's thoughts went the old, dreary round. Mark and his manager had been clever, no doubt about it, and she had been incredibly stupid. Coming back from the prenatal clinic, she had actually thought Mark would be pleased with the news.

"Twins?" She would never forget his look of horror or the appalling conversations that followed. Twins, it appeared, would be fatal to his "image." A teen-age idol with twins? It had a built-in absurdity. He explained it to her, first patiently, then with rising heat, finally called in his manager to "make her see reason."

Reason, it appeared, was an abortion or, when she pointed out that it was too late for that, even if she were prepared to consider it, a secret birth and adoption. Curious to think that when she fought for the twins' lives, she had been no older than they were now. The end had been inevitable. When she refused to budge, Mark had left her, as publicly as possible, apparently for one of the glossy young females who filled his world. It had been a "Great Romance" in the gossip columns; the unborn twins well lost for love. Interviewed, Mark had bared his heart to a sympathetic press. Naturally, that famous heart was breaking at the thought of leaving his wife and prospective family, but he must follow his star, and she led westwards. Predictably, when he was safely reestablished on the other side of the Atlantic, that particular star, having served her purpose, had set. Meanwhile, the twins had been born, and he had been quoted again. All he had was theirs. Was it too much to hope that they would be called Sebastian and Viola?

Mrs. Hilton was asking something. Marian roused herself. "Viola and Sebastian," she said.

"Ooh, how romantic," said Mrs. Hilton. The interrogation showed every sign of continuing until Athens, but Marian had had enough and pleaded headache.

"I thought you looked a bit ropey." Mrs. Hilton's sympathy flowed freely as her questions, but at last she lapsed into blessed silence, and Marian had time to be grateful that even the twins' names had called up no old association and to wonder, vaguely, who was sitting silently behind them, no doubt hearing everything they said.

She turned to look when the bus pulled up at long last outside the hotel and saw an elderly woman she had not noticed before, the kind of woman, in fact, that one tended not to notice, a small neat creature in what must be an unsuitably hot twinset and matching skirt. She, too, had been sleeping but now opened blue eyes in a surprisingly brown face and smiled muzzily up at Marian. "Catching up on my sleep," she said. "Did you get any last night?"

"Not much." Grateful for the excuse to escape from Mrs. Hilton, Marian paused to introduce herself. I'm Marian Frenche."

"How do you do." She spoke what Mark used to describe, with dislike, as University English. "Kay Spencer. Mrs. I hope you haven't got a burn."

"I don't think so. It takes me quite a while. You're lucky; you're brown already."

"Yes." She had a pleasant light laugh. "I'm a mad gardener. To tell you the truth, I come as much for the flowers as the ruins. Did you see the mullein at Sounion?"

"No." Turning to lead the way down the emptying bus, Marian did not confess that she would not know a mul-

lein from an aspidistra. They walked into the hotel together, chatting idly, and Marian, picking up her key at
the desk, had a prick of conscience, remembering Miss
Oakland's instructions to keep Stella away from the
other members of the party. But Mrs. Spencer was turning briskly away at the foot of the stairs. "I'm in the
annexe." She lifted a friendly hand.

It was well after seven, and by the time Marian had
made a quick change into a light cotton and terylene
dress the queue was already forming in the lobby. Once
again she dived through, with a faintly apologetic smile
for Mrs. Spencer, and again found Stella in the little bar,
but this time alone, reading a book and sipping an
ouzo. She looked, for her, relaxed and almost cheerful.
"Are you having one? You'd better. You look whacked."

"I am. Yes, thanks, I think I will. And it was worth it,"
she added firmly, as Stella rose to get her drink.

It took a little time, and taking her first, reviving sip,
Marian heard commotion in the lobby. "Oh, dear, the
dining room must be open already."

"Never mind," said Stella firmly, "Drink up. You need
it." She laughed. "Even if it does mean Useless and
Glamour-puss again." And then, as Marian looked her
question, "Oh, well, Cairnthorpe and Edvardson, if you
must have it. But I like them better as Useless and
Glamour-puss. I ask you, though! Birds! With a face like
that he ought to be one of those iron-willed TV heroes,
but it must be all surface. I expect he's soft as butter
inside. Look at the dear little dicky-birds! Ugh—"

"You young are so ruthless."

"Just honest, Mrs. F. And you're not exactly a grandmother yourself."

The silent wound bled a bitter drop. What use would
grandchildren be in America? Not for the first time, she
found herself wondering if Mark had stopped her money
partly to make it impossible for her to visit the twins.
It would be like him. . . . She pushed back her chair.
Don't think about the twins. "I'm famished again. Shall
we eat?"

They found Cairnthorpe alone at the table that they

had had at lunchtime. Rising to greet them, "I think the professor must be revisiting old haunts," he said.

"Professor?"

"Yes. He was telling me after lunch. Classics at Harvard. I hope our guide knows his stuff!" And then, as an afterthought, "Do you think everyone knows about the early start tomorrow, Mrs. Frenche?"

"I didn't."

"Oh, dear . . . I hoped they'd pass the word on."

"Better make an announcement." Stella was suddenly brisk. She clapped her hands. "Pray silence for our courier," she said into a surprised hush.

"Just to say"—he was on his feet, his colour high but his voice steady—"that I'm sorry about the muddle this morning, and I hope you all enjoyed your afternoon. And to break it to you that we've an early start tomorrow. Breakfast at seven thirty; leave at eight thirty."

"Ouch," said one of the schoolmistresses louder than she intended, and he sat down amid a ripple of sympathetic laughter.

"You could make an announcement at the end of the bus ride every day," said Marian thoughtfully. "While you've got us captive."

"Yes, I'd thought of that. The trouble is," he confided, "I don't know how the microphone works. And the driver doesn't speak a word of English. That's why I didn't know about the bus moving to the car park today. I must learn some modern Greek. . . . I feel a fool."

"Yes, isn't it tiresome?"

"*Kalemera,*" said Stella surprisingly.

"I beg your pardon?"

"Good morning," she explained. "And *kalespera* is good afternoon. It's all is the phrase book, but it actually works. I tried it on the chambermaid."

Seven thirty seemed very early, and eight thirty not much better. It was a subdued party that climbed into the bus to be greeted, once again, with muddle. Someone, it seemed, had decided that they must rotate ("like crops," whispered Stella crossly) so that everyone had his fair share of front windows and wheels. But, naturally, since not everyone had gone to Sounion the day before, there was considerable confusion about who should be sitting where. When they were finally sorted out, the schoolmistresses were sitting en masse in front of Marian and Stella, and the professor and Mrs. Spencer behind them. She looked hotter than ever today, in another twinset, this time blue to match her eyes. Had no one told her, Marian wondered, about the Greek climate? The professor had stood in the aisle for a moment, looking puzzled. Now he sat down beside her. "Funny," Marian heard him say, and then, "I guess I was tireder than I knew."

"Kyriae kai kyrii." A new voice drew all attention to the front of the bus.

"Wow," said Stella.

He was beautiful as only Mediterranean young men can be beautiful: brown skin, dark hair, flashing teeth all adding up to the glossy look of perfect health and, Marian thought, perfect self-confidence. His gleaming smile was an impartial benison. "Ladies and gentlemen," he went on. "Let me introduce myself. I am your devoted guide, Mihailos Angelou. You will call me Mike of course; everyone does, and we will be dear friends before many days. You will help me with my English"— his accent was sometimes difficult—"and I will teach you many things about our beautiful Greece, birthplace of the gods and of democracy." There was a challenging sparkle in his eye now. He laughed. "Do you know what one of my ladies said to me last year? "What is your Greek word for politics?" she asked me. And, 'Madam,' I said, 'Politics is our word. What is yours?' And that," he went on, "is all the politics we are going to talk. We have a proverb, here in Greece, that if you have two Greeks, you have two political parties, and if you have two of *them,* you have a quarrel. So, we shall not quarrel, you and I." Once again, the warm smile embraced them. "This is a classical tour, and we have more interesting things to do. We shall talk of Zeus and his cross wife Hera, and I will tell you tales of the old days, when gods were jealous and men were heroes." He turned and spoke rapid Greek to the bus driver. "Now we start. Our driver is Andreas, and he bids you *kalemera*, which is good morning. You will all say, '*Kalemera,* Andreas.'"

They did, rather sheepishly, and Mike beamed approval. "Now our first stop is at Eleusis. Most tours, as perhaps you know, go first to the ancient Byzantine church at Daphne, but it is not ancient as we are going to think of antiquity." The bus had pulled away from the hotel, but he still stood, swaying to its motion, the microphone in his hand. "We are going far far back into the dark past, and now, if you please, you will shut your eyes to modern Athens, and your ears to its noise, and you will imagine yourselves as pilgrims, torches in hand, walking, in the dark, the Sacred Way to Eleusis. Perhaps you are an initiate and know what is to come. Perhaps not, and you are afraid of what awaits you. And do not ask me what it is, for no one knows. The mystery of Eleusis has never been solved. The initiates swore a terrible oath not to reveal what they did and saw, and, my friends, they kept it. So this is a mystery story, if you like, with no ending. Only we know that the great goddess Demeter, the earth mother, was worshipped there, because it was there, while she searched for her lost daughter Persephone, that she taught her host, King Celeus, the art of husbandry. The first corn grew at Eleusis, ladies and gentlemen. I am afraid you will find no corn there now. The sacred site lies between an aerodrome and some very useful modern factories. But if you keep looking to your right, you will see the votive niches in the rock, where once stood statues, no doubt of gold and precious work, and presently, the sacred lakes of Rhiti. And if you look to your left, ladies and gentlemen, you will see the island of Salamis, where the Persian king sat on his golden throne to watch his fleet destroy the Greeks. As your poet says,

> *He counted them at break of day—*
> *And when the sun set where were they?*

The united Greeks beat him, ladies and gentlemen, and sent him back to Persia, where he belonged." He smiled once more. "And now, remember, you are pilgrims, torchbearing, on your way to the Great Mystery of Eleusis."

He sat down in his seat beside the driver, and a little buzz of conversation broke out in the bus. "I know another quote from Byron." Marian recognized Mrs. Duncan's brisk voice.

> *The mountains look on Marathon—*
> *And Marathon looks on the sea;*
> *And musing there an hour alone,*
> *I dream'd that Greece might still be free.*

"Apposite," said the professor quietly from behind Marian, "but perhaps not tactful? I reckon we've had our warning about politics. Let's take it, shall we? After all, we're here to enjoy ourselves, and I'm sure we don't want to make trouble for anybody."

"No, no, of course not." She sounded surprised at the idea but subsided into silence.

"How did Demeter come to lose her daughter?" asked Stella.

"I'm sure I don't know." The knife twisted once more in the wound. "It does seem careless." She made her voice light as she turned round to speak to Professor Edvardson. "Can you tell us?"

"About Persephone? Well, there are dozens of stories, but the gist of it is that she had a loving mother who didn't want to part with her and kept her safe in a garden, maybe on Crete; only unluckily Hades, King of the Underworld, happened to see her, fell in love and carried her off. Poor Demeter hunted all over for her, and in the end she only got her back for part of each year. That's why we have the seasons, you see. It's winter when Persephone's underground with her husband."

"It sounds like an awful warning to mothers," said Stella. "But I'm not quite sure what kind."

Marian clenched her hands on the strap of her bag.

Is it better to lose your daughter to a husband or a father? And how should one be warned? What should one have done? Her head was beginning to throb: the bad night, the hurried breakfast, the confused start, and now this. . . . Soon, she knew, the throb would be an ache, the ache a migraine. She closed her eyes and tried to make herself relax. "Just relax," Dr. Brown would say. Relax? You might as well say it to someone on the rack.

The bus was slowing down. "Here we are, ladies and gentlemen." Mike was on his feet again, microphone in hand. "This way for the Mysteries."

More talk about Demeter and Persephone? About lost daughters? Viola . . . Sebastian . . . I can't. She was in the window seat. Just stay there? Why not? Stella, surprisingly, had already pushed her way forward down the aisle to speak to Cairnthorpe. The professor and Mrs. Spencer were moving out to follow. Marian leaned forward. "I say." She spoke to both of them. "Would you very kindly tell Miss Marten that I think I'll sit this one out. I've got a bit of a head."

"I'll stay with you." Little Mrs. Spencer spoke with surprising authority.

"No, please. . . . I just need to rest. . . . It's very good of you."

"Migraine." The professor's eyes were kind under the bushy brows. "You'll be much better on your own. Come along, Mrs. Spencer; we don't want to miss young Mike on the Mysteries. I hope he's got another genuine homegrown Greek proverb for us." He shepherded her, firm but polite, forward down the bus. It was quiet at last. Marian leaned back in her seat and closed her eyes. Her conscience told her that she should have gone with Stella; her reason replied that in that case she would have been useless for the rest of the day. Traffic hummed; a factory siren sounded; voices drifted past as other buses let out their loads of tourists. It was nothing to do with her; it was peace. For a few minutes, exquisitely, she slept.

"You poor thing." Mrs. Hilton's voice jerked her back to wakefulness. "I came back the minute I heard. Fancy leaving you all on your own. Why! Anything might have happened to you. The driver's over at that bar, drinking God knows what with a lot of friends. I had to make him unlock the bus to let me in. No Greek, mind you, but I managed. So here I am, the little nurse, and here's a glass of water and a pill you're going to take."

Not a small woman, she loomed surprisingly large in the corridor of the empty bus. "No!" It came out with a vehemence that surprised Marian. "Thank you very much. But all I need is to be quiet for a bit."

"Nonsense." Mrs. Hilton sat down in the seat beside her. "I know those heads; they go on forever if you don't take something. My doctor gives me these—" She held the pill firmly in one hand and offered the water with the other.

"No, really. It's very kind of you." Marian searched wildly for an explanation for her deep irritational reluctance to accept the kindly proffered medicine. "I've got an odd kind of allergy." She found the perfect formula. "My doctor told me never to take anything without his permission. It brings me out in the most dreadful spots."

"Ooh, how frightful. Where?" Mrs. Hilton was putting the pill back in a little bottle.

"All over. Ought you to take the glass back?" Anything to get rid of this friendly, intolerable woman.

"Mr. Cairnthorpe can, when he gets back. After all, he's supposed to be in charge of us." She poured the water out of the window and went forward down the aisle to deposit the glass on Cairnthorpe's seat. "That was a proper turn-up between him and your Miss Marten, wasn't it?"

"What?"

"Ooh, didn't you hear? She's mad as fire because of this moving round business. In the bus, you know. Seems like common sense to me, but it won't suit her nohow. So hard on the singles, she says. Stuck with the same person all the time. Proper narked she was when he stuck to his guns and said it was all settled. There's more to that young man than meets the eye, if you ask me; I thought he was a dead loss yesterday, but I'm not so sure today. The guide chipped in, too, that Mike, and took your Miss Marten's side, but Cairnthorpe wasn't having any. 'You're the guide,' he says, 'but I'm the courier.' And that was that. I don't reckon Mike liked it overmuch, and I'm dead sure Miss Marten didn't. Oh— here they come."

She moved up to her own seat, which was now two forward from Marian's, owing to the clockwise movement of the passengers. At least, Marian thought, if they must resign themselves to the same people in front and behind them, there would be a constant change in those across the aisle.

"Well." Stella plumped down irritably in the aisle seat. You didn't miss much, Mrs. F. How's the head?"

"Better, thanks." Surprisingly it was true. Equally surprisingly, and much to her relief, Stella said nothing about the argument with Cairnthorpe.

"Corinth next," she said. "Are you game to walk across the canal, Mrs. F.?"

Chapter 4

MIKE WAS an admirable guide. By the time they reached the Corinth Canal, they knew it had been planned over and over again through the ages, by Nero amongst others. He had actually dug the first earth with a golden spade, before trouble in Rome called him home, but what with one thing and another the project had not been finished until the nineteenth century. They also knew a good deal about Corinth, city of wealth and courtesans, where the famous Lais charged ten thousand drachmae a night, but gave her favours free to ugly Diogenes, the philosopher who told Alexander the Great to get out of his sun. " 'It isn't everyone who can afford to go to Corinth,' " Mike quoted to them, and when their visit to the Temple of Apollo was over and they were back in the bus, Stella summed up what might well have been many people's feelings: "It isn't everyone who'd want to. They can keep it for all of me, Doric columns and the lot. I never did go much for architectural terms."

"No." Marian was happy to agree with her. "But I'm looking forward to Mycenae."

One last look up to the towering citadel of the Acro-Corinth, where, the professor leaned forward to tell Marian and Stella, the Turkish garrison had held out all through the Greek War of Independence, and the bus began to climb up out of the coastal plain.

"God, I'm hungry," said Stella. "Thank goodness it's lunch first and Mycenae afterwards."

Lunch at the Belle Hélène was stuffed vine leaves again, and delicious. Only the professor was disappointed. "They've changed the place a whale of a lot since I was here last. Progress, I suppose. But I liked it the way Schliemann saw it."

"Schliemann?" asked Stella.

"The man who found Mycenae and all that gold. I expect Mike will tell us about him on our way up to the site."

Mike did, but Marian was not listening. She was back in her own deep past, those lonely days at school, before she met Mark, when all her life was books. A day girl at an Oxford boarding school, she had somehow belonged in neither the world of school nor that of home. The school library, and later the public one, had been her refuge, secondhand bookshops her pleasure. She would never forget discovering the tattered grey translations of Aeschylus' three plays about the doomed House of Atreus. A cold little shiver ran down her spine. Agamemnon had sacrificed his own daughter, Iphigenia, to get a fair wind for his fleet to sail against Troy. He had got it, too, and conquered Troy, after ten years, by the meanest of tricks, only to come home, bringing the unlucky prophetess Cassandra with him, to his own doom, and hers. And could you blame his wife, Clytemnestra, who had sent her daughter off, as she thought, to marry the great Achilles and then learned of her death on the sacrificial altar? No wonder if she took a lover, and if the two of them, alerted by the beacon fires that announced Agamemnon's triumphal return, planned and carried out their deed of blood. Daughters. . . . What was Mark doing with Viola? Sebastian would be all right. It was his nature, all too like his father's. But Viola. . . .

Would Mark be taking care of her properly? Or sacrificing the two of them on the publicity altar of his career? They had been a liability eighteen years ago. Now, eighteen, similar, beautiful, they had proved, suddenly, an asset. Would he even have the sense to take care of them as such? And, if not, would they be wise enough to come home? Suppose they decided to, cabled her and got no answer, because she was here, on this mad venture, in Greece?

Mike's voice aroused her, and she was glad of it. This kind of aimless worry was a self-indulgence she could ill afford. They had reached the gate to the inevitable wire-mesh fence, and Mike was striking an attitude by it as Cairnthorpe handed out tickets. "Ladies and gentlemen, we are here, at the entrance to the palace of the doomed Atrides. Can you hear the Furies howling up the wind?"

"Grue," said Stella, and then. "We actually seem to have the place to ourselves."

It was true; theirs was the only bus below them in the car park, but now, looking back, Marian saw a small red car being deftly parked beside it. Two young men emerged and came up the hill with the long, swift strides of practised walkers. Marian wondered for a moment if they intended to hang on the edges of their party and get the benefit of Mike's guiding, but as they passed, they were talking in what she assumed to be Greek. Quick glances at all the younger females of the party suggested a more likely interest. They were handsome enough themselves to get several covert sideways looks as they loped past, up the hill and out of sight.

The Mercury party, straggling more slowly up the slope, struck Marian as disgustingly cheerful. Had they no sense of history? Probably not, she thought. Even the schoolmistresses were giggling happily together, having shared their first brave bottles of wine at the Belle Hélène. Only Stella was silent, deep in her own thoughts, and Marian was glad to walk, just as silently, beside her, up the hillside resplendent in the appropriate royal purple and gold of a thousand vetches and small, strange daisies. And then, turning a corner of the path, she saw ahead the great gateway, with the two headless lions guarding the entrance to Agamemnon's palace. Her first feeling was complete disappointment. She had imagined, for some reason, a kind of cross between Trafalgar Square and those extraordinary lions on Delos that turned up in all the picture books.

Stella, too, was looking at the stone figures with less than enthusiasm. "I don't see how their heads fitted in," she said.

"I think they were gryphons." Mrs. Duncan had joined them.

"I never saw a gryphon." Stella's tone was so rude that Mrs. Duncan moved away with a quick, at once surprised and sympathetic glance for Marian.

Mike was saying his piece about the weight of the huge stone lintel, interrupted from time to time by the necessities of the various photographers of the party. "The light's hopeless." One of the schoolmistresses had given it up. They moved forward raggedly through the great gate to see the rough path leading still upwards.

"Ouch!" Mrs. Hilton, just in front of Marian and Stella, turned an ankle and swore. "These damned shoes. Hey, you, Mike!" And as he turned back towards her. "Do we come back this way? I've half a mind to stay here."

Mike shrugged. "As you please. But the shaft graves where Schliemann found the golden death masks are just at the top here. You could sit and rest there, if you like, while the rest of us go down to the hidden spring."

"Come on, Mrs. Hilton." Cairnthorpe had stayed behind buying their tickets at the gate but now caught up with them and took her arm. "It's worth the climb, I promise you."

"Oh, very well, if you say so." Leaning on Cairnthorpe's arm, she flicked a quick, spiteful glance at her husband. "That's what I needed."

"We'll get you some espadrilles in Nauplia," said Mr. Hilton.

Stella wanted to take a picture back through the lion gate, and Marian was glad of the excuse to let the Hilton's get on ahead. She was beginning to find Mrs. Hilton's whining voice and perpetual grumbles an increasing irritant, and worse still, it was all too obvious that Mrs. Hilton intended to make friends with her.

The professor, too, had lingered and now came hurrying up through the gate. "Ah." He moved sideways to keep out of Stella's picture. "I was beginning to wonder if I'd lost you. There's supposed to be a bird here that croaks the doom of the House of Atreus. I've never managed to get a proper description of it from anyone, but I keep hoping to hear it every time I come."

"I shouldn't think it would do much croaking with us chattering all over the place." Stella had taken her picture and slung her camera back over her shoulder.

"No," he agreed. "I'd give my eyeteeth to stay here one day and come up in the evening."

"Ugh." Stella shivered. "I bet it really would feel haunted then."

"It does now." Marian surprised herself. It was curious; she had not quite realised how much she had felt it, the strange, heavy atmosphere of the place. It was like, and yet unlike, what she had felt back in London, the feeling of being always watched that had sent her to Dr. Brown. But there the haunting had been particular to her; here she felt it as general, heavy in the air, the breath of the Furies?

"Imagination," said the professor robustly. "Come on up, Mrs. Frenche. I want to hear what that glib young man has to say about Schliemann."

"Glib?"

"Well." Fairly. "It's splendid stuff, for the purpose, but I wouldn't give him an A for the course. I wonder if he'll even mention that Homer speaks of Agamemnon as from Tiryns, not Mycenae at all."

They found Mike haranguing a rather silent group scattered round a circle of stones deeply planted in the earth. "Not Agamemnon, of course," he was saying. "Much earlier. And so is what they call his tomb—the beehive one we'll be visiting presently." Behind Marian, the professor grunted approval.

"But what an extraordinary place." She turned to him as the rest of the party moved on up the hill. "It's like Stonehenge."

"Only different." The tension of the place seemed to have got into Stella. Once again she spoke with a brusqueness that was very nearly rude.

"Which came first?" Marian turned to ask the professor but found that he had drifted away, binoculars at the ready.

"Bird watching." Stella gazed after him with contempt.

Marian fought irritation and won. "Let's go on up." She made her voice a little extra cheerful. "I want to know if Mike will show us the bathroom where Clytemnestra killed her husband."

"Bloodthirsty, aren't you, Mrs. F.?" Had Stella noticed the strain in Marian's voice. Certainly the place was doing something very strange to her. Could she really be wishing that she had, simply, killed Mark all those years ago? It would have been easy enough, looking back on it. He was always taking pills. Pills to make him sleep, and pills to wake him up. Pills that combined well with alcohol, and pills that were poison with it. One of those times when he had been in session and had called upstairs, "Hey, Mari, throw me one of those blue torpedoes," she could so easily have thrown him the wrong one. She would have been a wealthy widow; the twins all hers. Horrible. She looked out over the rolling plain. How had Clytemnestra and Aegisthus felt when they faced each other over the knowledge of what they had done?

There was no fatal bathroom. The site of the palace was open to the sky, and one must imagine the great hall where Clytemnestra and her lover feasted Agamemnon and Cassandra before they killed them.

"But Orestes' stair still exists," Mike told them. "And the postern by which he escaped after he killed his mother. You can go down if you want to, but it's a long way, and besides, the Furies might get you the way they did him. I'd recommend the stairs to Perseus' spring, myself; that's really interesting, so long as you don't mind the dark." He felt in his pockets, produced an electric torch and a handful of candle stumps and gave a Greek exclamation that was evidently an oath. "I'm a fool. I forgot to get new ones. But these will do if we share them. Who's for the long stair to the secret spring that made the palace of the Atrides impregnable?"

"What do you think?" Marian turned to Stella. "I'm not mad about the dark myself." Passionately, she hoped that Stella would agree with her. Even the entrance to the secret stair looked sinister, black against the bright sunshine.

But Stella was already moving forward. "Oh, come on, Mrs. F.," she said impatiently. "You can't come all this way and then welsh out on the horrors."

Something odd about her tone? No time to think about it as Marian reluctantly joined the slowly shuffling queue and collected a candle stump from Mike. "That's it"—he was cheerfully matter-of-fact—"one to four of you, follow my torch, and I promise you won't get lost." He laughed. "No room for that on the secret stair. And no time to waste, either, if we are to see the beehive tomb of Agamemnon."

"*Not* Agamemnon," said Edvardson, from behind Marian, but Mike had already led the way into the dark cavity. There were exclamations, little gasps, giggles, as pair after pair vanished into the darkness.

Cairnthorpe gestured Marian and Stella to go ahead of him. "I'm the rear guard," he said. "I've got a torch."

"Good." Marian did not think there was anything good about it, but she was certainly not letting Stella go down that dark stair alone. In the end, she saw, the whole party had decided to go, although both Mrs. Esmond and Mrs. Hilton had shared her own qualms at first. But Cairnthorpe was waiting, polite, patient, almost, she felt, relentless. She took a deep breath of thyme-scented air and followed Stella into the dark.

For a while, sunlight, filtering down from above, made the candles absurdly useless, then, gradually, their flickering light was the only guide down the rough, half-seen steps. Somewhere in front, Marian could hear Mrs. Hilton's voice raised in a steady grumble, while Mrs. Adams, who seemed to be trying to cling to her husband's arm, kept up a shrill, unnerving squeak. It made Marian think, uncomfortably, of bats, and she wondered where the professor was in the now rather silent group of people who picked their way, awkwardly, downwards and still downwards in the thick dark. Far ahead, she could see Mike's torch from time to time, vanishing round a bend in the tunnel, then reappearing rather farther off than she liked. But it was not the kind of going over which one could hurry. She sympathised with Mrs. Duncan, who was now muttering crossly to herself. Suppose the candles did not last the trip? It was not a possibility to think of.

It seemed a very long way, in the heavy darkness that was beginning to feel damp. Somewhere ahead, there was a scuffle and one of the schoolmistresses spoke. "I don't much like this," she said. "OK if I go back, Mike?"

And, from what seemed a good deal farther down, Mike's voice, apologetic. "Sorry, miss. Down here, in the dark, we must all keep together. It is a rule with us guides. You will understand, I am sure. But not much farther now.

"Oh, very well." The scuffling below was more pronounced, as, presumably, the group of girls started moving downwards again. Marian and Stella, who had kept moving, had almost caught up with them in a place where, Marian thought, the stairway must widen. Could it be a passing place, from the old ways, when men under siege went to and fro with vital flagons of water? Certainly, voices echoed strangely here, and she was aware of the other members of the party, some moving forward, others, apparently, still waiting, perhaps hoping that Mike would change his mind and take them all back.

But his torch was moving, and candles flickering after it. Marian thought, from the voices she heard, that the more eager members of the party had seized the chance to get ahead. The going was easier, here, where the stairway widened out, and Marian stopped concentrating on her feet to congratulate herself that, in fact, she was bearing this ordeal by darkness better than she had feared. Curiously, it was Stella who seemed disturbed. Her breathing came quick and shallow, and the hand that held their candle was not quite steady.

Ahead, someone else was in difficulties. A candle went out. There was violent movement, for a moment, and a terrified scream echoed back to them, stopped suddenly, and was caught up by Stella. "What is it?" Marian took the candle from her now uncontrollably shaking hand. "What's the matter down there?"

"Let me pass." It was Cairnthorpe, with his torch, and Marian was glad to stand close against the cold stone and let him by. A babble of voices was coming up, now, from the darkness. Mike's, anxious; Mrs. Spencer's; Mrs. Duncan's; and then above them all, Mr. Hilton's, high with fright, "Martha! Martha! Where are you?"

No answer. Mike's torch swung back up towards them, its beam pitifully weak, but still strong enough to show a dark something on the stair, a little above where he stood. Mrs. Spencer spoke, with authority. "I've done some first aid, let me get to her."

More scuffling, and Cairnthorpe's voice, also surprisingly authoritative. "Please stand still, everyone but Mrs. Spencer. I'm afraid there's been an accident."

"Martha!" There was a sob in Mr. Hilton's voice now. "Is it Martha? I only stopped to tie my shoelace. Is it Martha?"

"I'm afraid so." Mrs. Spencer's voice was sober. "I'm afraid she's hurt herself. Badly."

Dead. That tone could mean nothing else. Marian put out a firm hand to take Stella's trembling one. "Do you want us to start back up? she called down to Cairnthorpe. "Or can we help?" it was interesting, she thought that in this moment of crisis, it was Cairnthorpe who had taken command, not Mike.

But, now, incredibly, a furious argument broke out between them as to who was to stay and who go for help. Common sense surely suggested that Mike, the Greek speaker, should go for help and Cairnthorpe stay with what was now tacitly admitted to be the body. But Mike refused, point-blank. He was responsible, he said, for the group. He must stay and organise the appalling task of getting Mrs. Hilton back up the dark stair.

Here another voice broke in. Mrs. Duncan's, Marian thought. "She should be left where she fell," she said. "For the police."

"Nonsense," said Mike robustly. "The candles won't last much longer, for one thing, and what have the police to do with an accident like this?" But, somehow, the argument was over. Cairnthorpe said something under his breath, then turned and started back upwards.

As the sound of his careful footfalls and the light of his torch dwindled together, silence fell on the party below, broken only by the painful, smothered sound of Mr. Hilton's sobs. "Those shoes," he said. "I shouldn't have let her come. Oh, Martha. . . ."

"Someone had better take him up." This was the professor nearer to the scene of the accident than Marian had expected. "And then I think between us, Mike, you and I and Mr. Adams might. . . ." Straining her eyes, Marian saw Mike's torch swing round to illuminate Edvardson, who was bending over the huddled figure on the stair. "Yes," he said, "she lost her right shoe, poor woman." He raised his voice a little. "Mrs. Frenche, are you there?"

"Yes?"

"Do you think you and Miss Marten could help Mr. Hilton up? You've got a candle, haven't you? And then perhaps the rest of the party would follow you, and leave the three of us. . . ."

"Yes, of course." It was obvious sense, and Marian was only surprised that it was Edvardson who had suggested it, not Mike, whose job it was. But then, just because it was his job, it was understandable that Mike should be badly shaken. "Wait here," Marian told Stella, I'll fetch poor Mr. Hilton." But he was already on his way up to them, being passed carefully from group to group, with light, sympathetic touches and murmurs of would-be consolation in the dark. His face, in the dim candlelight, looked ghastly, but, mercifully, he was now in some degree of shock. Tears trickled uncontrollably down his cheeks, but when Marian took his hand and began to lead him upwards, he followed in silent obedience.

Just the same, it was a horrible and difficult journey, with Stella, following behind silent and, it seemed to Marian, oddly unhelpful. Turning back to light Mr. Hilton over a specially rough bit of stair, she cut short an impatient expostulation with Stella when she saw that silent tears were running down her face. Stupid to have forgotten that it must be the child's first sight of death.

Mike had been right about the candles, she was just beginning to look anxiously at the stub she carried, now flickering low in its socket and threatening, soon, to burn the hand that held it, when she saw, blessedly, the faintest hint of light ahead. "Thank God," she said. "We're almost there."

"But where's Martha?" said Mr. Hilton.

The unanswerable question brought them in silence out into the warm sun that showed Hilton as ghastly as Marian had expected. We ought to have hot tea, she thought, and brandy. As it was, she spread her plastic raincoat on the grass and made him sit on it. "Do you smoke?" she asked.

"Martha didn't like—" He choked on it.

"Have one now." Stella, at least, had pulled herself together and took the cue to produce a battered package. She and Marian registered, with a relieved exchange of glances, that he was speaking of his wife in the past tense.

He must have noticed it himself. He looked up at them. "It can't be true," he said. "Just a fall; a little fall like that? They'll bring her up. She'll be all right, won't she?"

"We must hope so," said Marian. Let him take his time; better so.

"If only my shoelace hadn't come undone." He was reliving it now. "But it wasn't safe, down there in the dark. And hard to tie." He looked down at his right foot where the lace of a surprisingly good brogue looked indeed as if it had been tied with fumbling hands. "She shouldn't have gone," he said. "If only that young man— Cairnthorpe—if only he'd only not urged her not to, she'd never have come. She didn't mean to. But she was always one for a dare, was Martha." And then, aware of the past tense again, he crumbled helplessly into tears.

Stella was prowling restlessly about on the springy grass. "God," she said, "this is horrible. How long, do you think?"

"Cairnthorpe, or the others?" Marian was sitting beside Hilton, holding his hand and stroking it gently, as she might, once, have done for one of the twins in one of childhood's moments of despair.

"Both, I suppose."

"Well"—Marian did her best to make her voice sound matter-of-fact—"at least, here come the others. I hope they have some sense. . . ."

Mercifully, they did. The subdued babble of voices she had heard, doubtless exclaiming with relief, as she had, on sight of daylight, was stilled when the first of the others emerged and saw Hilton's crumpled figure. Mrs. Duncan, in the lead, blew out her candle and took charge. "Over here," she told the group who followed her. "Out of the way." They looked, understood and moved dutifully away. Only Mrs. Duncan came over to lean close to Marian and say, softly, "Should we move him? They'll be up in a moment."

"Yes." Marian looked up at her doubtfully. "I know, but I'm not sure. . . ."

"You may be right," said Mrs. Duncan. "Anyway, he's got to know."

Mr. Hilton took no notice of anything. He was staring at his own shoes, as if hypnotised. "Here they come," said Mrs. Duncan, and moved forward to spread her neat grey raincoat on the short grass as far as she could from where Mr. Hilton sat.

Mrs. Esmond and her son had just emerged from the dark stair with Mrs. Adams. Mrs. Esmond, as was her habit, was talking loud and angrily. "Badly organised . . . asking for trouble." She saw Mr. Hilton and fell suddenly silent.

From behind and below came the professor's voice. "Careful here," he said. "It's always tricky when you hit the light." And then, "That's it." He emerged first, moving half-backwards, and Marian found herself thinking it was like him to take the most difficult place. One look at the inert figure that the three men laid gently on the grey raincoat told her that she had been right not to let Mr. Hilton hope.

Suddenly, horribly, Mrs. Adams went into hysterics. "What do we do now?" she wailed.

"I'm afraid we wait," said Mike. "For the police." And then, quickly. "Even for an accident, like this, they must of course be summoned."

"Of course," said Mrs. Spencer, and moved forward quietly to lay her white handerchief over the dead face.

Chapter 5

THEY NEVER did see the beehive tomb. By the time the police arrived the hills were casting heavy shadows across the valley. And when the inevitable questioning was over at last, dusk was in the air, and the level of hysteria in the party rising.

The police had insisted on holding their examination up on the hill, where the body had lain until it was, mercifully, removed by a capable pair of young men with a stretcher, and Marian had found herself wildly imagining that these modern-looking Greeks in their neat uniforms perhaps believed in some primitive form of ordeal. Did they expect that poor little body to gush blood from nose and ears at a murderer's approach?

This was merely lunatic fantasy engendered by the grim hillside. In fact, it all seemed straightforward enough. Everyone knew that Mrs. Hilton had been staggering about in unsuitable shoes. Several people were sure that it was her candle that had gone suddenly out, presumably in some unexpected down draught. Everyone had heard her scream and fall, and if no one admitted to having been

near her at the time, well, the police shrugged their
shoulders. Down there, in the dark, it was hardly surprising. Mr. Hilton, coming slowly out of shock, explained
about his shoelace and how he had momentarily lost
touch with his wife before the disaster. "Very risky, down
there," he said, and went first red, then white.

It was a very subdued party that checked in at the
strikingly inappropriate modern hotel that loomed over
Nauplia. Resigned now to waiting to the last to be assigned
a room, Marian joined the professor, who was gazing out
at an astonishing view of cliff and sea. "What do you think
will happen?" she asked.

"Nothing, I should think. The tour must go on. That
kind of thing. After all, tourism's just about Greece's
number one industry. And it was so obviously an accident. I imagine poor Hilton will stay here and be flown
back with the body, if he wants, and, for the rest of us, it
will just be pleasure as usual."

"It seems heartless."

"But practical. Like life. Aside from anything else, I
heard Mike telling young Cairnthorpe that this hotel is
booked solid for the whole season. We can't stay on here,
even if we want to."

"Oh." She hadn't thought of that. "Where is Mike?"

"With the police still." It was odd how his smile trans-
formed the craggy face. And how had she failed to notice
the clear blue of eyes that seemed to see right through
her? What did they see?

Monstrous to be thinking so frivolously at a time like
this. And anyway Edvardson's eyes had moved away
from her. "Damnation!" he said. Behind them in the
lobby, Hilton had been confronted, suddenly, with his
wife's luggage as well as his own and burst totally, uncontrollably into tears. "Someone should have thought of
that." Professor Edvardson moved forward, took Hilton's
arm and guided him away after the pageboy with the bags.

Stella had been totally silent on the drive down from
Mycenae, hunched in her corner seat, biting her nails.
Now she was standing on the other side of the lobby
gazing out of a huge plate-glass window. At last, to Mar-

ian's relief, she came slowly across to join her. "What gives?" she asked.

"Business as usual, the professor thinks."

"You mean pleasure." Unconsciously, Stella echoed his word. "I suppose it makes sense, in a horrible kind of a way. After all, it was just a ghastly accident, wasn't it?" She sounded oddly like the young Viola, wanting to be reassured in some child's disaster.

"Well, of course." And, oddly, Marian found herself remembering her own macabre thoughts up there on the cooling hillside, about the police and the ordeal by blood. It was a relief to hear Cairnthorpe call her name. "Shall I wait for you?" she asked Stella. Something about her apparent composure nagged at her.

"Don't bother. If you're like me, you're dying to get upstairs. All rooms with bath here, by the look of the place. See you in the bar?"

"Right." Marian turned to follow her pageboy. Upstairs, he accepted her apologetic handful of unknown coins with a beaming smile and said something rapid and incomprehensible in Greek.

"Oriste?" She had learned this useful all-purpose word from the professor.

The boy smiled, closed the room door and went to open the other door on to the small balcony. Wind rushed into the room, and somewhere down the corridor, another door, banging violently, made his point. He closed the balcony door carefully, then opened the one into the hall, beamed again and left. Investigating quickly, Marian found that Stella had been right. She had her own tiny, typically Greek bathroom, with square tub, shower, and slightly defective plumbing. She made sure the hall door was firmly shut, then opened the one onto the terrace again, wincing at the force of the wind. But it was cleansing, somehow, purifying after the grim ordeal of the afternoon, and so was the wide view of the sea, ruffled to whitecaps by the wind. She shivered, not altogether with cold. Poor, silly Mrs. Hilton and her high heels. . . . What an ill-omened start for the tour. And then, how monstrously selfish to think that. Selfish, too, to realise, now, that in the horrible excitement of the day's events, she had quite forgotten her own horrors.

Disliking herself, she remembered that Cairnthorpe had warned that their dinner would be early. With one last, clean breath of sea-tasting wind, she went inside to pull her most respectable dress out of her case and get herself into it as fast as possible. It was a dark, becoming shade of blue, and quickly combing her hair, she found herself wondering whether the gesture was in respect for poor Mrs. Hilton or for this obviously elegant hotel.

As she let herself out of her room, doors were banging up and down the long corridor. Not everybody's pageboy had taken the trouble hers had. "God, what a gale." Mrs. Duncan emerged from the room opposite. "What kind of view have you got?"

"Marvellous. The sea. What's it like your side?"

"Marvellous, too. Come and see. Only for God's sake shut the door."

"Thanks." Marian obeyed, then moved over to the balcony door, which Mrs. Duncan had waited to open. "Oh, I say!" This side of the hotel looked down over tumbling red-tiled roofs to more sea, with an island, set, she thought, as carefully in the centre of the scene as an eighteenth-century landscaper might have set his "folly."

"We're on a peninsula," explained Mrs. Duncan. "No wonder if it's a shade draughty."

"What's the island? Do you know?"

"Yes. I read this place up in the guidebook last night. It's called the Bourdzi, or something of the kind. It's a bit gruesome, as a matter of fact. It used to be where hangmen lived. Safe from the vengeance of their customers' relations."

"Ouch."

"Yes. Well, never mind. It's a luxury hotel now."

"Hey!" Stella's voice summoned them from the next balcony. "How about that drink, Mrs. F.? I'm dying of thirst."

"Not a bad idea," said Mrs. Duncan. "I've been admiring you two. What is that curious stuff you drink?"

"Ouzo," Marian told her. "Come and try one?" Stella had already disappeared into her room, but surely she, too, would be relieved to have a new member for the inevitable foursome over dinner. With luck, Marian thought, they might get Professor Edvardson and be spared poor Cairnthorpe.

But when they joined Stella in the hotel's modernist, anywhere-in-the-world bar, her welcome was grudging in the extreme. "Oh, there you are." She spoke to Marian, hardly acknowledging Mrs. Duncan's greeting. "I should warn you that we're in civilisation here. Ouzo costs half again what it did in Athens."

"Never mind," said Mrs. Duncan cheerfully. "I bet it's still dirt cheap by English pub standards. Let me buy you one, to celebrate my first?"

Stella refused so ungraciously that Marian blushed for her as she accepted for herself. The drink arrived at once, but already cloudy, on ice. "Not half so good," said Stella.

"But a drink." Mrs. Duncan drank as if she needed it. "What a day." And then, "Poor Mrs. Hilton." She drank again. "If her husband hadn't suggested she stay behind, she'd never have insisted on coming. Crazy of Cairnthorpe to let her, in those heels."

"Yes," said Marian reasonably. "But what could he do?"

"Too young for the job." Mrs. Duncan summed it up.

"I don't know. . . ."

"I do." She overrode Marian's attempted protest. "Imagine letting that young Greek—too handsome by a half, if you ask me—send him for help. Crazy, the whole business."

"And frightening." The words slipped out almost unawares and surprised Marian as much as the others.

"Oh, for God's sake let's stop talking about it." Stella's voice held a dangerous note of hysteria.

"There you are." Marian turned with relief to Mike, who spoke from the door.

"Ladies, I beg of you; the manager is in despair; the Furies are after us. This hotel is—how do you say?—

crash full, and we are late. Ouzo is good, but punctuality is better."

"I suppose that's another of your Greek proverbs." Stella's voice held such animosity that Marian wondered whether the one, badly needed drink was making her imagine things.

"No, just a fact of living. This way, ladies, if you please. They are saving a table for you. Just."

It was indeed pleasure as usual next morning. The telephone shrilling by her bed, woke Marian at seven, with the news, in passable English, that breakfast was at eight and the coach would leave at nine. She replaced the receiver and turned over crossly. A whole hour of good sleep wasted. There was no need to pack today, as they were merely doing a morning tour to Tiryns and Epidaurus and returning to Nauplia for what was called a "Free afternoon's sight-seeing." But in the end, she gave up the idea of sleep, got up and threw back her shutters on to a crystal blue morning. Her sleep had been drug-induced and plagued by half-remembered nightmares. The Furies had been after her, their faces horrible travesties of members of the tour. Mrs. Duncan had been one, and Stella another, her hair, frightfully, a writhing of snakes. And someone had been trying to tell her something desperately important. Cairnthorpe? The professor? She could not remember, and what in the world did it matter? Dreams . . . just dreams. A walk before breakfast would do her good. She dressed quickly, went downstairs and encountered Mrs. Duncan in the main lobby.

"Morning!" Mrs. Duncan was brisk in pleated navy skirt and matching cardigan. "Barbarous hour to call us, wasn't it? You going for a stroll? Good. There are two fortresses here, the guidebook says, one on each side of the hotel. We can't lose."

"No." They emerged into the still-cool morning together and moved unanimously across the road to gaze down at white waves breaking in a little cove below.

"I thought the Mediterranean was always calm," said Marian.

"Not a bit of it. Frightful storms here in the Aegean. That's why I opted for a bus tour this time. Sick as a dog the time I went on an island cruise. No stabilisers. Which way shall we go? Palamede or Itchkali?"

"I beg your pardon?"

"The two forts. If I've got it right, Itchkali's the smaller one on the promontory. They shelled each other in the Greek War of Independence."

"That must have been fun. Which one were the Turks holding?"

"Oh, neither. Greek meeting Greek. It's a habit of theirs." She looked at her watch. "I suppose as we've only twenty minutes it had better be the Itchkali. There are eight hundred and something steps up to the Palamede. I'm rather thinking of doing it this afternoon. Good for the digestion after all this sitting in the bus."

"Yes." Glad to have her mind made up for her, Marian fell in obediently at the other woman's side, but when they turned the corner of the road, it was to discover that their way was blocked. A large notice, white lettering on red, seemed to discourage further advance.

"Do you read Greek?" asked Mrs. Duncan.

"Not a word."

"Nor do I, but I've got a dictionary." Her tone suggested that Marian had come on this holiday very ill equipped, and Marian was inclined to agree with her. She pulled a fat book out of her bag and consulted it, spelling out the Greek capitals slowly. "Alpha, pi, omega, gamma —got it!" Triumphantly. "I knew I'd seen it in the phrase book. Might have known it, I suppose. It means forbidden."

"No entrance, I take it. I wonder why not."

"Someone's entered just the same," said Mrs. Duncan, as the honeymoon couple rounded a bend in the road. "At least she seems to have got over her hysterics. I thought she looked like death last night."

"Well, it's not my idea of a honeymoon," said Marian. "Honeymoon with Furies, you might say."

"Imagination." Mrs. Duncan was disapproving. "I thought you looked as if you had too much. Good morning." She raised her voice in cheerful greeting. "What goes on up there?"

"It's a bit hard to tell." Mr. Adams looked infinitely older than his platinum blonde wife this morning, and Marian, looking from one to the other, decided it must have been the attraction of opposites. "Building work of some kind. They seem to be dismantling an old fort by the look of things."

"Shocking," said Mrs. Duncan. "No respect for antiquity."

"They'll probably build it up again better than ever," he told her. "*And* more convincing. Have you been to Lindos?"

"Yes." Enthusiastically. "Wonderful place. I'll never forget those columns against the sky."

"No?" His tone mocked her. "Did anyone think to tell you that they were put up by Mussolini when the Italians held the island?" He turned to his wife. "Come on, pet. If you want to do that face of yours in time for breakfast, we'd better get going."

"Yes, dear."

"Folly!" Mrs. Duncan was rather ostentatiously consulting her dictionary as the couple turned away. "That other word there means danger. Let's just go as far as the notice and see what we can make out from there. I'm not going on, I don't know about you. Couple of young idiots." She had turned to make sure that the Adamses were safely out of earshot.

"Not all that young," said Marian. "Not him at any rate."

"No, they're an odd pair, aren't they? I can't think what they see in each other."

"But one so seldom can," said Marian. What in the world had she seen in Mark? Glamour? The young idol coming down from his pedestal? Charm, of course. All that charm that she had seen, after their marriage, lavished so generously on everyone but herself. But then, was there, had there ever been anything underneath that charm? Was it not, really, when she started searching for what should have been there, for the real Mark (who, she now saw, had never existed save in her own mind)—was it not then that he had begun to turn away from her? Had the twins not really been a pretext for an escape he had already been longing to make? The twins, themselves a kind of miracle, when you thought of Mark's insomnia, his crowded days, the pills he must take . . . all the excuses he used to make for avoiding her.

She would never forget them, those nights when she lay awake, waiting for Mark to come up, to come to her, and then, at last, heard him—and heard him quietly opening the door of the little spare room across the hall. She could remember—it was horrible now—lying rigid, biting the sheet to stop herself from calling out to him.

All over now. Far away and long ago. And Mrs. Duncan saying something. "I beg your pardon?" said Marian.

"I said"—patiently—"that I must check up on that story of his about Rhodes."

"Rhodes?"

"Lindos is on Rhodes."

"Oh. You must think me absurdly ignorant, but you see I only came on this tour at the last moment."

"And anyway we don't go to Rhodes, not having wings." Stella's voice made them turn with a pair of starts. "You're up early, Mrs. F., but you're going to be late for breakfast just the same. If it's anything like last night, there'll probably be a maître d' waiting for us with a whip."

"Loathsome phrase," said Mrs. Duncan.

"Sorry I'm sure," said Stella. "It isn't given to everyone to go to Roedean."

Mrs. Duncan's enraged expression made it all too obvious that the shot had gone home, and Marian was relieved to hear Cairnthorpe's cheerful voice hailing them from the corner of the road. "Hi! Ladies, breakfast is served. Sorry about the early call," he went on, as they hurried downhill towards him, "but it was the only time the desk could manage. We're a bit on sufferance here, as you have probably gathered."

"I'll say," said Stella.

"What's the news this morning?" As so often, Marian found herself hurrying into the gap left by Stella's rudeness.

"Not too bad. Well, not all that good either. Poor Hilton's under sedation. And I'm afraid we're going to be without a guide this morning. Mike's got to look after the police formalities. But they *are* just formalities, so far as I can make out. There seems no question but that we'll be able to go on to Sparta tomorrow. It's luck—if you can call it that—that we were booked in for another night here anyway. But I feel badly about your missing what Mike would have to say about Epidaurus and Tiryns."

"Never mind," said Marian. "I bet you know quite a bit yourself."

"Robert Graves." Stella's voice was scornful.

Cairnthorpe, who had flushed with pleasure at Marian's remark, turned on her with sudden venom. "On the contrary," he said, "Pausanias."

Stella yawned. "Who's he?"

"If you care to listen, when we get started, you'll find out."

"I hope you've learned to manage the microphone." Stella had the last word.

David Cairnthorpe had learned to manage the microphone. When they had all found their places in the bus, with its three gaping empty seats, he stood up to speak to them. "Good morning, ladies and gentlemen. I'm sorry to say that owing to yesterday's most unhappy accident, Mike cannot be with us today. But I know you will all be relieved to learn that Mr. Hilton is as well as one could hope and that the police have agreed there is no reason why this disaster should affect your tour. We leave, as planned, for Sparta tomorrow, but for this morning I am afraid you will have to make do with me as guide instead of Mike. Our driver, Andreas, has promised to slow down when we come to any place of interest, and I will do my best to stand in for Mike's splendid spiel. And that reminds me"—he turned, with a surprisingly charming smile to the driver—"Andreas bids you *kalemera.*"

It was to a relieved chorus of *"Kalemera,* Andreas," that they started out on their morning's excursion. "Tiryns first." Cairnthorpe was mastering the technique of swaying to the bus' movement. "I like to think that Heracles was born there. Of course you all know about the twelve labours he undertook for that rather tedius King Eurystheus, and quite a few of them happened here in the Peloponnesus. That is, when he wasn't off chasing the Queen of the Amazons or looking for the golden apples of the Hesperides, beyond the Pillars of Hercules. Which may or may not have been Seville oranges from beyond the straits of Gibraltar. But have you heard the theory that the labours were, in fact, a good deal more practical— or even political—than the myths let on? That when he killed the Lernean hydra, for instance, he was actually draining the marsh over there?" He pointed out of the window. *"Hydra*'s the Greek word for water," he explained.

"Then what was that Nemean lion he killed?" asked Mrs. Duncan. "The leader of the opposition?"

He had an engaging laugh. "There you have me, I'm afraid. And, luckily for me, here we are."

After Mycenae, Tiryns was, at first, disappointing: just a mild protuberance in the surrounding plain, with its disconcertingly adjacent prison, to which Cairnthorpe had, rather uncomfortably, pointed and drawn a sharp unintelligible Greek comment from Andreas, the driver.

Mrs. Adams hung back as they made the usual slow, awkward descent from the bus. "I don't believe I'll bother," she said. "I'm a bit tired after yesterday."

"Nonsense." Her husband's tone was surprisingly brisk, for a honeymoon. "It gets better as you go on, I expect."

"It does indeed," said the professor. "You'd better come, Mrs. Adams. And it's not much of a climb either."

In the end, they left the Adamses still arguing, and straggled after Cairnthorpe, in the familiar fits and starts of passing and repassing, as, one after another, people dropped out to admire a flower or take a picture. Turning to look back at the car park they had left, Marian saw a small red car pulling in beside their bus. "That looks like our friends from yesterday," she said, as two young men emerged briskly.

"Friends?" Stella's temper had not been improved by breakfast, when they had shared a table with Mrs. Duncan and the professor, and he had talked exhaustively about Greek birds.

Marian turned away from her impatiently and found Mrs. Duncan at her elbow. They exchanged the tolerant glances of the middle-aged over the temperamental young and moved onward, by silent consent, together. Doing so, Marian suppressed a quick pang of guilt. Miss Oakland at Jobs Unlimited had stressed that Stella should be protected from outside contacts. Well, she thought, Stella seemed to be able to protect herself pretty adequately. She had fallen back, on some pretext, and was walking, now, ostentatiously alone at the very rear of the party.

"Prickly young thing." Mrs. Duncan's eyes had followed Marian's.

"Yes, poor creature. She's had a hard time, I think." Marian had meant to end the discussion there but could not help an amused exclamation as she saw yesterday's two young men catch up with Stella and, apparently, attempt to engage her in conversation.

"Good-looking." Mrs. Duncan was watching too. "In rather a Greek kind of way, had you noticed?"

"No." It was true, she realised. "But I do see what you mean."

"Like a Greek with European top dressing," Mrs. Duncan summed it up. "You'll probably have your hands full fending off the local talent when we get out into the wilds."

"I should think she could take care of herself." She did not mean to expatiate on the precise nature of her relationship with Stella and was relieved to find that they had come to the top of the site and that Cairnthorpe was already speaking, rather inaudibly, against the wind.

"Hopeless," Mrs. Duncan summed it up. "Let's read it up in the guidebook afterwards. I'd rather save my strength for Epidaurus anyway. Now that's a place I really do long to see. It's why I came on this trip, as a matter of fact. You can have Delphi—we did that from my cruise, and a very exhausting day it was—but I've always wanted to see Epidaurus. Here"—she settled herself on a patch of flower-sprinkled turf—"come and have a second breakfast with me. I don't know about you, but I could do with it after that travesty of a first one." She opened her capacious bag and produced a small hoard of chocolate and biscuits. "I saved the biscuits from the plane." She unwrapped the cellophane packet and put it carefully away in her bag. "You never know when you'll need a little something. Pretty soon we'll have learned to live off the country. I mean to go shopping in Nauplia this afternoon, after I've done the Palamede. Do you want to come too, by the way?"

Teach Stella a lesson in good manners? Why not? "Yes, I'd like to."

"Good. Looks like we're on the move again."

Tiryns, like Mycenae, it seemed, had had its secret postern and concealed spring, and Cairnthorpe, leading them through an arched tunnel greasy with the wool of centuries' sheltering sheep, admitted with an engaging honesty that he had no idea what it had been used for. "Storage, perhaps," he suggested. "But no one knows, and what with the shepherds using it through the ages there wasn't a thing left as evidence." Wisely, he did not pause in this darkling spot, with its inevitable memories of yesterday's tragedy, but hurried them back into the sunshine. "And now for Epidaurus." He led the way down towards the bus, and Stella rose from a lump of rock to greet Marian.

"I hope it was worth it." Her tone held almost an apology. "I decided I couldn't be bothered."

"We're all a bit tired this morning," said Marian. "You got rid of your followers all right?"

"Followers?" Stella looked puzzled, then laughed. "Oh, them! No trouble at all. Their English! You should have heard it. But you were quite right, Mrs. F. They were the ones from Mycenae. What d'you bet we meet them at Epidaurus, too?

The red car was still parked beside their bus, but its occupants had vanished somewhere up the hillside. Marian looked around. "What happened to the Adamses?"

"Oh, didn't they catch up? They meant to. After a brief matrimonial discussion, they decided unanimously that it would be a pity to miss a single bit of a trip that cost so much. Or rather he decided, and she agreed—unanimously."

"They must have missed us up top somewhere. There's much more to it than it looks. I'm sorry you didn't see it."

"Never mind," said Stella. "There will be plenty more."

It was their turn to move forward in the slow, inevitable queue and climb the high step of the bus. Andreas was waiting, as usual, with a beaming smile and an outstretched hand for any lady who needed help. Cairnthorpe was already in his seat, counting them in. He turned round, as the professor appeared, last and hurrying. "Is that the lot?"

"No." It was a chorus. "The Adamses aren't back yet."

"Oh, dear, nor they are. I thought they stayed behind here."

"Miss Marten says they changed their minds."

"Blast," said Cairnthorpe, winning the sympathy of half his flock and shocking the other half. He turned and made gestures to Andreas, who grinned his comprehension and leaned obligingly on the horn.

"Horrible noise," said Stella.

"But useful," said Marian. "Look!" Two small, distant figures had appeared at the top of the hill and were waving with what must be accepted as apology.

"I'm sorry, ladies and gentlemen." Cairnthorpe looked at his watch. "But we'll just have to wait for them."

"Tedious." From the seat behind Marian and Stella, Mrs. Spencer voiced the feelings of the whole party. "But not your fault," she added fairly.

"Thanks." Cairnthorpe coloured. "While we wait, has anyone any questions?"

"Yes." It was the schoolmistress called Pam, egged on by her companions, who occupied a whole block of seats in front of Marian and Stella. "Where's the fountain of Kanathos?"

"You've been reading your guidebook." Cairnthorpe's colour rose a little higher. Then he laughed. "Mike would tell you about it so much better. The fountain of Kanathos, ladies and gentlemen, is the one where Hera used to bathe every spring and thus renew her virginity. I believe the Greek guides make a good deal of play with the story. Well, you can see its possibilities. . . . But in fact, the difficulty is that no one quite knows which spring it was. Otherwise, no doubt, there would be special spring-time conducted tours."

"You can just bet there would be," said Stella. "This way for the fountain of eternal virginity." To Marian's relief it was Mike's voice she was imitating, not Cairnthorpe's.

"Yes." He entered into the spirit of the thing. "Like the monastery on Rhodes you read about—the one women go to"—he paused, but then went bravely on—"when they want a child. You can imagine what a time the guides have with that. But luckily it's way up on top of the mountains, so they just make their jokes and drive by."

Stella laughed. "With a bunch of disappointed tourists. And talking of driving, here come the Adamses."

"At last," said Cairnthorpe, and leaned over to open the door for the couple, who climbed in brimming over with apologies.

"We met such a charming pair of young Greeks up there," explained Mr. Adams, "that we quite forgot the time."

Their guidebook was in Greek," said his wife. "It all seemed quite different. Ooh, dear"—she was working her way down the silent aisle—"have we kept you all waiting? I'm ever so sorry."

"What I would like to know," said Stella, *sotto voce,* as the bus started to move, "is how they talked to those 'charming young Greeks,' who couldn't get beyond "beautiful miss' with me."

Chapter 6

MARIAN WOULD always remember Epidaurus as the high point of that disastrous tour. From the moment that they filed out of the bus into a pine-scented grove, she felt the special quality of the place and felt it, too, begin to take effect on the rest of the party. The Adamses, who, she suspected, had spent their time at Tiryns in one of those first, terrifying quarrels of married life, were arm in arm again, her fake blond curls snug against his shoulder. The loud voices of the schoolmistresses hushed suddenly as a cuckoo called, somewhere away among the trees.

"It's a short walk," Cairnthorpe explained. "They've very sensibly kept the car park away from the site. We come back to the café over there, so anyone who gets exhausted can always come on ahead, but I doubt if you will want to. I've always felt there was something special about Epidaurus. The Greeks knew what they were doing when they made it into a place of healing." He had told them, in the bus, about the cult of Aesculapius, the great healer, who was struck down by Jove for his temerity in bringing the dead back to life, but finally became immortal himself, his shrine a kind of classical Lourdes.

"Except they seem to have been much more practical about it," said Stella, as she and Marian set off side by side through the grove. "I mean, you just go to Lourdes and pray for a miracle, don't you? While here you really got some treatment."

"Exactly." Cairnthorpe, who was just ahead of them, turned eagerly to agree with her. "It was a kind of psychoanalysis, when you come to think of it. If you were ill enough, the priests actually let you sleep in the sacred site, and then, in the morning, discussed your dreams with you."

"Oh, God," said Stella. "Freud. I bet the journey did them as much good as anything. And getting away from home."

"Very likely. That must always have been part of the point of pilgrimages, mustn't it?"

"A change is as good as a rest," put in Marian.

"Mike would tell us there was a Greek proverb for that," said Stella.

"Or if there wasn't, he'd undoubtedly make one up," agreed Cairnthorpe. They turned a corner of the path. "Well, here's the theatre. Is it worth the pilgrimage, Miss Marten?"

"I wish you'd call me Stella." Cross tone contradicted friendly words. "It's ridiculous for us all to be so formal with you and calling Mike 'Mike.'"

And, "Well worth every step of it," said Marian. "May we call you David?"

"I wish you would." He moved forward to the centre of the theatre and began to explain about its amazing acoustics. The schoolmistresses were already hurrying up the tiers of seats ready to hear him strike a match from the bottom.

"I'll take their word for it," said Stella. "What do you think, Mrs. F.?"

"I think it's the most heavenly place I ever saw. Let's find a quiet corner and just enjoy it."

It was easier said than done, since two other parties were already scrambling up and down the great amphitheatre, but they settled at last in two of the surprisingly comfortable stone seats. "Heavenly sun," said Stella. "There's that cuckoo again. I wonder if the professor will see his wet-winged warbler or whatever it was? Lord, didn't he go on at breakfast?"

"I found it very interesting," said Marian.

Stella laughed her short, surprising gurgle. "*Touché*. And apologies. Not your fault if he talks a blue streak to you and treats me like something out of kindergarten."

"Oh, but. . . ." Marian began to protest, but was laughed down.

"I believe you hadn't even noticed. Really, Mrs. F., you're incorrigible. Do you honestly think he goes round imparting all that information to every stray female he meets? If you ask me, he finds you a good listener. Fatal!"

Fatal indeed. How often, in the past, had she sat, interminably listening as Mark made up his own mind about a new act. And her reward at the end? A quick pat on whichever bit of her came handy, a loving phrase and a dive to the telephone for one of those equally endless talks with his manager. Sometimes, bitterly putting herself to bed while the eager voice went on and on in the next room, she had wondered what Mark wanted with a wife. . . . Strange how this tour was bringing back the old, unhappy memories she had managed to keep battened down for so long. But perhaps time they were faced?

The cuckoo called again. Stella was sitting moodily throwing little stones at a spiky plant that grew out of the seat below them. "Don't." Marian put a gentle hand on hers. "It might spoil David's demonstration."

"Oh—" Stella swallowed the next word. "Sorry, I'm sure." She reached for a more friendly tone. "I really *am* sorry. To tell you the truth, I had rather a hellish night."

"Oh, dear. . . ."

"A dream for Aesculapius. Do you think if I take him an offering he'll send me the interpretation?" She stood up and began to climb the few remaining tiers to the top of the theatre. "Come and help me look, Mrs. F.?"

It was, unmistakably, an olive branch, and Marian followed with an inward sigh of relief. "What kind of offering?" She caught the spirit of the thing.

"Goodness knows." Stella threw back her head. "Oh, Aesculapius, send me a sign."

"You'll be expecting an eagle next," said Marian.

"No, no," Stella corrected her. "That's at Delphi. And, don't you remember, the professor says they're vultures anyway."

"Very disillusioning." Marian thought that Stella must have been paying more attention at breakfast than she had let show. "How about a pine cone?" She bent to pick one up.

"Pretty." Stella took it and tossed it thoughtfully in the air, caught it again, then threw it away with one of her swift violent gestures. "But I must find my own thing."

"Of course." They had reached a path that circled the top of the amphitheatre, then curved down its side. "Shall we go down this way? I find steps a bit exhausting. Specially downwards." Marian turned to lead the way. "I must say I rather wish I hadn't said I'd go up to the Palamede with Mrs. Duncan this afternoon. Do you want to come? It's eight hundred and something steps apparently. There ought to be quite a view from the top."

"There certainly should. But, no, thanks. I thought I'd go swimming. It's the last chance till Aegina."

"You'll be careful? It looks rough to me." But it was a relief to have Stella's afternoon so pleasantly taken care of.

"Don't worry. I swim like a dolphin. It's my talent. But why struggle up all those steps with that dreary Mrs. Duncan if you don't want to? If you ask me, you'd do much better to rest for a while. You look as if you'd had about the same kind of night I did. Why don't you do that, and then when I get back from my swim, we could go down and explore Nauplia?"

"I'll see." Marian was touched by the suggestion. "I must admit it's tempting."

"Just to be alone," said Stella. " 'And the sound of the hollow sea.' "

"It's marvellous, isn't it?" Marian recognised the mis-quotation with pleasure. "I'd like to come back to Nauplia sometime, on my own." Or with the twins, went her mental parenthesis. "And come over here every day."

"Why not stay here? There's a tourist pavilion, I believe."

"Is there?" Marian was surprised at this sudden bit of local knowledge.

"Somebody said so. Oh, look! There's my offering." Stella bent down to pick a flower from beside the path. "What is it, do you think?"

"I haven't any idea." Marian examined the exotic-looking flower with careful ignorance. "I'm afraid I'm as bad at flowers as I am at birds. But it looks like a bee."

"Yes, doesn't it? One of those ingenious dodges plants get up to, I suppose. Anyway, I'm sure it's just the thing for Aesculapius. Isn't there something a bit magic about bees?"

"You have to tell them things, I know."

"I'd hate to try it."

Thank God, thought Marian, she's cheering up. "Me, too," she said. "Oh, look." They had emerged from a thicket of pine and blossoming Judas trees at the bottom of the slope. "They're moving."

"This way for the museum," said Stella.

But when they reached the museum, it was to see the tail end of a crocodile of blue-clad Greek schoolgirls vanishing into the entrance. "Blast," said Cairnthorpe for the second time. "Perhaps we'd better go down to the site first."

"By all means." Mrs. Duncan was positive as usual. "We wouldn't be able to hear ourselves think with all those noisy children in there." And then, "Where in the world did you find that?" She was looking with apparent rage at the flower in Stella's hand.

"On the path above the theatre. Why? Do you know what it is?"

"Of course I do. It's a bee orchid. A Very Rare Flower." She gave each word capital letters. "And if you pick one, it doesn't flower again, or seed again, for seven years."

"Well," said Stella reasonably, "I suppose if it didn't flower, it would be bound not to seed."

"Intolerable ignorance," said Mrs. Duncan between her teeth.

"I believe they aren't quite so rare here as they are in England." Cairnthorpe intended, obviously, to pacify.

"They will be if every ignorant tourist who sees one picks it," said Mrs. Duncan.

Suddenly, amazingly, David Cairnthorpe lost his temper. "Personally, I think people are more important than plants." In anger, he went white, rather than red, and looked a good deal older. "Of course"—belatedly he remembered his position—"you're perfectly right, really."

"Ecology and all that," said Stella cheerfully. "Consider me in disgrace. So help me, I won't pick so much as a buttercup from now on."

"There aren't any buttercups," said Mrs. Duncan, and Marian saw David and Stella exchange delighted glances behind her back.

The schoolmistresses had clustered round to examine the rare flower, and they all moved forward together, while Marian found herself between Miss Gear and Miss Grange as they straggled along the path to the rest of the site. "Lot of nonsense," said Miss Gear.

"Well, I don't know." Miss Grange was judicious. "She had a point, of course, but there was no need to make it so rudely. And just as that poor child of yours was looking a bit better, too. Frankly, Gear and I have been a bit worried about her. Looks a bit schiz to us."

"Schiz?"

"Ophrenic," helped Miss Gear. "We're psychiatrists, Grange and I. You can't help noticing things when you're in the trade. Of course, we'd rather die than interfere, but we've been wanting a word with you, just to offer help if it's needed."

"Has she anything to take?" asked Miss Grange.

"Take?"

"Medicine." Miss Grange was patient. "Tranquillisers.

You take them, don't you? If you don't mind my mentioning it."

Marian found that she did, very much. Her every instinct was to evade this merciless, courteous probing, but they were walking along in a kind of loose crocodile through the ruins, and escape would be impossible short of open rudeness. "Sometimes," she admitted.

"But you're perfectly normal," said Mrs. Gear heartily. "Anyone can see that. I'm not so sure about Miss Marten."

"Very odd changes of mood," said Miss Grange.

"We'd thought about drugs, but the symptoms aren't right."

"I'm glad to hear it." Marian's tone was dry to the point of fury, but the two women were too happily launched on what was obviously a well-tried discussion to notice.

"Naturally," agreed Miss Grange. "But there could be worse things." The idea appeared to give her pleasure. "You don't share a room with her?"

"No."

"That's something. We thought you couldn't be when we saw her sitting up to all hours last night, drinking with that young Greek."

"Greek?" This, Marian realised, was what they had wanted to tell her.

"That Mike, who's so handsome and knows it. We rather hoped she wouldn't get—well, too involved with him."

Divided between being worried and annoyed by this doubtless well-intended bit of information, Marian was still searching for the right reply when Mrs. Spencer spoke briskly from behind her. "Mr. Cairnthorpe's started to speak. Poor man; it's the least one can do to listen."

"He wants us to call him David," said Marian gratefully following through fallen pillars to where Cairnthorpe had taken his place on a block of stone to talk of the cult of Aesculapius and the various theories about the mysterious circular ruin, or tholos, that they were about to see. She found she could not listen, could not care what the curi-

ous labyrinth under the circular building might or might
not have been used for. Serpents . . . a very small mino-
taur. . . . Cairnthorpe was enjoying himself, she thought,
and so had Miss Gear and Miss Grange been. Disgusting,
but true. "Power corrupts." . . . "We murder to dissect."
. . . Quotations buzzed in her head like angry bees. . . .
Bees. She would not let two prying women spoil this heavenly place for her. She moved a little away from the crowd,
sat down on a stone, closed her eyes and tried to make
her mind a blank. The cuckoo called again. . . . The
magic of the place was coming back. . . . Let them go,
the thought grew in her mind, unexpected, like a green
shoot in the desert. Let it all go. The remembered bitterness; the terrible feeling of inadequacy, of failure; those
desperate months after Mark left her, when the only
thing that kept her going, kept her out of the enticing
river, was the fusillade of kicks with which the unborn
twins reminded her of their existence. And now—she lay
back in the warm sun—now she must let the twins go, too.
They had been her life for eighteen years, and then, at a
nod, at a ring of the doorbell, at a brief cable from
America, they had left her. Grown up. Gone. And in
their place a great emptiness. A great peace? Why had
she never thought of it like that before? And the cuckoo,
singing of spring.

"Daydreaming?" A heavy hand fell on her shoulder.
"You'll miss the museum if you don't get a move on."
Miss Gear and Miss Grange had found her again.

This time it was Stella who rescued her. "There you
are!" She hurried towards them, picking her way nimbly
among fallen stones. "Come along, Mrs. F., you have
to help me make my offering to Aesculapius. In the tholos,
don't you think? It's the most magic place."

"The museum closes at one." Miss Gear looked at her
watch.

"We wouldn't keep you for anything." Stella's voice
was honey-sweet.

"The carvings are supposed to be quite extraordinary,"
said Miss Grange.

"So is this place." Stella watched them move away, then

hurry to catch up with the rest of the party, talking eagerly together as they went. "Prying old pussies." She reached down a hand to pull Marian to her feet. "What did they say about me?"

"They don't think you're on drugs." Marian surprised herself with her answer.

Stella threw back her head and laughed. "Handsome of them. I'm just mad, I suppose. Come on, Mrs. F. Let's behave like the lunatics we are and leave our gift for Aesculapius."

She insisted on climbing down into the ditch that surrounded the little circular building and working her way into the centre of the labyrinth, where, she reported, coming back flushed and smiling, she had left her offering on a most suitable stone. She looked, Marian thought, rather like a child who knows it has been naughty, as she reached up a hand to be helped out of the deep ditch. "Now, Mrs. F., must it be the museum, or shall we cheat and go and have an ouzo? I liked the look of that café."

"So did I." Marian was hardly paying attention. When she had thought of Stella as looking like a child, she had just thought of children, not of her own children. I'm free, she thought. I'm free of them. "Wait a minute." She stopped. "Oh yes, the café, of course. But I want to leave something, too." She looked about her. No pine cones here. Only the ordinary flowers. "It's the thought that counts." The trite words mocked her. She opened her bag. "Stella?"

"Yes?" Something in her tone had brought Stella's attention full on her.

"Could you bear to go back and leave something for me?"

"Of course." But she looked swiftly up from the photograph Marian handed her. "Your children? Are you sure, Mrs. F.?"

"Quite sure." Don't let her say anything. Not anything at all.

Stella said nothing. She climbed quietly down into the ditch again, vanished into the labyrinth, and returned, after a surprisingly short time, to hold up a hand once more, for help, and say, "They're there, Mrs. F. Under my flower. Aesculapius has had a good day. And now, how about that drink?" She took Marian's arm, in a curiously protective gesture. "I think we could get across this way."

They could. Emerging from a lower entrance to the site, they found Andreas leaning comfortably against his bus. *"Kalemera,* Andreas," said Stella.

"Kalespera, kyria," corrected Andreas, with his beaming smile.

"Crushed again," said Stella cheerfully, leading the way up to the shady terrace of the café. "Ouzo, Mrs. F.?"

"Yes, but it's my turn." She handed Stella her purse. "You're spoiling me abominably, bless you. I can't tell you how restful it is to have you do all the coping."

"Even to making your offerings for you?" Stella had ordered their ouzos from a hovering waiter by the simple expedient of raising two fingers and uttering the one essential word. "Seriously, Mrs. F., are you sure about that? The photo? I could easily go and get it back for you?"

"You're an angel." Marian was enormously touched. "But it's not absolutely the gesture it may seem. I've got a bigger one at the hotel, and the negative at home."

"Oh, well, in that case." Stella smiled and raised the glass that had just been set before her. "To Aesculapius," she said. "And to your children. Do you feel like telling me about them, Mrs. F.?"

"Yes." Surprisingly, now, she did. "They're a bit younger than you. Eighteen. Twins. They took their A levels last summer. Not very brilliantly, I'm afraid. Personally, I thought the school pushed them too hard. . . . That they'd have been better to have taken another year. But I suppose that's the kind of thing mothers do think. Anyway, they were mad to get out of there. . . . They'd had it, they said. And of course no university would look at them: not with their A levels."

"And they wouldn't try again?"

"No." In retrospect, the bitter, useless argument seemed a complete waste of time and strength. "Viola had had

all kinds of holiday jobs. Well, she wanted the money."
Had Mark been mean on purpose?

"For clothes." Stella was quick. "I suppose she's pretty,
like you?"

"Me!" Marian did not quite like the sound of her
own laugh. How many light-years was it since Mark had
called her beautiful? And of course Viola had wanted
clothes, had gone to work in a big shop where she could
get them cheap. Easier to talk of Sebastian. "My son
never meant to go to college," she explained. "He said it
was the tyranny of the mediocre. Or something like that."
How long ago it seemed.

"So they got jobs?"

"Yes." How they had hated them. "Not very good ones,
I'm afraid. And—different firms. They'd never been separated. They were wretched. But what could I do?"

"Nothing. They're grown up, aren't they? Eighteen.
Voters."

"I know. But just the same. . . ."

"You feel it's all your fault, of course." Stella's voice
was tolerant. "Really, mothers! And then?" She was a
child, wanting the end of the story, and Marian, who had
meant to, found she could not deny it to her.

"Their father sent for them. He's in America, doing
very well. He left me before they were born."

"Rugged."

"Well, it was a bit. But he supported us. Lavishly. For
a while."

"Past tense?" Stella was too quick for comfort.

"It got less . . . and stopped when they left. They
don't know, of course. I can tell from their letters."

"They're happy?"

"Blissfully. So far." She looked anxiously into the
future. "He lives a very interesting life," she said fairly.

"And you were just little mother?"

"I suppose so. My fault."

"Your job."

"Actually"—Marian was amazed to find herself ready
to probe this old, old wound—"I didn't do it. Not properly.
I failed them when it mattered most. At least that's what I

think now. You see, when we met—their father and I—I was just going up to Oxford. It was September." Could the sun really have shone all the time? It certainly had at the fête in that green village whose name she never could remember. She had gone, unwillingly, with her mother, who was on a committee—several committees? Certainly, having got her there, her mother had abandoned her to drift round, aimlessly, from stall to stall. And then—Mark. Mark, coming suddenly up from behind her and taking her hand. "All alone, beautiful?" Trite enough words, if one had ever thought of oneself as beautiful.

But from Mark, beauty personified, they had been the incantation that woke the sleeping princess. The mad, ecstatic weeks that followed were preordained from that moment. Why was it only now, recollecting it all, for the first time, in tranquillity, that she recognised that Mark, that day, had not been his normal self? He had been ruffled—frightened? Certainly in what he would later, in their brief married life, refer to as "one of my states."

"So you never got to Oxford?" Stella's question brought her back from the lost, baffling past.

"Well, yes, actually, I did." She was proud of the casual note she struck. "When he left me, next spring, they offered me my place again. We lived in Oxford," she explained. "My mother helped with the twins. I think half the time they didn't know which of us was which."

"So they had a mother *and* a grandmother, and your heart is bleeding because they were so deprived! Honestly, Mrs. F., I would have thought you'd have had more sense. No grandfather?"

"No. That's why my mother was so glad to have us. The trouble was, all our ideas were so different. I read Dr. Spock." She said it as if it explained everything.

"I know. And your mother believed in discipline? They sure must have been two crazy mixed-up kids. And if you say it's all your fault, Mrs. F., I'll clonk you. You managed to raise them, didn't you? You didn't leave two tiny bundles in the snow anywhere? You did the best you could. Right?"

"I suppose I did."

"Then, for God's sake, stop suffering about it. You've done your best; now you can relax and enjoy yourself. You never thought of remarrying?"

"No." After Mark? But was that all the explanation? "I was too busy. I got quite a good degree," she explained. "Mother thought I ought to go on to a D. Phil."

"Mother liked having the twins." Stella summed it up with her usual devastating accuracy.

"I suppose so. Well, she was better with them than I was. It was hell for a while after she died."

"When was that?"

"Halfway through my D. Phil. Suddenly. Overstrain, the doctor said. She hadn't told me anything."

"So you're carrying round a great load of guilt about that, too? Honestly, Mrs. F., you need a psychiatrist."

"Miss Gear and Miss Grange?" She looked quickly round, but their party must still be in the museum. "No, thanks. I've tried that. To tell you the truth, they were the ones who made me feel it was all my fault."

"Don't they!" Something absolutely basic had changed in Stella's face. She leaned forward eagerly. "Just because you're what they've got to work on, they want to find the root of all the trouble in you. And if it's not there, why, then they plant it and sit back and watch it grow. I'll tell you about me some time, Mrs. F., and that's a promise. But just now I can see the others coming down like a wolf on the fold. Shall we nip back and do a quick tour of the museum while they're having their elevenses? The carvings really are rather super, I believe."

"But the museum will be closed." Marian looked at her watch. "More lunch than elevenses. I imagine David will be rounding us up pretty smartly to get us back to the hotel."

"Oh, Lord, yes. I don't quite imagine them tenderly keeping it warm for us. Well then, let's just go sit in the sun, shall we? And listen to the cuckoo?" While they were talking, she had competently paid and tipped the young waiter. "Remember, Mrs. F., 'Privacy is the last resort of the human spirit.' "

"The trouble is, it's true." Marian rose and walked

across the café's terrace with her, wondering what it was that nagged at her about Stella's quotation of Miss Grange. Or had it been Miss Gear?

Lunch was cold, and so was their welcome. David Cairnthorpe, marshalling them like an anxious hen, urged them straight to the ground-floor cloakrooms at the hotel and so into the dining room. "The staff must have their afternoon off," he explained. "It's all my fault. We took a bit longer than was planned."

"And enjoyed it enormously." Marian followed him into the dining room. She had meant to ask Stella, in the re-laxed atmosphere that had followed their talk about the twins, which of the various combinations of table partners she looked on as the lesser evil, but David Cairnthorpe had rounded them up so smartly for the bus that she had never got round to it. She hung back a little to let Stella lead the way and was surprised and pleased when she crossed the floor to join Cairnthorpe and the professor, already settled in an inconspicuous corner.

"May we?" Stella pulled out a chair as she spoke.

"Delighted." Cairnthorpe was on his feet to help Marian. "I'm sorry you two missed the museum."

"We'll have to come back someday." Marian was impressed that he had noticed. For all his casual air, he must be contriving to keep a closer eye on his charges than she had realised.

His next question confirmed this. "And what are your wild plans for the afternoon?"

"The Palamede for me. Mrs. Duncan says we have to climb more than eight hundred steps."

"And I'm swimming," said Stella. "But I still wish you'd rest, Mrs. F. Don't you think she looks tired, David?"

He flushed with pleasure at her use of his first name but refused the gambit. "It's too fine a day to stay indoors. Just don't be tempted to go to the other fort, Mrs. Frenche, I'm told they're dynamiting there. You're a strong swimmer, I hope, Miss—Stella? It's pretty rough down in the bay."

"I know. That's how I like it."

Eight hundred steps were too many. Mrs. Duncan seemed made entirely of muscle and went up without pause, while Marian panted after, stopping obstinately from time to time to admire the developing view. But Mrs. Duncan pausing irritably a little higher up to wait, made it impossible to enjoy it. At last, reaching a corner where the steps turned away from the sea for what looked like a last steep ascent, Marian jibbed. "You go on." She settled on a convenient parapet. "I've had enough. I'll wait here."

"But we can't be any distance from the top."

"I don't care." At least, alone, she could enjoy such view as she had.

"Oh, very well." No doubt Mrs. Duncan was delighted to be able to go at her own ruthless pace. Marian sat peacefully for a while, enjoying sun, and breeze and small birds the professor would have identified. She had picked, in fact, a point with a sea view and ramparts rising steeply behind her on the landward side and wondered whether to climb a little higher, in the hope of a landward prospect. But the backs of her legs, already aching, decided her against it. This was quite far enough for anyone not made of steel like Mrs. Duncan.

She settled herself more comfortably on the warm stone and gazed out to sea, her mind, after the morning's self-exploration, a blessed blank. Would this be how an Elysian spirit would feel? Her eyes closed, for a moment, then flashed open at the sound of falling rock. A huge boulder from the wall above roared past her and dropped, in a scurry of smaller stones, over the cliff edge towards the sea.

She was on her feet, shaking all over. It had been a very near thing indeed. An accident? She looked upwards. No sign of life, but then the tourist who had dislodged the stone might easily not have realised the near disaster he had caused. Or, face it, if he had, he might easily have lost his nerve, hurried to join his party and pretended that nothing had happened.

The wind felt cold. Two accidents in two days were too many. It was more of a relief than she liked to admit

when she saw Mrs. Duncan appear, unmistakable in the
navy blue windbreaker that was so like Marian's own, and
come hurrying towards her down the steps. Was she going
to tell her about the boulder? She rather thought not. If
she had made an uncomfortable connection between it and
Mrs. Hilton's accident, so might other people, with deplorable effects on the morale of the tour. And of course,
she told herself briskly, it was all her imagination.

"Sorry to have been so long." Mrs. Duncan shouted
down to her. "It's fascinating up there . . . much bigger
than you'd think. You ought to have come."

I'm afraid I've had enough as it is," Marian said. "Look,
don't wait for me on the way down. I'll be happier going
my own pace. But what's the matter?" Mrs. Duncan was
looking back over her shoulder. Something, surely, had
disturbed that calm self-confidence. Her heartiness rang
just a trifle false. Marian was not the only one who had
had a fright.

"Oh, nothing." And then, "Well, actually, something
rather odd. You'll think me a fool, but I could have sworn
someone was following me round up there. It's all so
complicated. You know, with bastions and different levels
and bits of wall you don't quite understand. I'm not an
imaginative type." She was proud of it. "But I actually
found myself keeping away from the edges of things.
Ridiculous. That's partly why it took me such a long time
to get back. There was a way I didn't want to come. Oh,
well, all nonsense, of course. But if you really don't mind,
I think I will go on down. What I need is an aspirin and
a good rest." She had settled it to her own satisfaction
that she was suffering from nervous fatigue. "These coach
tours are a bit more tiring than one expected, aren't
they?" And then, "You won't tell the others, will you?
I'd feel a fool."

"Of course not." Marian was glad she had kept quiet
about her own experience. Mrs. Duncan was close enough
to panic as it was. But at least she had started down
without waiting for an answer. Marian followed her at a
slower pace, unable to help casting a nervous, backward
glance from time to time. Absurd, of course, to think of

the Ancient Mariner and wonder if some frightful fiend might close behind her tread. But impossible not to be pleased to meet a cheerful party of young Greeks, grinning and greeting her as they started on the long climb. After that, she felt able to go as slowly as she wanted.

Reaching the hotel terrace, she forgot her own fright in the scene she found raging. Stella, dripping wet in bathing suit and towel, stood furiously in the middle of a small, exclamatory crowd. Mike was there, shirt and trousers soaked, his normally curly hair clinging to his head, and Cairnthorpe, dressed and dry, both looking shaken and, Marian thought, angry. "Absolute nonsense." As Marian approached, Stella's voice rose towards hysteria.

"You were pretty far out," said Cairnthorpe. "I was coming back along the cliff path. I admit I was a bit worried."

"But at least you didn't come diving in like a bloody Leander." Stella turned from him to Mike. "And you know as well as I do you nearly drowned me with your damned 'lifesaving.' Quite the little hero, I don't think. When I want to be rescued, I'll let you know."

"A million apologies." Mike was shivering in the sea wind "But how was I to know you swim like a Nereid?"

"I should have thought you could bloody well have seen. I was no more in danger than I am now. And a lot less than I was when you were hauling me into shore. I'm only grateful you didn't decide to knock me out and do it that way." She turned angrily away from him and saw Marian. "Oh, glory be. Come and tell these idiots I'm not a suicide type." And, back savagely to Mike. "Oh, yes, I know that's what you were thinking. And you couldn't be more wrong. I'm going to do something before I die."

"I bet you are," said David Cairnthorpe surprisingly, and got a grateful look. "Anyone can see you're far too obstinate to think of suicide," he went on.

"Yes." Marian was surprised and pleased at the perceptiveness of this. "But one thing I do know is that it really is suicidal for you two to be standing about in those wet clothes. Come on in and change."

"Thanks," said Stella, as they turned towards the hotel,

and then, "Blast." She had seen Miss Gear and Miss Grange, on a farther level of the terrace obviously taking in everything avidly. "Now we're for it." She wrapped her large beach towel more closely round her and led the way into the hotel.

Marian, following, was aware of Charles Esmond gazing, all eyes, at Stella and of his mother saying something angry and being ignored. Safe in the privacy of the lift, she asked, "Were you very far out?"

"No farther than I usually go. I really can swim. But I suppose it was stupid of me." She admitted it now. "I'd told David I knew what I was doing. I never thought Mike would turn up and get in a flap."

"Gallant, I suppose." Marian was remembering what Miss Gear and Miss Grange had said about last night's tête-à-tête.

"Bloody stupid," said Stella. "He nearly drowned me."

"Aren't you overworking that word a bit?" Marian stepped out as the lift door opened.

"Bloody?" Stella laughed. "Sorry, Mrs. F." And then, warmly, "My God, you do do me good. I'd never have gone out so far if you'd been being anxious on the shore. But then, you wouldn't have been. How was the Palamede, by the way?"

"Exhausting—and a bit odd. But you need some dry clothes. I'll tell you about it later."

They were soon on their way down into the little town, since Stella insisted that she was none the worse for her experience. "Just a bit full of Aegean. What I need's an early ouzo, so let's go and find one out of doors somewhere. Away from all this. . . ." Her descriptive gesture had included both the hotel and its guests.

It was pleasant to be off on their own, working their way down steep, narrow lanes, full of hens, cats, children and the occasional motorbike. As always, in Greece, plants bloomed lavishly out of petrol and olive-oil tins, washing flapped in the breeze, rich smells of cooking teased the senses. Stella was leading. "Well, now—" she had stopped to admire a huge, fisherman's pullover—

"what happened to you Mrs. F., while I was being half drowned by our Mike?"

At what point in the walk had Marian decided not to say anything about the boulder that had so nearly killed her? She was not sure, only certain that she was right to keep entirely quiet about it. Mrs. Duncan's experience, which was odd enough in all conscience, she described as casually as possible, making a point of Mrs. Duncan's request for secrecy and feeling guilty as she did so.

"Funny," said Stella. "I wouldn't have thought she was the type to imagine things."

"No, nor would I." Marian was able to say this with perfect truth. She was afraid she did not think Mrs. Duncan had been imagining things. The two of them had been wearing similar windbreakers. A cold shiver ran down her spine. What was the matter with this tour? And then, nonsense, she told herself briskly, if one middle-aged lady could imagine things, why not two? But that boulder had been real enough. . . .

"Come on, Mrs. F.," said Stella. "You need that drink. And so do I." She laughed. "What a busy afternoon. And what do you think Gear and Grange would say about it?"

"I hate to think." Marian was relieved at least that she had not communicated her own feeling of disquiet to her companion.

Chapter 7

THEY SETTLED, at last, at a small waterfront café, where Stella procured their ouzos with her usual cheerful competence, then paid up fast at sight of Miss Gear and Miss Grange striding purposefully towards them along the quay. "I don't know about you, Mrs. F."—she rose to her feet—"but I suddenly find myself simply longing to get back to the hotel."

Marian laughed, drank up and rose, but it was too late. The two psychiatrists were upon them. "None the worse for your experience, I'm glad to see," said Miss Gear. And, "Drinking again," said her expression.

"We're going to walk back round the point," said Miss Grange. "Why don't you come, too? I'm sure you need a good warm-up after that fright."

"Which fright?" asked Stella. And then, "I'm fine, but Mrs. Frenche has been right up the Palamede. I'm taking her straight home while she can still walk." She watched the two sensibly clad figures move briskly away. "I hope that was right?"

"I should say so. Actually, I don't think I'll do the point, but would you like to sit here a while and go on your own?"

"No, thanks. Being rescued is damned hard work. I wouldn't mind a sit before dinner either. Let's just hope it's edible." Stella stepped quickly back on the narrow pavement as a small red car nosed past them on its way to the quay. "It's those men again."

"So it is." Marian could not muster much interest. "I suppose one's liable to meet the same people over and over."

"At least it makes a change from our own lot. Let's get into dinner early tonight and try and bag us a couple of spare schoolmistresses. I have the most sinister feeling that Gear and Grange will be laying for us with a lot of casual questions. Which I am not prepared to answer."

Marian had meant to seize just such an opportunity for some casual questions of her own, not so much about the "drowning" episode as about Stella's tête-à-tête with Mike the night before, but found she could not bring herself to do it. Best let sleeping problems lie?

In fact, Miss Gear and Miss Grange did not appear until dinner was nearly over. Sitting, as planned, with Meg and Pam, Marian and Stella had a good view of their hurried entry to the dining room. Both looked white and shaken, and Miss Gear had a professional-looking bandage round her head. "What on earth?" said Stella.

"I can't think." Marian watched the two psychiatrists join David Cairnthorpe and the professor, talking hard. "Some kind of accident, poor things." Another accident?

They learned after dinner that this was an understatement. Walking round the cliff path, the two ladies had heard an explosion above them and had huddled against the cliff just before a shower of rocks came hurtling down. One of them had struck Miss Gear a glancing blow on the head, and it had taken Miss Grange some time to get her back to the little town and find first the police and then a doctor. The police had been understandably appalled at this accident and had sent at once up to the site of the fort. "They're going to report back here." Miss Grange had settled Miss Gear in one of the hotel's uncomfortably modern armchairs and was standing over her protectively.

"And here they come," said David Cairnthorpe. "And, Mike, too, thank goodness." Mike had vanished after the scene with Stella and had not appeared for dinner.

He had been dining, he explained now, with a friend of his who was a member of the police, and had come along at once when he heard of the accident. "Most regrettable." He and the policeman told the story between them. The workmen up at the fort had been impatient to get their day's stint finished—they were working late as it was. "Our people are not very sensible about explosives," explained the policeman. In short, they had tried to hurry things up, to make one explosion do the work that should have been spaced out over two. "The usual foreman was off sick," Mike pleaded in extenuation.

"They gave themselves a terrible fright." The policeman's English was almost as good as Mike's.

"Not half such a bad one as they gave us," said Miss Grange dryly. "None of them was hurt, I take it."

"Mercifully, no. They send their most abysmal apologies to you two ladies." The policeman turned to Cairnthorpe. "The doctor's bill will of course be taken care of by the town of Nauplia. Is there anything else we can do to make amends?"

"We'll have to see," said Cairnthorpe. "It depends rather on whether these two ladies feel up to coming on to Sparta tomorrow. If not, I will have to ask you to find them somewhere to stay here in Nauplia."

"That's no problem," put in Mike. "Of course the ladies will wish to rest. I have already had a word with the manager here. In these circumstances, he says, a room will certainly be available for them."

"Two rooms," stipulated Miss Grange.

"No need," said Miss Gear. "An early night tonight and I'll be right as rain tomorrow. It was only shock." She spoke with a rather daunting professional competence. "Not concussion."

"We'll see in the morning." Cairnthorpe did his best to end the discussion.

But, inevitably, it continued as word of this new accident spread through the party. More and more of them gathered in the steel and plastic bar, where the drinks might be expensive but the atmosphere was reassuringly that of any bar anywhere. Safely settled in a corner, Marian and Stella watched the Adamses order scotch and soda. Mrs. Adams' colour was high already. "They've been quarrelling again," said Stella.

"Poor things." Inevitably, Marian's thoughts harked back to all the humiliations of her own "honeymoon."

"Oh, God," went on Stella, "here come the Esmonds." Charles Esmond was making towards them when his mother took him firmly by the arm and steered him over to join the Adamses. "Mother's good boy," said Stella with relief. And then, as Mike appeared in the doorway. "Do you know, I think I'll make an early night of it. OK?"

"Of course." Marian, who had not finished her own drink, sat where she was and watched Stella pass Mike with a quick exchange. A drink offered and refused? Or an assignation for later? Impossible to tell and disconcerting to find herself worrying a little about Stella.

"May I join you?" She looked up with a pleasure that surprised her at the sound of Edvardson's voice. "And may I get you another drink?" He had his own in his hand.

"No, thanks, but do sit down. Stella's gone to bed, and I've got a touch of the grues." And how odd, she thought, to find herself admitting this to a total stranger.

"Well, no wonder," he said cheerfully. "Anyone would think we'd got the Furies on board that bus. But, tell me, Mrs. Frenche, did you see anything of the sinister figure that is supposed to have chased after Mrs. Duncan this afternoon?"

"Oh, dear," said Marian. "I did hope she wouldn't mention it."

"She thought it was her duty." The professor's voice was dry. "After what happened to Miss Gear and Miss Grange."

"Ridiculous," said Marian, and changed her mind. She

had actually been tempted to tell him about the boulder but did not want to risk his using that tone about her.

"Yes." He looked round the crowded room. "Panic makes strange friendships." The Esmonds were still with the Adamses, and Mrs. Duncan was talking, low and quick, to Mrs. Spencer.

"Panic?" The word gave her an odd twinge.

"Pretty close to it. I'm glad I'm not in young Cairn-thorpe's shoes."

"He's doing very well, don't you think?"

"Yes." His laugh was the youngest thing about him. "Much better than I expected. In every way." He was facing the window, with its view of windy terrace. "I was backing young Mike to get your ewe lamb, but I suppose she doesn't take to being half drowned." And then, seeing her puzzled look. "She's out walking with him. Cairn-thorpe, I mean, not Mike."

"She said she was going to bed."

"Well, maybe she was, until she met Cairnthorpe. And maybe not. They all lie when it suits them. Well"—cheerfully—"who doesn't?"

"They?"

"The young. Which, thank the Lord, you and I are not. There"—he laughed again—"I knew that would get you bristling. If you were a cat, you'd spit."

"Lucky for you I'm not."

"Yes, indeed." And then, with an abrupt change of tone, "Now, forget about that child you're mothering, and tell me about yourself for a change and why you're doing it."

"Money," she said, and knew it for an inadequate answer.

"Useful stuff." He rose politely as Mr. and Mrs. Adams came over to join them, and Marian felt a pang of disappointment.

The Adamses were in need of reassurance. "The little woman wants to cut the tour," explained Adams. "What do you think, sir?"

"Nonsense," said the professor, and Marian could only hope that he was right.

Next morning's was another early start, but Miss Gear and Miss Grange appeared at breakfast, Miss Gear pale, composed and quite ready, she said, for the long drive over the mountains to Sparta. It was their turn to sit over the wheel at the back, but the two schoolmistresses who sat in front of Marian and Stella volunteered to change places with them, rather to Marian's dismay. She had enjoyed the two girls' cheerful comments on everything they saw, from overloaded donkeys to equally burdened women, and was not at all sure about Miss Gear and Miss Grange as substitutes.

Mike was back in command of his microphone and had begun the day by announcing briefly that Mr. Hilton was already on his way back to Athens. "They will fly home today." Presumably the reference was to Mrs. Hilton's body. It made for a rather muted start, and he did not speak again until they were passing the acropolis of Argos, where, he told them, forty-nine brides had killed their grooms, on their father's instructions. The fiftieth, he explained, spared hers and became the mother of Perseus. After that, he was silent again until the bus was nearly at the top of the long zigzag climb up through the mountains, when he made them all turn round for one last look at the promontory of Nauplia, stretched like a lion with its paws out to sea.

"I'm glad to be away from there," said Miss Gear, and Marian, thinking of all the events of the day before, could not help silently agreeing with her. She was not so sure, now, that she wanted to go back to Nauplia.

In the window seat, Stella was very quiet, as, indeed, she had been all day, so that Marian could not help wondering if she had had a late-night session with David Cairnthorpe or, indeed, with Mike, or just another bad night and, possibly, nightmare. But today there were no jokes about Aesculapius. She sat hunched together, gazing broodingly out at the changing views forward and back as Andreas swung the bus round one dizzy hairpin bend after another. It was impossible not to remember the two psychiatrists' remarks about her changing moods, and it was tiresome to have them sitting just in front, very probably aware of silence behind them and drawing their own conclusions.

They stopped for midmorning coffee at Tripolis, a depressing modern city, flat on its plateau. "You will find no classical ruins here, ladies and gentlemen," Mike warned them. "The town was ruthlessly sacked by the Turks when they retook it during our War of Independence."

"Having been just as ruthlessly sacked by the Greeks when *they* took it." The bus had slowed down on entering the town, and even without benefit of microphone, Cairnthorpe's voice came over surprisingly clearly. It was not the first time that Marian had wondered a little about how guide and courier were getting on behind the scenes. There had certainly been antagonism sparking in the air after Mike's "rescue" of Stella, but then that was understandable enough. She had been frightened and angry herself.

The bus had stopped, and the usual half-polite, halfpushing queue was working its way off. "Don't let's bother with coffee," said Stella as they finally emerged. "It's too early for ouzo; I don't think I could face that sickly Turkish—and I'm sick of Nescafé. I don't know about you," she went on as they walked up the undistinguished street. "But I'm getting claustrophobia. Shall we opt out tomorrow?"

"We could, couldn't we?" The idea was tempting. And they were to spend two nights in the hotel at Sparta, so as to take what Mike called a coachman's holiday to Mistra. "No classical ruins," he had explained. "But every other kind."

"Do let's." Stella spoke with surprising vehemence. "I know Mistra's supposed to be full of marvellous Byzantine stuff, but it gives me the willies just to think of."

"Oh? Why?"

"Didn't you know? There was a frightful massacre there after the last war. You *must* know about the Communist rebellion, Mrs. F.?"

"Well"—shamefacedly—"I do remember reading something. In a life of Churchill, would it be?"

"Very likely. He flew out at Christmas, 1944, to try and settle it, but it went on for ages just the same. There was a time when the Communists held most of southern Greece." Stella looked up and down the placid street. "Odd to think this might be a Communist country now."

"Thank God it's not. But what happened? At Mistra, I mean."

"The Communists holed out there in the ruins after the tide had turned. They'd"—she paused for a moment—"they'd been pretty bloody. I suppose they knew what was coming to them. The army moved in, and hunted them down, like animals. I don't know where they buried them, but I'm sure the place must be haunted. God! Isn't this a dump! Shall we try one of the side roads?"

"Might as well." Marian, too, had seen Mrs. Duncan just ahead and sympathised with Stella's wish to avoid her. But it was too late. Mrs. Duncan had turned, seen them and waved.

"Blast," said Stella.

"Never mind. It must be about time we got back anyway."

Mrs. Duncan, too, had found nothing of interest in Tripolis, and they turned to walk back towards the centre of the town together. "Not even any shops." She dismissed the place as hopeless. "I like to get a small souvenir everywhere we stop—something characteristic for choice—but what on earth would one get here?"

"A Turk's head?" suggested Stella. "But it would be even more awkward to pack than your corn dolly." Mrs. Duncan had bought one of these when they stopped by the Corinth Canal and had been tenderly carrying it about ever since.

"Gruesome child." Mrs. Duncan shuddered. "Interesting to have young Cairnthorpe come out so strong about the first massacre, wasn't it?"

"Massacre?" Marian was thinking of what Stella had told her about the Communists at Mistra.

"Oh, he was too polite to use the word, with Mike right in front of him, but that's what it came down to. When the Greeks took Tripolis for the first time. In the

War of Independence they boast about so much. They were the ones who began the killing and sacking, and don't let anyone tell you different."

"What about Mistra?" Stella put in, adding still further to Marian's confusion.

"Oh, that first rebellion in the eighteenth century," said Mrs. Duncan. "That was doomed from the start. Poor things," she added perfunctorily.

"What about Mistra?" asked Marian. "And what first rebellion?"

"It was the Russians," Mrs. Duncan explained. "They liked to stir things up down here, to keep the Turks busy. They sent a naval force to encourage a Greek rebellion in 1770 and then changed their minds and took it away again just when the thing had got off the ground. Meanwhile, the Greeks had taken Mistra, and, no doubt, killed off a lot of Turks while they were at it."

"And then the Turks came back," said Stella, "retook Mistra and killed the lot of them. It's been in ruins ever since. Not my idea of a lucky place."

"But beautiful." Mrs. Spencer had joined them from a side turning. "It really is worth seeing, Mrs. Frenche." She fell into step beside Marian, leaving Stella and Mrs. Duncan to follow behind. "Come with me if Miss Marten doesn't want to."

"Thanks." It was a useful reminder that whatever one said in the bus was inevitably heard by the people in the seat behind. Well, Marian thought, it was not too bad to have Mrs. Spencer and the professor there. But she had a question for Mrs. Duncan as they all came to a halt beside the bus. "How on earth do you know so much about Greece?"

"I read it up, of course, before I came away," said Mrs. Duncan. "It's a waste of money to come on holiday without doing one's homework first."

"Crushed again," said Stella *sotto voce* as Mrs. Duncan reached up a hand to be helped on board by Andreas.

"But you know all about it too." Marian had been impressed by this.

"I did it at school. God knows why. Or why I remember, come to that. But one couldn't help feeling sorry for those poor Greeks. They were always being used as tools by the great powers. So called. Really it's no wonder they're a bit difficult by now."

"It's time we got back into the bus," said Mrs. Spencer.

It was a long way from Tripolis to Sparta. "We should have stopped later." Stella sounded cross.

"Yes." Marian had thought this, too. "But did you notice? Mike had friends to meet there."

"Oh? Did he?" Stella was profoundly uninterested.

Mike, in fact, was being surprisingly quiet. He used the microphone once to warn them to look out for the first views of the great snowcapped mountain of Taygetus ahead, then lapsed into a silence that was shared by most of the passengers. From time to time, someone would point out a round threshing floor or a donkey almost invisible under its load, and necks would crane in that direction, but mostly they all sat silent and, Marian thought, a little glum, a little anxious, even, as she was?

"I suppose we don't get the lecture on Sparta till this afternoon," said Stella.

"He's got a right to be tired, poor thing." They were far enough back in the bus by now so that there was no chance of Mike's overhearing what they said. And yet, once again, Marian found herself embarrassed by memories of what the two psychiatrists had told her. Had Stella and Mike, in fact, sat up again last night making it up after that odd "drowning" episode? But the professor had seen her with David Cairnthorpe. It was all very confusing. . . .

"I hope he's exhausted." Stella's cross remark cast little light on the situation.

Their hotel, which they reached in time for a late lunch, was on a hill outside Sparta, and Mike picked up the microphone as the bus slowed down to urge them to eat quickly and leave their unpacking until the evening. "Leonidas and his gallant three hundred and all their history await you, ladies and gentlemen:

> *Go tell the Spartans, thou that passeth by,*
> *That here, obedient to their laws, we lie.*

I will tell you more about them this afternoon, when we will visit first the museum, where you will see Leonidas himself, and then the shrine at Amyclae, where Apollo killed his beloved Hyacinthus by an unlucky throw of the discus." He jumped lightly down from the bus.

Stella stood up and stretched herself. "Do you know. I believe he actually likes the Spartans."

"Why not?" asked Marian.

"A dreary lot." Stella dismissed them with one of her angry shrugs.

"Sordid." Charles Esmond had been standing in the gangway, trying to catch her attention. "I wonder if we'll get to see the theatre where they whipped the Spartan boys."

"Better than actually sacrificing them," said Professor Edvardson from behind.

"Come *on*, Charles," said his mother. "You're holding everyone up."

"After you." Charles made way gallantly for Stella, then fell in behind her, leaving his mother and Marian to follow as best they might. Letting Mrs. Esmond go first, Marian thought she looked far from pleased at this development. In fact, she was not altogether happy about it herself. And she was appalled, when she and Stella entered the dining room ten minutes later, to find that they were the last and that the two inevitable vacant places were at the Esmonds' table.

Received with little enthusiasm by Mrs. Esmond, and with too much by her son, Marian wondered whether this could possibly have been arranged between him and Stella. If so, it seemed extraordinary, considering that Stella, with her gift for inventing nicknames for their fellow tourists, had so far christened him, aptly enough, "Mother's Boy." Now, however, she was listening patiently while he expatiated on the rigorous training of Spartan boys, the swims in the icy Eurotas, the barrack life, the blood brotherhood of youths who lived and died together.

"You're as bad as Mike," she said at last, but quite tolerantly. "You don't care that I'd probably have been exposed on Taygetus."

"Of course I care." He put far too much feeling into his voice, and Marian felt his mother stiffen beside her and rather suspected herself of doing the same. How very tedious if Mother's Boy was going to develop a first passion for Stella, who, wretched girl, seemed to be egging him on. How many conquests must she make? Yes, now she was agreeing that they should all four visit the museum together. "I want you to see the Leonidas," said Charles eagerly. "I came here with a party from school— a long time ago," he hurried to add. "But our classics master was super; he told us"—he coloured, aware of his mother's baleful glance—"oh, all kinds of things."

It was an uncomfortable afternoon. There seemed no way of avoiding the unwelcome foursome, and Marian, listening to Mike explain that the Spartans had not gone in for noble buildings like the Athenians, hence the paucity of remains, rather wished that she had pleaded headache and stayed behind. She could not like Mrs. Esmond, to whose company she was reduced, nor could she like the sight of Stella so obviously leading young Charles on. After having been silent to the point of glumness all morning, Stella now seemed in tearing spirits and was really, Marian thought, flirting outrageously. She was aware of Mrs. Esmond's increasingly irate reaction to this and also of an occasional glance from Cairnthorpe. At least Mike seemed to be taking no notice. Presumably, the relationships between the tourists were Cairnthorpe's affair, not his, and he was busy singing the praises of Spartan simplicity.

"They lived their own life, ladies and gentlemen, keeping themselves to themselves and avoiding foreign trade as much as possible. The simple life was their ideal."

"Yes." Professor Edvardson spoke from behind them. "The simple life, with paederasts and slaves."

"Oh." Marion turned to him. "Tell me!"

"And a secret police," said Edvardson. "You look tired Mrs. Frenche." They were straggling after Mike from the museum towards the bus. "Can I persuade you to cut the rest of Sparta? It's honestly not worth seeing, still less hearing about from that young enthusiast." His dismissal of Mike was firm but kind. "I thought I'd walk up the Eurotas a bit and see what I could see in the way of birds. How about coming, too? It's pretty there, and quiet."

"Oh, I'd love to." She spoke impulsively, then directed a quick, anxious glance to where Stella was walking between the two Esmonds, her entire attention fixed on Charles. "I don't know," she began doubtfully.

"I do. Let it work itself out. The best thing you can do. She'll be bored to tears in a day or so."

"That's what I think," said Marian gratefully. "As long as his mother. . . ."

"I don't suppose she'll actually take a hatchet to your protégée, though I admit she looks as if she'd like to. You tell them, and I'll tell young Cairnthorpe. We should be back about the same time as they are. I don't suppose your ewe lamb can get in much trouble between now and then. No sea here, at least."

Of course he had heard about yesterday's "rescue." One must face it, gossip would spread like wildfire in a group like this. No doubt there would be gossip, too, if she went off for the afternoon with the professor. For some curious reason, this decided her to do it, and she caught up with Stella to announce her decision.

"Really? You don't want to see the grove where the hyacinths grow?" Stella looked disconcerted and pressed her hard to change her mind, but having made her decision, Marian was firm. It would do them both good, she thought, to have an afternoon apart, and, after all, it was Stella who had initiated it by involving them with the Esmonds. Besides, with luck, a whole afternoon of them might well hasten the cure the professor had predicted.

She found him wonderfully pleasant, easy company. He talked a good deal about birds and insisted on her trying to see a golden oriole through his binoculars. "It's no good"—she handed them back to him—"I can never use these things. It's like opera glassses at the theatre. Hopeless."

"You like the theatre?"

"Love it."

"So do I." He turned out to be surprisingly knowledge-able. "I always make a point of going when I'm in London," he explained. "And a few weekends a winter in New York. You can have the movies," he added.

She laughed. "I don't want them." Would the twins miss going to the theatre with her? Why should they? They had their father and all his glamour. They would be going to first nights, no doubt. "I'm sorry?" She had missed something the professor said.

"Not important." He had a kind face, she thought, in its craggy way. "Lonely people like you and me do a lot of our talking to ourselves anyway."

"Are we lonely?"

"Of course we are. And I often find a crowd makes it worse."

"Well." She thought about it. "Certainly a crowd like ours. Goodness, I'm grateful to you for getting me away for a while." She paused to listen to the rush of the Eurotas, a surprisingly lively river.

"It's a pleasure." It was formally spoken, but he sounded as if he meant it, and she felt an unaccustomed warmth steal through her. It seemed a long time since her company had been a pleasure to anyone.

"Thank you." She too spoke formally, and yet it did not come out quite as she had expected. "They're a curious mixture, aren't they?" She hurried it a little.

"Not quite the usual," he agreed. "I come on these tours—ones like this—all the time," he explained. "And I must admit some of our fellow travellers baffle me a little. Those Adamses, for instance. They're the most unusual honeymoon couple I ever saw."

"They've had some ups and downs," she agreed. "But then—" She stopped. She had been going to say, "One does," but—had he ever been married? Extraordinary how little she knew about this man who was now holding out a helpful hand to get her over a rough bit of the path.

"Oh, yes." He was no fool. "I've been through it. I know what you mean. She died."

There was a little silence, then, "Children?" asked Marian.

"No. That's why I come on tours like this. Look! There's a bee-eater."

"Where?" She recognised the subject as closed.

"They nest in riverbanks," he explained. "Look! Down there. Come on, try the binoculars. I'll adjust them for you. There." He put a steadying hand on her shoulder as he held the glasses to her eyes. "How's that?"

"Oh, my goodness!" Was the exclamation for the tiny, fast moving bird or for the extraordinary, long-forgotten surge of emotion that rose to his touch? "I wish I'd brought my glasses." She was babbling and knew it. "I'm all right for a museum, but when it comes to birds, I really need them."

"You're not nearly so bad as poor Mrs. Esmond." The professor had clearly felt nothing. His voice was matter-of-fact as he put the binoculars back in their case. "I can't think why she doesn't wear glasses—or even contact lenses. Have you noticed?"

"No." Her voice was under control again.

"She can't read a notice or recognise a face at more than a few yards. I think it's partly why she clings so to that unfortunate son of hers."

"Much better to wear glasses." Marian wondered whether, if he had seen her with Sebastian and Viola, he would have thought she clung to them.

She was considering the temptation to talk to him about them, when they heard a shout from behind and turned to see Stella and Charles hurrying along the little path by the river. "Caught you," said Stella. "We got bored with old Sparta, too, and Mike very kindly dropped us off at a convenient corner. Seen any good birds, Mrs. F.?"

"No, alas. I was just telling Professor Edvardson. I'm not much good without my glasses."

"Just like my mamma." Charles looked guilty.

"She'll be all right," said Stella bracingly. "That competent Mrs. Spencer is looking after her."

"Amazing woman," said the professor. "I don't know how she endures this heat in those woollies of hers."

Stella laughed. "I call her 'Twinset a Day.' I suppose nobody told her about the Greek climate."

"It's odd about her," began Edvardson, but Stella interrupted him.

"I say, what's that?" She pointed at a black and white bird, large enough so that even Marian could see it hovering over the water, its long beak at the ready.

"Good God!" said the professor. "It's a pied kingfisher. I never saw one before, but it must be; look at the way it's watching the water! There it goes!" The bird had plunged swiftly into the water and emerged with a small, wriggling fish. "I do congratulate you, Miss Marten." He turned to her warmly. "I never even hoped to see one of those."

After this stroke of luck, their slightly odd quartet proved more of a success than Marian had feared. Stella seemed genuinely interested, now, in what Edvardson could tell her about the birds she spotted with her sharp eyes, and Charles was apparently prepared to take an interest in anything Stella cared about. Enjoying themselves, they walked farther than they realised and got back to the hotel a good deal later than the rest of the party, to find Mrs. Esmond sitting like a thundercloud in the hotel lobby.

She looked at them muzzily for a moment, then her eyes focussed on Charles. "There you are at last." It was the scolding tone appropriate for a small child. "I was beginning to be afraid of another accident."

"Another?" asked Stella. "You don't mean—"

"No, no," Mrs. Esmond interrupted her rudely. "Nothing new. But you could hardly say this was a lucky tour, could you? Not so far. That poor Miss Gear's beginning to look like death. I thought she was crazy to insist on coming today. Much better to have stayed at Nauplia the way that guide suggested." Marian had noticed that she refused to call Mike, or anyone else, by his first name.

" 'Hermes means death,' " quoted Charles light-heartedly. "Do you think the old thing's going to kick the bucket?"

"Charles!" said his mother.

Chapter 8

STELLA WAS very late down that evening. Marian had finished her ouzo, and the rest of the party was already in the dining room, when she appeared. "Sorry, Mrs. F., we'd better go right in, hadn't we? I wonder what our doom will be tonight."

In fact, they found a whole empty table awaiting them and dined, restfully, alone. Miss Gear and Miss Grange were absent, and an empty place at another table caught Stella's eye. "Mike's out on the tiles again. Let's be devils and have a bottle of wine, Mrs. F. After all, I missed my ouzo." She caught a hurrying waiter's eye and ordered white Demestica. "I warn you, in a night or so I'm going to make you try the retsina."

"That pine-flavoured stuff? Must I?"

"You'll like it in the end. It's like oysters—habit-forming. And good for you. What about Mistra tomorrow, by the way?" She had waited until the wine arrived, been poured and happily sipped. "Do we still think we'll opt out?"

"Well—" Marian had been thinking about this. "What

117

do you think? Granted that we went off on our own this afternoon, perhaps we ought to go along tomorrow? Unless you'd really hate it, that is."

"Ghoulies and ghosties?" She thought about it. "Better to face them, perhaps? And Mistra does sound quite a place. Besides, what would we do here all day?"

"I know." Marian had thought of this, too. "We could go back to the museum, I suppose, but really, Sparta—"

"Just so. I gather most coach parties stay in Mistra itself. Mrs. Spencer did last time. She says it's a heavenly little place—the new village, that is, with a stream flowing out of a tree. I'd quite like to see it."

"In that case—"

"Yes." Stella settled it. "Let's go. And let's go to bed early, too. I don't know about you but that long drive this morning has left me stiff as a post."

"Me, too." Marian could not help wondering if Stella, after seeing her to her room, meant to go down again and keep some assignation—With Charles? With Mike? With David? She flicked an apologetic mental backward glance at Miss Oakland and Jobs Unlimited. But how in the world could she chaperone Stella's every waking minute? Besides, it had been coming over her since halfway through dinner, that old, horrible feeling from which she had been free since Epidaurus. Why, suddenly, here, should she be plagued by the illusion that hostile eyes were upon her? She drank the last of her wine quickly. Absurd to give way to it. But, "Let's go for a quick stroll—" Anything to get out of this crowded, hostile room. "And then bed."

Since it was only a few miles from Sparta to Mistra, they made a blessedly late start next morning, but even so Miss Gear and Miss Grange failed to appear. The long drive the day before had, predictably, been too much for Miss Gear, and Miss Grange was staying behind to nurse her. "Poor thing," Stella summed it up as they settled in the bus. "What on earth's going to happen to her when we go over the mountains tomorrow?"

"Let's hope a day's rest will fix her." They were over the wheel today, and Marian was grateful for Stella's insistence that she take the most uncomfortable seat by the window.

"We're in luck," Stella pointed out. "There's hardly any driving today, and tomorrow we'll be on the back seat." She laughed. "It's really hopelessly unfair."

"But restful." The polite pushing and making way were tiresome enough, Marian thought, without an unspoken, perpetual battle for the best seats.

Mike had picked up the microphone. "Ladies and gentlemen, today you are on your own. I am a classical guide, and Mistra, as you doubtless know, is Byzantine. So—get out your guidebooks, or ask Mr. Cairnthorpe to tell you about the emperor who was crowned here in Mistra and which of all its many churches are worth visiting. He will tell you, I have no doubt, about Christ the Pantokrator, and no one needs to tell you about the views of the valley and of Taygetus, for they are there for all to see. But as your loving and devoted guide, I do beg that you will be careful how you go. It is a long time since they repaired the roads in Mistra." This was a joke; he waited for their laugh. "The walking is not easy. And when you get toward the top, watch yourselves; there are no guardrails there to protect the unwary. It is not a place to which I would bring my children." He beamed at them. "If I had any children."

The bus stopped outside a small café, where, Mike told them, they would all meet for lunch. "You are in luck. Most tours come from further; you have the place to yourselves, probably until about twelve o'clock. So, enjoy yourselves, my children." He jumped out of the bus, was greeted warmly by the heavy-jowled proprietor of the café and disappeared into its kitchen with him.

"Mike's got a friend in every port," said Stella.

"Poor Cairnthorpe." It was restful being so far back in the bus and able to speak freely. "I wonder if Mike warned him."

"It doesn't look like it." Cairnthorpe, too, had alighted and was already surrounded by a small crowd of eager questioners.

"At least he's got a proper guide," said Marian. "My Fodor only gives the place a couple of paragraphs."

"Never mind." They were out of the bus now, and Stella took a great breath of mountain air. "Why don't we just wander and enjoy ourselves, Mrs. F.? I don't know about you, but I feel unsociable today. And it's not going to break my heart if we never do see where that emperor was crowned."

"Nor mine." Marian was delighted at this outbreak of unsociability on Stella's part. The professor had already announced his intention of going right up to the fortress at the very top. "After all," he had explained from behind them, "it's a foothill of Taygetus. My first chance at the mountain birds. Who knows? If I'm as lucky as you, Miss Marten, I may even see a bearded vulture." He had not suggested that they accompany him, however, and had gone off with the long, loping stride of the practised walker.

"It looks as if we must have held him up a bit yesterday, poor man," said Stella. "He travels the fastest who travels alone, and all that."

"Yes," said Marian irritably, surprised at her own sense of abandonment. "Let's go." The Esmonds were on the other side of the group round Cairnthorpe, who was doling out tickets. "Get ours, would you, and let's get on ahead."

"OK."

Marian watched with amusement as Stella made her ruthless way through the crowd and collected the tickets. Charles Esmond, she could see, was watching, too, but helplessly. His mother was leaning heavily on his arm this morning.

"Mrs. Esmond's afraid of turning an ankle." Stella returned with two tickets and a mischievous grin. "Onwards and upwards."

They were quite high already, since the bus had been climbing steadily since they passed the small, comparatively modern village of Mistra, and Marian paused to admire the view across the olive-studded plain below. "Heavenly day," she said.

"Yes, but do come *on*, Mrs. F." The impatience in

Stella's tone was so out of proportion that Marian gave her a quick glance. "Well," said Stella in explanation, "you don't want one of the old tabbies for the day, do you?"

"I'm an old tabby." Marian fell into step beside Stella on the rocky path.

"You're a honey," said Stella, and then, "Oh, damnation."

"Hullo there." Mrs. Duncan was waiting for them at a turn in the street of grey, ruined stone houses. "Did you decide to go it alone, too? But you'll never get anywhere without the guide." She held out her own. "We mustn't miss the frescoes in the Perivleptos." She turned to lead the way, making it impossible for them to do anything but follow.

Aware of Stella simmering beside her, Marian found it hard to listen to Mrs. Duncan's competent readings from the local guide. She did notice the double-headed eagle in the Metropolis, where, it appeared, the last Byzantine emperor might or might not have been crowned, and she could not help enjoying the constant views out over the valley. The churches, Mrs. Duncan told them, had been carefully built so that in most cases a cloister or arcade would take advantage of this extraordinary vista.

"A vista from Mistra," said Stella, and got quick looks from both the older women for her bitter tone. But of course, Marian reminded herself, she must be remembering the bloody history of the place. She was broodingly silent for a while, and when they got up, at last, to the palace that loomed above the ruined streets of the town, she broke rudely into Mrs. Duncan's remarks about the unusual oriel windows. "I've had it! I'm going to pass out here in the sun."

"Not going on to the top?" Mrs. Duncan's voice was shocked. "Think of the views across to the heart of Taygetus."

"This is near enough its heart for me." Stella had found a patch of short grass among the high, grey-pink flowers that filled the palace yard, almost like sea in a bay. "We'll wait for you here. Right, Mrs. F.?"

"Right," said Marian, with relief. "It's so beautiful. . . ." She sat down on the grass beside Stella. "What's this extraordinary flower?"

"You don't know asphodel?" Mrs. Duncan sounded as if it were a crime of the first water.

"The Common Asphodel," said Stella.

"There's nothing common about it." Marian lay down so that she could look through delicate flowers towards blue sky. "Now I know what the blessed spirits felt like."

"You're lucky." Once again, Stella's tone reminded Marian of the Communists who had hidden here, among these bleak, waterless, ruined houses, and been hunted down. "Like animals," Stella had said. Horrible. Had they come up here, higher and higher, in panic-stricken flight, to plunge, at last, over the cliff edge beyond the palace?

She shivered in the hot sun but was silent. No need to remind Stella of this, if she was merely in one of the sullen fits Miss Oakland had predicted. They lay there silent and apparently peaceful for a while until a rising babble of sound warned them of the approach of the rest of the party.

"Oh, damn!" Stella sat up with a jerk. "What now?"

"Nothing," said Marian. "Just let them wash over us."

"Like this sea of flowers?" It was not the first time that Stella had surprised Marian by the almost psychic sharing of an idea. She lay down again. "Very well then. Let's lie doggo."

"Eternal sleep," Marian closed her eyes. "Like Cleobis and Biton."

"Horrible story." Mike had told it to them the day before. "Think of asking for the best thing for your children and having them killed. Honestly, Mrs. F., don't you think those Greek gods were a nasty lot?"

"Very." The story of the mother who had asked for the best thing for her sons had shocked Marian too.

" 'As flies to wanton boys, are we to the gods,' " quoted Stella surprisingly. " 'They kill us for their sport.' " And then, "Have you ever wished you were dead, Mrs. F.?"

"No." And then, "Yes." Impossible to lie about this. "The sin against the Holy Ghost. If you believe in all that." And then, "Here they come. I'm asleep." She rolled over on her face, burying it in the short, sweet grass, and Marian, feeling like a middle-aged fool, did likewise. They were a little way from the path, in a clear patch among the glimmering asphodel. No reason why anyone should disturb them.

Voices passed. Cairnthorpe, talking earnestly, and the schoolmistresses plying him with questions. As they moved away, a new group of voices took up the theme.

". . . Higher up." That must be Mrs. Spencer, but for a moment Marian could not think who the man was who answered her.

"Better spread out," he said.

"My feet hurt." That was Mrs. Adams, so presumably the man had been her husband.

"Fuck your feet," he said.

And, "Hush," said Mrs. Spencer.

As well she might, thought Marian, looking down a whole depressing new vista of the Adamses' honeymoon. "A vista from Mistra." Stella was very still and quiet beside her. Well, it was embarrassing to have put themselves in this position of unintentional eavesdroppers. They must be less visible from the path than she had realised; probably some piece of fallen masonry was just high enough to hide them. More voices: Charles Esmond, angry. "I tell you, I mean to go on to the top. You sit here, if you like, and I'll pick you up on the way down. And, by the way you've been limping on the wrong foot ever since we stopped to look at that blasted Pantokrator."

"Fancy your noticing," said his mother imperturbably. "Very well, go off on your wild-goose chase if you must. I just hope you find the little bitch and she spits in your eye." Alone with her son, Mrs. Esmond let her voice slip several degrees down the social scale.

"Good-bye." Charles's voice was both angry and farther off.

Now what? thought Marian. How intensely uncomfortable it would be for them all if Mrs. Esmond were to look about for somewhere to await her son and happen on them. But, thank goodness, here must be Cairnthorpe and the schoolmistresses returning to join her.

"You're not going up to the top?" Cairnthorpe's voice. "Not likely."

"Then come up to the chapel with us. It's only a step, and I believe there's another Pantokrator you might like to see. Extraordinary place, isn't it?" His voice was dwindling as he led his little party off in a new direction.

Silence again for a while, and then two men's voices speaking, by the sound of it, in Greek. Beside Marian, Stella stirred restlessly for a moment, then was still again. There were plenty more of their party still to come. Or had the others boggled at even this much of a climb? It was possible. There was a large indeterminate group of middle-aged ladies given to soft shoes, plastic macs and a habit of opting out and sitting on them at a fairly early stage of any climb. Marian rolled over and sat up cautiously.

"They've all gone." Instinctively, she spoke low. "Shall we move on a little? I wouldn't mind seeing that chapel David was talking about. If there really is another Pantokrator. I think they're magnificent. Why, Stella!" She looked down in amazement at her companion. "What's the matter?"

For a moment, she had thought that Stella's shoulders were shaking with laughter; now, horrified, she realised that it was silent tears that wracked her. She put a tentative hand on the shaking shoulder. "Do you want to talk about it, pet?" How strange to use Viola's endearment.

"No!" The voice came, muffled from between Stella's arms, which encircled her head. "No! But—please—you won't leave me, Mrs. F.?"

"Of course not. Gently now; gently. . . ." She kept her hand, comfortingly, she hoped, on the still-shaking shoulders and felt them gradually quieten. "Handkerchief?" She felt in her bag with her left hand and produced one of the large ones she found invaluable when travelling.

"Thanks." One of Stella's hands groped for it. Her voice sounded steadier. She raised herself just enough to use the handkerchief on her invisible face, then subsided again with a long sigh. "I'm so sorry, Mrs. F. I haven't done that for ages. The ghoulies and ghosties got me, after all. Didn't you feel it?"

"A little," Marian admitted. The trouble was, she felt so many things. Stella's hysteria had brought on a bout of her own horrors, and she could feel the cold sweat that meant the onset of one of her worst attacks, doubly unpleasant, somehow, in the hot sun. Passionately, desperately, she wished she was at home, safe in the London house, with Dr. Brown round the corner to tell her it was all nothing, all nerves. . . .

But she was here, on a Greek hillside, gold with sunshine, silver with asphodel, and the girl beside her needed help more than she did. No doubt Stella's explanation of her tears was part of the truth, but it was most certainly not the whole. But best, perhaps, to accept it for the time being? Thinking of Stella helped her own trouble. She was less certain, now, that hateful eyes were watching her from behind that gaping oriel window, that door opening on vacancy. All absurd. The sun was comforting; the cold sweat had passed. And Stella's shoulders had stopped shaking. Marian took her hand off her shoulder to open her bag. "I think Cairnthorpe and Co. are coming back." She could hear their voices from above. "I don't know about you, but I feel a wreck."

Stella turned over and sat up, showing a surprisingly calm face. "Thanks, Mrs. F. I said you were a honey." She gave back the crumpled handkerchief and pulled a mirror out of her bag. "You're fine, you always are, but I look like hell." She began an expert elaborate rescue operation on her face.

"You don't, you know." Marian was surprised at how little damage that dreadful crying bout had done to Stella's eye makeup.

"Hysterics," said Stella angrily. "I'm ashamed. You won't tell anyone. . . . No"—with apology—"of course you won't. Hullo, here comes the professor. I say! What's the matter?"

They both jumped to their feet, as Professor Edvardson came hurrying down the hill towards them. He had lost his hat and was carrying his binoculars by their broken strap. Everything about him spoke of crisis. "Where's Cairnthorpe?" he shouted as he approached. "I've been attacked."

"Attacked?" said Marian.

"Who?" said Stella.

"I don't know. I was quite close to the edge. I'd seen a blue rock thrush and thought I might even find its nest. I didn't hear a thing, but suddenly someone was trying to push me over. And, boy, was there some over to go." Telling it seemed to make him feel better. "I'd have been clear down in the valley by now."

"But what happened?" asked Marian.

"I guess I surprised him." The professor was pleased with himself. "I was in the army once. I still remember a trick or two they taught us. And he thought he had a pushover." It had shaken him more, Marian thought, than he would admit. "Very literally a pushover," he went on. "A long, long way down. Only I didn't want to go, so I walloped him one with my binoculars—broke the strap, dammit. Excuse me—" To Marian.

"Him?" asked Stella.

"I think so. Can't be sure, though; not when you girls all wear trousers, and the young men grow their hair. But if he was a girl, he sure had some muscles. We had quite a tussle there, for a minute. Then I guess he gave up. He got out of there so quickly I never did see more than lots of dark hair and blue jeans."

Instinctively, Marian looked at Stella. Dark hair and blue jeans. Absurd to be grateful they had been together all the time. But the professor was speaking again. "Where's young Cairnthorpe?" he asked. "I have to warn him, round up the party. It has to be a maniac," he explained. "No chance of robbery; not with me a goner down in the valley. We ought to get the hell out of here and report it."

"Here he comes." But Marian's heart sank at the thought of Mrs. Duncan, Mrs. Spencer and the Adamses, all, so far as she knew, wandering about on the upper reaches of the mountain. And Charles Esmond. Who had dark hair and was wearing blue jeans. Horrible. She listened quietly while Edvardson retold his story to Cairnthorpe and his horrified party.

"A madman," Edvardson summed it up. "It can't be anything else. I mean, why me? Not robbery. No reason. Don't you have any way of calling the others back?"

"How could I? Go out looking for them? No." He dismissed it at once. "It would only add to the risk. We'd best stay here, all together, until the others come back."

"If they come back," said Pam, and then burst into a nervous, apologetic giggle.

But she had voiced everybody's hidden fear, and it was a subdued and gloomy group that settled on stones and patches of grass, almost uncomfortably close round Cairnthorpe and Edvardson, who were still standing and canvassing possibilities.

"At least I could go down and get Mike," said the professor. "Was he planning to spend the morning with his friend at the café?"

"I don't know. He said he'd be there for lunch. But, yes." Cairnthorpe made up his mind. "I would be grateful if you'd go on ahead, Professor, and if Mike's not there, find someone who can understand your story—there's always your German. I'm afraid it means the police again, whatever happens."

"I'm damned sure it does," said Edvardson grimly. "That was no joke up there, believe me. Not by a long shot. And I'd like to have a look in the parking lot, as soon as possible, and see what else there is in the way of transport."

"Absolutely." Unspoken between the two men was the possibility that the attack had been committed by a member of their own party. "There's a second one, a little farther up," David continued. "You might take a look there if you get the chance. And watch yourself, going down." He thought about that for a moment. "I think someone should go with you. There are plenty of places among the ruins. . . ."

"Yes." The two men looked consideringly at the anxious group around them.

Their problem was obvious. Who was safe company? Jeans and dark hair covered about half the younger members of the party. Any one of the loose, inchoate group that had accompanied Cairnthorpe could have slipped away for long enough to attack the professor, who had, he had explained, been on his way back when it had happened.

Marian spoke up. "Miss Marten and I were together the whole time. I'm afraid we've just been lying here in the sun."

No need to say more. David Cairnthorpe's face cleared into obvious relief. "Then you're the ones to go down with the professor. And, perhaps, Mrs. Frenche, while he's reporting what happened, you could go and take a look at the other car park. Only, keep together, won't you? On the way down."

"We certainly will," said Marian.

Chapter 9

MIKE WAS not at the café but the proprietor turned out to speak very passable French. "Just as well you came," said the professor as Marian succeeded in establishing this. "I only had a year of French, and damn little good it did me. Tell him what happened, would you, and ask him to send for the police? Oh, and you might ask him where Mike went, too."

Jeans and dark hair again. But that was impossible. Marian put the question and learned that Mike had gone down to the hotel in new Mistra to make arrangements for another party. "He'll be back any moment." She interpreted the man's answer for Edvardson, then quickly told him what had happened. The man pantomimed amazement, pulled three chairs up to a table on the quiet little terrace behind the café, produced a bottle of ouzo and three glasses and disappeared into the interior. They could hear his voice, strident and incomprehensible on the telephone.

"Trusting." Edvardson poured lavish shots of ouzo for

them all. "I'm afraid we'd better forget that other parking lot, don't you think?"

"Yes." Stella had moved over to the edge of the terrace. "But I'll tell you one thing, there's nothing here but our bus and a red car."

"The same one?" asked Marian.

"God knows. It looks the same."

"Same as what?" the professor asked, and Marian had just finished explaining their previous encounters when the café proprietor returned to tell them the police would be coming— *"Vite, vite,"* from Sparta.

"I wonder how long the others will be," said Marian. "And come to that, what's become of the rest of the party? The ones who didn't even get as far as the palace?"

"That's a good question," said the professor. "No, no," he hurried on, noticing that Stella had gone very white. "I don't seriously think there's been a wholesale massacre, but it is peculiar. Ask the man, Mrs. Frenche."

Asked, surprisingly, he spat, then burst into an explosive torrent of words, part Greek, part French. "Oh, I see." Marian got the gist of it at last. "There's a new café up the road. It's always happening, he says. There's another way out of the site there, and they've got a menu as long as your arm, and—oh—I'm not quite sure what else, but anyway people who are supposed to come here go there instead."

"So what do we do about that?" asked Edvardson.

"Nothing, I should think. Mike and David will have to sort it out. Just so long as we know they're somewhere."

Stella finished her ouzo and looked a little better. "I was really beginning to think the earth had opened and swallowed them." She was laughing at herself or, Marian thought, trying to.

"A kind of mass Persephone." Marian could not help a smile. "Just think of all those good ladies turning up in hell."

The professor refilled all their glasses. "I bet the boss would run for it. Well, here's to survival."

"Everyone's," said Stella, and caused a cold little silence.

The police came first, and this time the professor was

able to tell his story in English. Finishing it, he asked the inevitable question and got the answer Marian had feared. They were the only tour on the site so far, but there were, it appeared, a few private cars at the upper park, as well as the red one down here. No one was being allowed to leave. "For the moment," added the policeman, and began, patiently, to take Edvardson through his story all over again, point by point. It came out exactly the same as before, and he turned politely to Marian. "You will forgive me, *kyria,* since I can see you are all friends, but when the gentleman told you this story the first time, was it the same?"

"Just the same."

"And you did not think, at all, that he might, perhaps, have imagined this attack? It is a strange place, Mistra," he hurried on. "A place where one might, just possibly, imagine things."

"Ghoulies and ghosties," said Stella.

"Not me," said the professor.

"You had heard, perhaps, of what happened here after the war?" The courteous voice made it at once a question and a suggestion.

"Yes, I know about that. But if you think it made me try and push myself over a cliff, you're crazy."

"Oriste?" For the first time the courteous voice was puzzled. "I beg your pardon," he amended, and Marian found herself wondering what rank he held. A high one, she rather thought. Higher than one would have expected?

"I meant," the professor explained patiently, "that I don't make a habit of imagining things." He reached into the pocket of his shabby windbreaker, produced a wallet and surprisingly, a card. "I am a professor of classical studies." He handed over the card.

"And you do not speak Greek?"

Edvardson laughed, threw back his head and recited a magnificent, incomprehensible speech. "You understand it?"

The young man smiled politely. "Homer, I think. The catalogue of ships, perhaps? I take your point, Professor. We have come a long, hard way since Homer, we Greeks."

He looked at his watch. "How long since you came down? I think we must admit that the rest of your party are a long time coming." He spoke quickly to one of his two men. "Whatever has happened, they should come down now, and I must telephone."

"It's bad, isn't it?" Marian had waited till he had left them alone with only the other man, who spoke no English.

"I'm afraid so. They should have been here long ago."

"Not necessarily," said Stella. "David didn't set any time. He just said, 'back for lunch.' Any of them might have decided to stay up top all morning. And of course he'd wait."

"That's true." Marian jumped at it.

The professor looked at his watch. "It's one o'clock now."

"And here they come." But one look at Cairnthorpe's face confirmed their fears.

"Mrs. Duncan," he said. "There's not a sign of her. We split up into pairs, and called, and searched. Nothing."

"There's another way out," said the professor, but they all knew it for a forlorn hope.

The chief policeman, returning at this point, listened to Cairnthorpe's story and took this point at once. "The rest of your party were at the other café," he said. "They are on their way here now. Then we will know."

But none of them expected Mrs. Duncan to be among the group who came grumbling down the road. They had been comfortably settled at the upper café and were not at all pleased to be dragged away—and by a policeman, too —to this, in their opinion, inferior place.

"You will find the food delicious," said the young policeman firmly. "My friend here is ready to serve you, if you will all be so good as to be seated."

"And a drink all round first, on Mercury Tours," said Cairnthorpe. "If you wouldn't mind organising it, Mrs. Frenche? I gather you can communicate with the boss?"

It was a good idea, Marian thought, as she moved between the anxious little groups, where Cairnthorpe's party were telling the others what had happened. There was agitation so far, but no panic. If they were lucky, if the police, who had now arrived in force and spread out to search the hill, were to find at best Mrs. Duncan with a broken ankle or at worst some local lunatic responsible for whatever disaster had happened to her, the party might survive, as a party. But it seemed horribly unlikely to Marian. Only she knew what had happened to her on the Palamede, and she was deeply grateful that she had made so light, to Stella, of Mrs. Duncan's fright there. For the unpleasant fact was that once again she and Mrs. Duncan had been wearing their almost identical blue windbreakers. It was a thought to chill the blood, but one she meant to keep to herself. After all, she might so easily be wrong. And Cairnthorpe had enough on his hands as it was. She felt horribly sorry for him and watched with surprised respect as he moved among the party, settling them at tables, giving a word of reassurance here and there, where it seemed most needed.

Mrs. Esmond was on the verge of hysterics. "Just think." She said it over and over again. "Charles insisted on leaving me alone up in that horrible palace. If I hadn't met you, Mr. Cairnthorpe, God knows what would have happened to me."

The fourth time she said this, Marian, sitting at the next table, could stand it no longer. "Actually"—she leaned across— "you weren't alone. Miss Marten and I were there; we heard it all."

"I didn't see you." Suspiciously.

"We were lying among the asphodel." Marian felt more foolish than ever.

"Have you told the police chief?" Cairnthorpe, who was helping the owner hand out the drinks, paused behind her chair.

"No."

"You should, I think. When he comes back. In the meantime, here is food, and very good it smells." The proprietor and his two bright-eyed, dark-haired daughters were busy handing out plates of grey-looking meat with great mounds of potatoes and the mixture of carrots and peas that seemed to be the only vegetable served to tour-

ists. Cairnthorpe moved quickly through the small indoors
of the café to look out at the members of the party who
had settled on the other terrace at the front, then returned to the table where the professor was still sitting
with Marian and Stella. "May I?" He pulled out the
fourth chair. "Everyone seems to be settled, thank God."

"Except Mrs. Duncan," said Stella, and Marian could
have kicked her. Why on earth did she tease poor Cairnthorpe so?

The meat was fatty but delicious, strongly flavoured
with garlic and rosemary. "This needs retsina," said the
professor. "And I certainly do. It's been a long morning.
And if we're not lucky, the afternoon will be worse."
He caught the eye of one of the smiling girls and gave
his order. "Basic Greek," he said.

"The classical is so different?" Anything, Marian
thought, for a neutral topic.

"It looks the same, but it sounds different as hell. And
of course, all the meanings have slipped."

"Like boy into knave?" asked Marian.

"Right." He smiled at her as on a bright pupil and dis-
coursed for a while about language changes. Marian was
intensely grateful to him. Cairnthorpe was understandably preoccupied, and Stella had plunged deeper and
deeper into one of her impenetrable silences. And no
wonder. This shock, coming on top of that bout of hysteria
up in the palace, would be enough to shake anyone. And
there must, almost inevitably, be worse to come.

The young policeman, returning as they disposed of the
inevitable choice of apples or oranges, confirmed this. His
face was grave. "We have found her, I am afraid," he told
Cairnthorpe. "Or rather a goatherd has, down in the
valley. She had fallen a long way. Poor lady. Too long a
way."

"From the top?" Cairnthorpe had gone very white, but
spoke with a calm that Marian respected.

"No. We think not. Probably from not much higher than
the upper chapel. There are many places there where
an accident could easily happen." He was looking almost
pleadingly at the professor.

"If it was not for my story?" Edvardson returned look for look. "I'm sorry, sir, but it happened just the way I told it, and, remember, I told it before any of us knew Mrs. Duncan was missing."

"Unless *you* knew," said the policeman.

"That's not stupid." Edvardson might have been conceding a point to a bright student. "You mean, I went mad or something? Pushed the poor woman over, and then made up my story as a cover? But it wouldn't have been all that smart, would it, because without my story it would have been taken for an accident, just as you said."

"One is not always very wise when one has just committed murder," said the policeman quietly.

"You can't be serious." Marian looked from one to the other with horror.

"No need to look so worried, Mrs. F." The professor had never used Stella's nickname for her before. "Though I take it kindly. Cross my heart, I didn't do it, and they'll find out soon enough. But it's damned queer whichever way you look at it."

"I'm afraid so," said Cairnthorpe. "'Oh—Mrs. Frenche, I think you should tell the officer where you and Miss Marten were and what you overheard."

"I didn't hear anything," Stella intervened rudely. "I was asleep."

"I see." The policeman looked at Marian thoughtfully. "It's crowded here, *kyria*. Would you mind coming out to my car?"

"Not at all." It should have been a relief to get away, but there was something very unpleasant about feeling the combined eyes of the party on her back. And in fact there was little enough to tell.

"I have it, I think," he summed up for her. "First you heard the courier, Mr. Cairnthorpe, with, you think, the group of schoolmistresses. Very charming young ladies. Many of whom wear jeans and have long black hair. Then a lady called Mrs. Spencer, with a newly married couple. Adams you said?"

"Yes. They were talking about going higher up. Mrs.

Adams didn't want to: she said her feet hurt. There was something—I don't know—odd about them." She had a feeling she had got something wrong when telling him about them but could not think what it was.

"Mr. Adams, too, has black hair and jeans. And so does Charles Esmond who quarrelled with his mother and left her at the palace. And then, later, two men, you think, speaking Greek. Thank you, Mrs. Frenche, you have been most helpful."

"But it proves nothing." She ought to tell him about what had happened on the Palamede. Why was she so reluctant to do so? The answer was obvious. If the professor could be accused of imagining things, or worse, what chance had she of being believed? Remembering Dr. Brown, she was not even sure that she believed herself.

"I'm afraid not." He got out of the car and came round to open her door for her. "But here, perhaps, is something." He was looking down the hill to where three men had just rounded the corner, talking eagerly. Mike and two others.

"But those are the ones—" said Marian.

"Which ones?"

"Well," she temporised. "I think they are. I think they own the red car over there. If so, we've seen them before —two or three times. We thought they must be doing more or less the same tour. They're talking to Mike—that's our guide—now. They might have been the ones I heard speaking Greek."

But the three men, surrounding the policeman, all talked to him at once in rapid Greek. He listened intently, interjecting a question from time to time. At last he turned to Marian. "Forgive us. But it's good news for you. As good as possible in the circumstances. These two men saw it happen."

"What?"

"Yes. You were quite right. They say they have visited the same sites as your tour several times and have noticed your party. They say that they wished to see Mistra alone —they had all day, you see—so they hurried to get beyond you all and up to the top. It was from there that they saw."

"What?"

"Mrs. Duncan—they did not, of course, know it was she, but a middle-aged lady in a skirt and blue jacket, hurrying, they say, as if, like them, she wished to be by herself. And, turning a corner too quickly, missing the path, falling. . . ."

"An accident?" Impossible to keep the relief out of her voice and impossible not to be ashamed of it.

"Just so."

"But what about the professor's story?"

"Ah," he said. "That is rather the question, is it not?"

By evening the professor was the most unpopular member of the party. If he would only have admitted to a brief hallucination, a temporary aberration, anything, they could all have relaxed. As it was, the free afternoon that was to have rested them for the next day's long drive to Olympia was spent in anxious, hard-talking groups, that broke up and re-formed, dropping their voices when a less well-known member of the party came near.

But the police at least, were satisfied. The bona fides of the two young men who had seen the accident had been checked by telephone with Athens. One of them had lived there all his life and worked, respectably, in a bank. The other was his cousin from northern Greece, having his first sight of the Peloponnesus. He worked in a chemist's shop in Yannina, and his employer, interviewed by telephone, spoke highly of him. And their story, too, made sense. Having seen Mrs. Duncan fall, they had hurried down, by the shortest way, through the convent and so down to new Mistra to report the accident. Meeting Mike, they had recognised him as the guide they had seen with the party, had broken the news to him and had let him do the telephoning.

"Funny they didn't come back and pick up their car," said Marian. The four of them were sitting together at dinner; unspoken between them the fact that no one else would wish to join the professor.

"I expect they panicked a bit," said Cairnthorpe. "They looked pretty young to me."

It came comically from him, Marian thought, but, in fact, he seemed years older than the blushing young man who had not known what to do at the airport.

"So—what next?" asked the professor.

Now Cairnthorpe did flush. "I'm afraid you have to accept it, Professor, that the police think—" He ground uncomfortably to a halt.

"I'm subject to delusions? Right? And the rest of the party would much rather think so."

"That's about it." Cairnthorpe was grateful to him. "Mike and I have been talking about it. After the police left. He feels, very strongly, that for the sake of the rest of the party, you should—if you don't mind my saying so—say no more about it."

"Until someone else gets pushed over a cliff?" The professor was not letting him off as easily as that.

"What we thought was"—Cairnthorpe leaned forward to press his point—"that I would make a little speech when we start out tomorrow. Explaining that the matter of poor Mrs. Duncan is all cleared up, but asking that, in future, people do not wander off by themselves. For their own sakes."

"But what about couples," objected Edvardson. "Suppose you picked the wrong partner?"

"You really stand to it?"

"I'm afraid I do. Look, David, you've got to face this. If something else happened, because I'd agreed to hush up, I'd never forgive myself. Now would I?"

Cairnthorpe almost groaned. "Very well," he said. "I'll suggest larger groups. After all, it makes sense." He was discussing it with himself. "If someone was to turn an ankle, there should be one to stay with them and one to go for help."

"Or if they fell over a cliff." Stella spoke for the first time, out of a silence that was becoming portentous. "Or down a flight of steps."

"But that was an accident," said Marian. And then, uncertainly, "They both were."

"We seem to be a bit accident prone," said the professor.

"You could say so." Stella turned to catch the eye of a passing waiter. "I need another drink." She looked as if she did. "What's happened to Mike, by the way?" she asked David. "Don't tell me he's got another policeman friend here?"

"Friends anyway," said David. "He's staying with them as a matter of fact."

"Oh." It came out curiously flat, and she drank the ouzo that had just arrived as if it were water. After that, she was totally silent, and Marian, keeping up a rather random conversation with Cairnthorpe and the professor, was not sure whether to be glad or sorry when she rose suddenly, orange in hand, to say she was exhausted and would go to bed.

"Not a bad idea." David smiled up at her. "It's going to be another of our early starts in the morning, I'm afraid. I'd better pass the word round." He rose and moved from table to table in the crowded dining room, where people were still talking in uncomfortably low voices.

The professor peeled his orange and smiled at Marian. "Not afraid I'll slip a Micky Finn in your Nescafé?"

"No." She meant it. "But, Professor Edvardson, I *am* afraid."

"And quite right, too." Like everyone else, they were talking low. "Not to be afraid would be stupid, and you're not that."

"Thank you." It was years since she had blushed. Should she tell him what had happened on the Palamede? The temptation was strong. To unload the burden of her anxiety on to his capable shoulders. . . . But—she sipped weak coffee—might he not think her the kind of woman who made things up to draw attention to herself? Somehow she could not bear that. The time to tell her story had been earlier, when the police interviewed her. After Mike appeared with the two Greeks, she had felt she could honestly let herself off. And anyway, it would be no help to the professor, who, she remembered unhappily, had been looking for birds somewhere above Nauplia when she and Mrs. Duncan had their frights. And after all, what happened to Mrs. Duncan had been proved an accident. She probably really was imagining things. The boulder an accident; Mrs. Duncan, poor woman, perhaps suffering from some kind of premonition. That must be it. In her relief, she looked up, caught the professor's eye and smiled brilliantly.

"That settles it." He smiled back. "I was sitting here wondering if I had the gall to ask you to pass a one-woman vote of confidence and come for a walk with me. How about it?"

"I'd love to. Will I need a coat, do you think?" It was curiously natural to turn to him for advice.

He picked up the cardigan from the back of her chair. "This should do." His hands, helping her into it sent a shiver of such delight through her that she caught her breath and looked up at him wondering if he could have felt it too, that thrill Mark's caresses had never given her. Absurd . . . moonshine. Or rather, that damned imagination of hers working overtime again. He was laughing, looking back from the entrance hall into the dining room. "You should see their faces, Mrs. F. I guess they think I'm going to eat you alive."

"And are you?"

"My one friend. I think not. I'm going to show you the spring that comes out of a tree and find you some decent coffee."

They found it, served by a black-clad woman who put chairs for them on the narrow pavement, where they sat, and watched the light fade behind the huge tree, and talked, idly, happily, about everything except the tour. Much later, lying sleepless in bed, Marian thought how little, in fact, he had said about himself, preferring to talk of world affairs, about which he was disconcertingly well informed. "For an American?" he had teased her when she said this. "It seems to me, granted we have to carry the can, we might as well know what's in it."

He had not touched her again, and she told herself she was glad of it. After all the lonely years as mother, perhaps, at last, she had found a friend.

She slept in the end, restlessly, all the old nightmares back, with a new twist. Mark, sullen, angry even, because he knew he had not satisfied her . . . Mark chasing her down those terrifying corridors of dream and then, horribly, turning on her with the professor's face. She woke at first light and lay rigid for a while, cursing herself for a fool. She had let Mark blind her with glamour; was she now—at her age—going to blind herself with sex? When she got up, thirty-five felt like a hundred, and the early start almost more than she could face.

The others seemed to feel the same. Breakfast was a silent meal, and they started off, a little late, not one but three short. Miss Gear was worse, and she and Miss Grange had decided to give up the trip. Borrowing Enterovioform from Marian before breakfast, Miss Grange had explained, confidentially, that it was not so much, now, the effects of the blow that were bothering her friend but what she described as "one of those inevitable traveller's complaints. Brought on by the shock, I expect. It's something we don't suffer from in the ordinary way, Gear and I. But she could no more do that long drive to Olympia. . . ."

"No." It was an obvious problem of the long drives, and Marian thought their plan of staying a few days in Sparta and then making their slow way back to Athens to join the party for the flight home a very sensible one.

It meant that the bus, now five short of its original complement, felt rather pleasantly roomy, or should have. In fact, it made little surreptitious whispered exchanges possible. There were nervous glances, this way and that, but nobody mentioned Mrs. Duncan, at least not aloud, not even after Cairnthorpe had made his speech about keeping together in future.

Mrs. Duncan had sat with a middle-aged secretary who had emerged, the day before, as a very competent Miss

Thompson, and, granted the professor's general unpopularity, Marian had rather expected to see her pair off with Mrs. Spencer this morning, but, in fact, she found Mrs. Spencer already ensconced on the back seat that the four of them were to share today.

"You get such a fine high view from here." Had Mrs. Spencer noticed her look of surprise?

It was a long, gloomy, tiring day and made no easier for Marian by the fact that Stella sat almost entirely silent in the window corner that she had taken without apology. There were dark circles under her eyes, and not for the first time, Marian found herself wondering whether she had really gone to bed early or stayed up till all hours with—whom? Shocking, in retrospect, to have gone so lightheartedly with the professor. Guiltily, she looked up and down the bus and saw that David Cairnthorpe looked tired too, and Charles Esmond and his mother appeared not to be on speaking terms, which might mean anything or nothing. The same was apparently true of the Adamses. Only Mike seemed his cheerful self. He waited awhile until they were beginning to recover from the daunting effect of Cairnthorpe's announcement, then stood up, with his familiar, beaming smile to tell them that they had left disaster and the Furies behind in Lacedaemon. "Now we are for Olympia, ladies and gentlemen, the home of the first United Nations."

"And about time Greece was thrown out of the present one," said a muted, unidentifiable female voice from somewhere halfway up the bus.

Very sensibly, Mike pretended not to hear. "I have told you already how much that is political we Greeks have invented. Professor Edvardson at the back there would tell you much, I am sure, about the *Politics* of Aristotle, but I am only an ignorant modern Greek, so I will tell you how, when the great Olympian Games were held, every four years, it meant a truce to all the fighting between the competing states. Peace for their time, ladies and gentlemen. The heralds went out, far, far afield . . . to Asia Minor, to Egypt, to Sicily, proclaiming the Olympic truce.

All fighting stopped, while the athletes prepared for the great competition. They had to train for ten months, I must tell you, at Olympia itself, and all this time the truce continued, the crops could be harvested, men could walk abroad freely. And then, when the time of the games themselves came, more permanent truces could be signed. It was a chance, ladies and gentlemen, a chance for peace and a greater Greece."

"Like you've got now," said the same female anonymous whisper.

And beyond Mrs. Spencer, Marian was aware of Professor Edvardson, muttering something to himself. "I'm looking forward to Olympia," said Mrs. Spencer brightly. "I've never been there. Have you, Mrs. Frenche?"

"No." Marian rather hoped that the monosyllable would end the conversation, but once started, Mrs. Spencer went comfortably on and on. Her first trip to Greece. Marian's first trip to Greece? Her unsuitable clothes. "If only someone had *told* me!" And then, inevitably, poor Mrs. Hilton, poor Mrs. Duncan. Did Marian think they ought to get up a collection? For wreaths? Marian, explosively, did not, but wrenched her thoughts away from yesterday's disaster, from the arrangements Mike had made last night for sending home the poor, battered body, to listen to Mrs. Spencer, who had reached the subject of her children. "A bit young to be left alone, but such competent young things. I expect they'll enjoy themselves with old mum away. You have children, Mrs. Frenche?"

"Two."

Once again, the intended conversation stopper had no effect. "So have I. Very respectable these days. Avant-garde, that's us. You know: population control and all that."

"Quite."

" 'Hostages to fortune,' " said the professor, and earned a puzzled look, and silence at last, from Mrs. Spencer.

As the long day dragged on, the bus grew more and more silent. Once the schoolmistresses tried to sing, but faltered into silence when an anonymous voice said,

"Poor Mrs. Duncan." Mike seemed to have given them up. He was engaged in a rapid Greek conversation with the driver. Tomorrow, presumably, would be time enough to tell them more about Olympia.

But next day it was raining.

Chapter 10

WAKING TO the sound of steady rain on her window, Marian was tempted to turn over and fall asleep again; and, later in the day, trudging dutifully behind Mike through the Altis, or sacred grove, listening to him talk of altars made of burned bones, of races won and lost, of cheats and the penalties they paid, she rather wished she had.

Stella was in the blackest mood Marian had yet seen, and for the first time she found herself thinking that Miss Oakland had been right. If things went on like this, she would indeed earn her high pay. With Stella beside her, silent, shoulders hunched, hands in raincoat pockets, how could she take an interest in the story Mike was telling about Nero and the Olympic Games? Did she dare ask what was the matter? She thought not, and as they trailed farther and farther behind the rest of the party, her own spirits sank to match Stella's. It was a curious thing; this morning she did not feel haunted or spied on, as she had so often, so desperately, in the past. Instead, she felt, quite simply, afraid. In sunshine, perhaps, it would have been possible to shrug off that chapter of accidents as—just accidents. Today, in the rain and after what Edvardson had said, she could not do it, nor, she suspected, could the rest of the party. They clung together in groups, as David Cairnthorpe had advised, and few of them looked as if they were enjoying themselves.

The professor had opted out this morning, announcing at breakfast that he was going to look for water birds along the sacred rivers. Remembering that happy afternoon by the Eurotas, Marian had found herself ridiculously disappointed when he did not ask her to come too, though, of course, she could not have gone. His absence freed the tongues of the rest of the party, and Marian, catching snatches of conversation as they made their way by fits and starts from the workshop of Pheidias to the temples of Hera and Zeus, was surprised how angry they made her. The general view was that Edvardson was touched in the head. "He was in the army," she heard Mrs. Spencer say. "A head injury, I expect. That white hair and black eyebrows must mean something."

And Mrs. Adams, comfortably blood-curdled: "Ooh, do you think he's dangerous?"

"Nonsense," said Mrs. Spencer, and then, "Hush, Mike's talking."

They were in the stadium now, and Mike had begun a long story about a woman who broke the ban on her sex at the nude racing held there and nearly lost her life for it.

"Who'd be a woman?" said Stella crossly at the back of the crowd. "I don't know about you, Mrs. F., but I've had about enough. My feet are soaking, water's dripping down the back of my neck, and I don't care how many statues by Praxiteles they've got in the museum. Let's get the hell back to the hotel."

Marian was glad enough to agree, and in fact, about half the party decided against the museum and trudged back to the hotel together. The rain was coming faster than ever, and Marian's headscarf was soaked through.

Entering the hotel, she pulled it off with a sigh of relief and was amazed to see Professor Edvardson looking at her with a curious mixture of open-mouthed astonishment, and, surely, dislike? "What's the matter?" The question slid out.

"Nothing." His smile was an effort. "At least, the strangest thing. With your hair like that, you reminded me of someone I knew a long time ago. Forgive me. It was like a ghost walking, just for a minute."

"A pleasant one, I hope." There was too much talk of ghosts on this trip.

"Oh, come *on*, Mrs. F.," said Stella. "You're drenched, and so am I. We'll both be ghosts if we don't get into dry clothes." And then, upstairs, pausing for a moment outside Marian's room. "What do you bet you reminded him of his dead wife?"

"Oh." It was oddly disconcerting, and she was glad to be alone with it. In fact, it was a kind of relief that the rain went relentlessly on all day, and the most sensible thing seemed to be to spend the afternoon on one's bed with a paperback and a two-day-old *International Herald Tribune* picked up at the shop on the corner in one brief sortie before lunch. Stella had announced that she intended to write her entire quota of postcards for the trip, and had, indeed, bought a vast supply of postcards and stamps while Marian was getting her paper. It was odd, somehow, to think of Stella with so many friends. But then, Stella herself was odd today, and Marian was glad of the excuse to leave her alone. The friendship that had been quietly developing between them seemed to have stopped growing, like a plant without water. It was with an effort that Marian finally put down her book, changed her dress, brushed out hair now fluffy from its wetting and went down to find Stella drinking ouzo with Mike.

"Not our most successful day, alas." Mike jumped up gallantly to fetch Marian a drink. "But tomorrow will be better, and the next day fine."

"Guide, philosopher and weather prophet." There was

a disconcerting note of bitterness in Stella's voice as Mike left them. "I hope you slept, Mrs. F.?"

"No, actually I've been reading. I got started on *My Brother Michael* and couldn't put it down."

"Restful," said Stella. "I hope you don't mind, Mike's joining us for dinner; this seems to be the one place where he hasn't got a friend."

"Of course," said Marian vaguely. "How very nice." But it was disappointing to find that the fourth at their table was Mrs. Spencer, and impossible not to worry, just a little, when the professor never appeared. Altogether, dinner was a dull meal. Marian felt tireder and tireder, and when Mike, who had ordered Nescafé all round, suggested that they go out for another coffe and a liqueur, she refused almost without thinking, and then had a quick qualm of conscience when Stella accepted—rudely, brusquely, but still accepted.

But it was no use; she could not bring herself to go out again. Resisting the temptation to sit downstairs until the professor returned, she went to her room, undressed quickly and climbed with relief into her cold bed. She was too tired for anything but sleep and plunged down into it with a speed that surprised her when she woke, later, to moonlight, flooding through the window whose curtains she had forgotten to draw. Extraordinary. She could not remember ever doing such a thing. Darkness was essential to her sleep. She got out of bed and moved muzzily over to the window, which looked out onto the street. Down there, people were still moving about. It could not be as late as it felt. Strange to have slept so soon and so deeply, but no doubt it was the retsina, and Dr. Brown would be pleased with her. "Wine is better than pills" was one of his sayings.

Dizzy a little with the depth of her sleep, she pulled one of the curtains across, then paused with her hand on the other to look down into the moonlit street. Something, down there, had caught her rather fuzzy attention. A couple, of course, locked in a deep embrace just outside the hotel.

"Damn you!" The girl broke away, her voice unmistakably Stella's. "I want to talk to you! I don't want—"

"You don't know what you want my star, but I do." Mike pushed her away, semiresistant, to look down at her, his face, like hers, shadowed and blank in the otherwise revealing moonlight. But there was a smile in his voice as he broke into Greek.

"And what does that mean, pray?" Her voice was strained as she pulled a little away once more.

"You don't understand? It might have been written specially for you:

> *Gazing on stars, oh star,*
> *Star of my soul, oh, me,*
> *Would I were heaven that I might gaze*
> *With all those eyes on thee.*

"In short you want to keep an eye on me." Stella's voice held a strange note.

"I want to be near you always." He pulled her to him, fiercely, and Marian seized the moment of their total absorption to pull the second curtain gently across and tiptoe back to bed, more disturbed than she liked to admit to herself. Nothing in Stella's daytime behaviour to Mike had given the slightest clue to what was going on. In fact, a good deal of the time, Marian had thought, she rather disliked him.

And what now? Should she tell Stella what she had seen? Every instinct said no to this. For one thing, it is never pleasant to have to admit to eavesdropping, however accidentally; for another, bringing the situation out into the open might so easily make things worse. It had always been one of her firmest beliefs, as a mother, that interference in affairs of the heart, however well meant, usually had exactly the opposite effect to that intended. With a bit of luck, Stella was simply allowing herself a two-week flirtation with Mike as a salve for the hurt dealt her by that unknown young man back in England. Looked at this way, things could be worse. Mike would be careful; it was as much as his job was worth to be anything else, and Mike, Marian was sure, was a careful, ambitious young man. No, he might kiss Stella and quote poetry to her, but he would go no further.

Soothed, Marian slept deep and dreamlessly, haunted, for once, by none of those tantalising visions of the old life with Sebastian and Viola. She woke, reluctantly, to the sound of knocking on the door and the thought that dreamless sleep might easily be the best gift Aesculapius could give.

"Mrs. Frenche!" Stella's voice, high-pitched from outside. "Are you all right?"

Marian rolled over and saw her alarm clock's hands accusingly at eight o'clock. And today's was to be an early start for the long journey to Delphi. Incredibly, she must have forgotten to set the alarm.

"Mrs. Frenche!" There was almost a note of hysteria in Stella's voice as she vainly rattled the self-locking door.

"Coming!" Marian's voice sounded irritable even to herself as she rolled out of bed and hurried to open the door. "I've overslept in the most awful way." She was still heavy with sleep. "I suppose breakfast's over? Bless you for waking me. Tell David I'll be down in five minutes. Well." She looked at the chaos of her room. And she had intended to get a start on her packing the night before. What could have got into her? "Say ten minutes."

"Fifteen," said Stella. "I'll bring you a roll and some coffee. After all, we've waited for the others often enough. But how do you feel? You look exhausted still."

"I feel it. But I slept like a log. I'll be fine in a minute, but I would be glad of that coffee, if you can raise some."

She was dressed by the time Stella returned with the coffee and, still only half-awake, grateful to sit and drink it while Stella swiftly and competently finished packing for her. Now, if ever, would be the moment to speak of the scene she had witnessed the night before. And "never" was the answer. It was curiously touching to sit and watch Stella competently folding her nylon nightgown, carefully tucking the alarm clock among its folds and laying the good blue dress neatly on top of everything.

"You're an angel." She finished the coffee and looked at her watch. "Not so late as all that, after all."

"No." Stella lifted the larger case. "If you can bring the little one? The rest of the bags were down half an hour ago."

"Oh, *dear*!" Downstairs, Marian apologised profusely to David Cairnthorpe, who was standing in the hotel lobby, watch in hand.

"Never mind." He was taking it beautifully. "It must have been my fault for not knocking loud enough. That's the worst of these hotels that don't have telephones in their rooms."

"Goodness, *did* you knock?" She had always thought she could as easily sleep through a crying child as a knock on her door. But then, how long ago it was that one or the other of the twins would come knocking to report some midnight crisis of earache or nightmare?

"Never mind." David Cairnthorpe was shepherding them out to the bus. "Oh"—he handed two white boxes to Stella—"here are your packed lunches. It's a long day, I'm afraid."

"And I've made it worse." Marian climbed into the bus, glancing apologetically to right and left as she made her way to the left hand side of the back seat. The professor and Mrs. Spencer, she saw, had sensibly moved one forward, avoiding the seat over the wheel to take the one that had been occupied by Miss Gear and Miss Grange. Absurd to have been worried about Edvardson last night.

"It's not like you to oversleep." His smile did the strangest things to her.

"No, I'm properly ashamed of myself. Too much retsina last night, I suppose. I don't know when I've slept so sound."

"Do you good," he said as she passed him to settle in the corner of the back seat. "Though I must say you don't look exactly wide awake yet."

"I don't feel it." She smiled at Pam and Meg, who were

to share the back seat with them, and settled down for the long day. It was a cool, grey morning, with puddles in the streets as a reminder of yesterday's rain. "Surprising," said Marian, looking out of the window as the bus moved heavily off, "I thought it would be fine today after the moonlight night." And then, getting a sharp glance from Stella, wished she had kept quiet.

They caught the ferry at Aighion with ten minutes to spare. "And very satisfactory, too," said Edvardson. "I've spent hours sitting in the draughty little café on that quay being sold pistachio nuts by indigent Greeks."

"There aren't very many of them." said Marian thoughtfully as they filed on board the ferry. "I mean, not actual beggars."

"I expect the colonels have put them all in gaol." said Stella. "Beggars are so untidy." Either she had gone overboard with her eye makeup today, or that scene with Mike had given her a sleepless night. Judging by her obviously frayed state of nerves, Marian suspected the latter. She, too, still felt curiously exhausted, considering how long and hard she had slept, and was delighted when Stella suggested that they eat their packed lunches on the open, breezy upper deck of the ferry. It was crowded, of course, but mainly with Greeks, and they were able to eat their highly flavoured cold chicken and hard-boiled eggs in what felt like a companionable silence.

The professor joined them as the ferry drew in towards the quay at Itea. "I'm going to try and get off one of the first," he said. "I've always wanted to look at this place—it's a bit of a naval headquarters, you know, and looks like genuine living to me. One gets so little of that on these tours. Would you like to come?"

"Yes, do let's." Marian was aware of Mike farther along the deck, apparently beginning to marshal his party ashore. "I'm sick of walking in crocodile like a good girl. Coming?" she asked Stella, with one of her usual qualms of conscience.

"I suppose so." Stella, too, had a quick glance for Mike. Perhaps she needed to demonstrate independence today. At all events the three of them worked their way down to the narrow catwalk that ran along above the deep central space where cars and lorries were stowed. Their bus, as a last arrival on this rather primitive ferry, would be off among the first.

"But that proves nothing." Edvardson looked down to where Andreas sat relaxed in his cab, a Greek newspaper spread over the steering wheel. "We're bound to lose some of the old dears. There'll be time for a quick walk down the front and back. There's a shop I've heard of— There! We're in." The ferry had touched, bounced a little and steadied, as men up and down the wharf worked fast and skilfully with huge ropes. Now the great ramps were letting down onto the quay with an accompaniment of the revving of car engines. Little groups of people stood at the front of the catwalks, waiting for their chance to climb down the few metal steps and edge ashore among the cars.

It was a rather disconcerting free-for-all, Marian thought, watching group after group jockey their way through the slowly advancing stream of vehicles. Now their chance had come; they waited for a moment at the bottom of the catwalk steps. "Now," said Edvardson, and then, "Christ!"

It all happened so fast. Afterwards Marian could be sure of nothing. There had been, unmistakably, a pause in the movement of cars; she had noticed that their bus was next in line as she stepped out on to the ramp, with the professor on one side of her and Stella on the other. People were surging down from the opposite flight of steps, and others pushing rather harder than she liked from behind. Her last steps from the metal stairway on to the ramp were taken, helplessly, too fast, and it was then that the screams began. Looking up, she saw their own bus bearing down on them. A hand pulled her violently backwards; she saw the professor falling forward, blacked out for a moment and came to herself still, incredibly, alive, the centre of an hysterical crowd. The front of the bus was over the professor's prostrate body.

He lay there, horribly still, and Marian's world spun black about her. Nothing in her life had ever felt like this. . . . Nothing. . . . Silent tears streamed down her face. Stella had her arm, was crying and swearing and trying to comfort her all at once. Mike, miraculously appeared from nowhere, was kneeling beside that too-still body. Andreas, white-faced and shaking, was climbing down from the cab of the bus.

"God blast all wheeled vehicles." It was a miracle: the professor's voice. His legs moved, turned over; he wiggled out from under the huge front of the bus, black with dirt, his jacket torn, his sunglasses hanging over one ear, his face white with shock—or was it rage?

"You're not hurt?" Mike was helping him up.

"No, by the grace of God. And no one else?" He looked back to Mike. "Ask that damn fool what he thought he was doing. He might have killed us all."

This view was obviously shared by a good many Greeks, who had surrounded Andreas in a threatening noisy crowd. Mike spoke through them, loud and angry, and Andreas pushed forward, answering, as rapidly, in Greek.

Mike dismissed whatever excuse he had made with one explosive Greek monosyllable and turned to the professor. "Reading the newspaper!" The scorn in his voice was nuclear. "Bad news of his home village. So—foot on the accelerator instead of the brake. And the last job he does for Mercury Tours. But for the moment, we're blocking traffic."

It was true. Angry hootings from farther back in the queue of vehicles spoke of everyone's impatience to get ashore.

"Yes." Edvardson pulled his torn jacket together. "No use crying over this lot of spilt milk. Come help me buy a jacket, Mrs. Frenche?"

Incredibly, it was all over. The angry Greeks had seen friends waiting on the dock. It was just one more episode in the long, sanguinary battle between man and the motor vehicle, and this time, in fact, no blood had been drawn. The curious stop-go, pedestrian-vehicular movement ashore began again, with Andreas, back in his cab, driving as if over eggs.

Safely on shore, the professor looked Marian and Stella up and down. "You look like the wrath of God," he said. "You need ouzo, not exercise. And this looks like the place. Stay here"—he settled them at the metal table of a waterfront café—"and for God's sake, don't let that maniac leave without me. This was my only jacket." He gave it a rueful glance.

"It's your only life, too," said Stella.

"Yes," he said, "that had occurred to me, Miss Marten."

He had just left them when David Cairnthorpe came hurrying across the quay. "You're not hurt?" The question was for them both, but his anxious look for Stella.

"Just shaken up a bit," Marian reassured him. "Someone grabbed us from behind."

"Mike," said Stella, with what sounded oddly like hatred. "But the professor nearly bought it. He's had to go and get himself a new jacket."

"He asked us to see that the bus waited for him," put in Marian.

"Of course. Thank God it was no worse. But"—he paused— "Mrs. Frenche, Stella, I know it's a lot to ask, but for everyone's sake, can we say as little as possible about this?"

"Yes." Marian had thought of this, too. "One more accident. . . . We don't want a general panic, do we?" Or did they? One more accident. Could she really believe it one? Might not the safest thing, for them all, be a general panic and consequent return home? But that was absurd. "This really *must* have been an accident." She was not quite sure whom she was trying to convince.

The bus, sedately parked on the quay, was filling up by the time the professor rejoined the party, wearing, to Marian's amusement, the kind of navy blue windbreaker popular with the younger Greeks. As he had bought himself a navy blue beret the day before in Olympia, to replace the hat lost at Mistra, he now looked, as she told him, every inch a Greek.

Thanks," he said. "You might call it protective colouring."

And what in the world had he meant by that, and why had Stella given him such a strange glance for it? But it was time to get back into the bus for the inevitable babble of question and exclamation. David Cairnthorpe had been optimistic when he hoped to keep the news of the accident quiet. But oddly enough, it had had the opposite effect to that which he and Marian had feared. Everyone was used to accidents involving motorcars. There was nothing strange or frightening about them. From being almost ignored, the professor had become a figure of rather affectionate fun, his blue jacket a kind of prize for survival.

But, "Odyssey with Furies," Marian heard Pam whisper to Meg, and was inclined to agree with her.

Andreas was driving as if he carried a load of Venetian glass, but Mike, picking up his microphone, made no reference to the near tragedy. "Now," he said, "at last we come to the high point of your Mercury Classical Tour. Now you are to see Delphi, where, for centuries, the oracle gave counsel wise and enigmatic; Delphi, the home of Apollo and of Bacchus, of wisdom and of divine frenzy. You are now on the Sacred Way, ladies and gentlemen. Once more you are to imagine yourselves as pilgrims, coming up through the olive groves to the place of the oracle. And, by the way, these are the largest olive groves in Greece, and some of the oldest. Who knows? A few of these trees may have been bearing fruit when St. Paul preached to the Corinthians, or when the oracle returned its gloomy answer to the Emperor Julian that the bright citadel had perished and Apollo's laurel bough was withered. The laurel may have withered, ladies and gentlemen, but the olive still thrives here in the valley of the Pleistos, and you will find that Delphi is coming alive again, with a new life, that of the International Cultural Centre that is being built here, to act, as Olympia did of old, as a meeting place for the nations of the world."

"And very ugly it is," said Professor Edvardson.

It was late by the time the bus climbed up through

the town's narrow one-way streets. "You'd have thought when the French moved the old town from on top of the site, they'd have had the wits to build wider," said Stella.

"But that was in the nineteenth century." The professor turned round to explain. "No one imagined this kind of tourism then. Nor the motorcar," he added thoughtfully.

"Still less the bus." Stella, too, must be remembering that frightening moment at the harbour. "Oh, well, I can see this way you get a kind of compulsory tour of the high points of the place." They were threading their way narrowly between gift shops full of the usual enticements of hand-embroidered Greek dresses and brilliantly coloured rugs. Now the bus slowed and stopped, on the right hand side of the road, outside the white-painted Hotel of the Muses.

"It looks all right." Stella hitched her patchwork bag over her shoulder and prepared for the slow struggle off the bus.

A few seats ahead of them, Mrs. Esmond and her son had decided to wait it out. Sitting, as usual, by the window, she was talking to him in a kind of angry half whisper, when Stella, passing by, lost her footing in the crowded aisle and steadied herself, with an apology, by a hand on Charles' shoulder.

It affected him like an electric shock. Ignoring his mother, he leapt to his feet, insisting on taking Marian's small case, which Stella had got into the habit of carrying for her. Following along behind, Marian got the full benefit of Mrs. Esmond's look of blind fury and felt compelled, in her turn, to offer to help her with the extraordinary accumulation of paraphernalia that Charles, as a rule, dutifully loaded and unloaded from the rack. Reaching down heavy raincoat, light plastic mac, umbrella, cardigan and a coloured bag full of lumpy unidentifiable objects, Marian was grateful that they were almost the last out of the bus. Meg and Pam, still collecting themselves on the back seat, could, she thought, be relied on to ignore

Mrs. Esmond's angry mutterings of "cradle snatcher" and "leaving his old mother to fend for herself."

At least Charles was waiting to help his mother down the steep step, but Stella was waiting with him. Marian had never seen an understanding arrived at so swiftly and was forced to the conclusion that this was some manoeuvre in Stella's complex, underground relationship with Mike. At all events, it seemed already to have been settled that the four of them would dine together that night. "I hope you don't mind, Mrs. F.," Stella had the grace to look conscience-stricken when they were alone at last outside their rooms, which proved to be in an annexe a little farther down the steep hillside on which the hotel was built. "I thought we were due for a change."

"It's not so much a question of my minding. I just hope Mrs. Esmond doesn't poison you. You should have heard her." And then, "What's the matter, child?" Stella was white as a sheet.

"Nothing." Stella put the key in her lock. "I'm tired, aren't you? Early bed tonight?"

It had an all-too-familiar ring, and Marian, opening her own door, resolved that tonight she would stay up, however much it went against the grain, both physical and psychological.

No use wondering what kind of words were being exchanged by the Esmonds, but at least when Marian and Stella entered the hotel dining room, Mrs. Esmond greeted them with stiff civility. She and her son were established at a table by the window, commanding an immense view of the olive-silver valley, and Marian could only assume that Charles had dragooned his mother into a very early position in the inevitable dinner queue. There was, perhaps, more in Charles than met the eye.

Mrs. Esmond was looking sourly round the dining room. "That professor's out on the tiles again. He's an odd one if you like. In every sense of the word. Fancy frightening us all like that!"

"He was nearly killed." Marian was frightened herself at hearing her own voice shake with anger. Had she been planning to stay up for Stella's sake or for her own? Had she really meant to sit in the hotel's tiny entrance lounge until Edvardson was safely returned? If she had, she changed her mind. "I'm going to bed." To her amusement, she sounded almost as curt as Stella.

Chapter 11

STELLA LOOKED more hagridden than ever over breakfast next morning, and Marian could only assume, gloomily, that Charles had proved unsatisfactory as a substitute for Mike. Or had the three perhaps met up somewhere in the small town? Granted the scene she had witnessed between Stella and Mike at Olympia, this could have had all kinds of unpleasant possibilities. But she soon learned that Mike had gone down to Itea the night before in the bus with Andreas, who had met friends there and decided to stay the night. Mike had returned in a flaming temper and a hired car, and so far Andreas and the bus had not returned at all.

"I'm so sorry." Cairnthorpe was passing the word round the dining room, where the members of the party were drinking unusually good coffee. "I'm afraid it means we are going to have to walk both ways to the site. Andreas is still not back." He looked anxiously at his watch. "Naturally, if anyone really doesn't feel up to it, Mercury Tours will be glad to provide taxis. Or"—more hopefully —"if we walk there—it's downhill all the way—I expect

Andreas will turn up in time to bring us back. Mike's down in Itea looking for him now, so I'm afraid you will have to make do with me as a guide."

It was an uncomfortable, straggling walk, over large paving stones apparently laid with complete disregard to the needs of the human foot, and they were a rather irritable party by the time they reached the Castalian Spring. There, Cairnthorpe surprised both them and, perhaps, himself. Mistra and Byzantine art had meant nothing to him, and he had by all reports been merely a parrot there, dutifully reciting the high points of the guidebook. Delphi was a very different matter. Delighted to be spared Mike's glib talk about being pilgrims on the Sacred Way, Marian listened with quickening interest as David took them back to the first, conjectural origins of this place of sacred prophecy. She had not known that it had originally been dedicated to a goddess, the earth mother, who had been deposed, back in the dark ages of myth, by the brilliant young sun-god, Apollo.

"Women's Lib," muttered Stella beside her, as they began the slow climb up from the sacred spring to the first of the ruins that marked the steady upward sweep of the Sacred Way. "I think he's better than Mike, don't you?"

"Yes." David had stopped to tell them that the little temple on their left was a reconstruction of the original treasury of the Athenians, built after the victory of Marathon, and Marian heard Edvardson, behind her, give a little grunt of approval as David went on to describe the competitive way in which the various city-states had put up statues. "Served them right when Nero went off with five hundred of them," said the professor. "But it must have been an awe-inspiring place just the same. In a vulgar kind of way."

"Vulgar?" Marian was amazed.

"Painted," said Edvardson. "It's what you always have to remember. The ancient Greeks liked bright colours just as much as the modern ones. Think of those handwoven rugs back in the village; imagine that kind of colour

painted on to the temples, outside *and* in, and then think
what it would have been like."

"Claustrophobic." Marian could not help a shudder at
the word.

They were up at the great ruined base of the Temple of
Apollo now, and David was telling them about the famous
ambiguity of the oracle. "Talk about having it both ways,"
said Stella. "It sounds like a modern psychoanalyst to me.
You know: If you dream, it's terrible; and if you don't,
it's worse."

"Give me Aesculapius any day," said Marian, and then,
by a logical transition, "I do hope Miss Gear is better."

"I'm sure she is." Something odd about Stella's tone?
But they were climbing again, up the narrow, difficult
path to the theatre, and it needed all one's concentration
to get safely from stone to stone, without cannoning into
another member of the party or, worse still perhaps, a
stranger.

And there, in fact, were two men who were not
strangers, the Greeks from Mistra, and Marian had a
sudden superstitious qualm and chided herself for a fool.
Naturally, as she herself had said, since they were apparently doing much the same tour, they would constantly
meet each other, but, passionately, she wished them away
and turned, for a moment, to watch with relief as their
blue-jacketed backs vanished down the rocky path.

Beside her, Stella had drawn a sharp breath. Was she,
perhaps, thinking much the same thing? There had certainly been no exchange of broken compliments here as
there had been at their second meeting—how long ago it
seemed—at Tiryns. "Come on," she said now, impatiently.
"I want to hear what David says about the theatre. He's
really good." It had obviously surprised her.

In the theatre, David was speaking already. It could
not compare, he said, with the one at Epidaurus, except in
its extraordinary position between the shining peaks of
Parnassus and the olive-green valley. The stadium was
higher up still, but—he looked at his watch—the walk
down from the village had delayed them; he thought those
of the party who wished had better come back inde-

pendently in the afternoon. There was an upper entrance which could be reached by climbing one of the step streets up out of the town. For now, they would retrace their steps and visit the little tholos of Diana, below the main road. And perhaps, hopefully, they would find Andreas and the bus awaiting them there.

When they emerged from the lower entrance to the site, it was to a curiously domestic scene. By now several other tours had arrived, and their buses were parked along the side of the road, being busily washed by their drivers in the stream that ran down from the Castalian Spring.

"Practical people, the Greeks," said Marian.

And, "No Andreas." Stella was looking worse than ever, the dark shadows heavy under her eyes and, something Marian had never seen before, a small involuntary twitch cracking this morning's unusually heavy makeup on her left cheek. Had she, perhaps, waited up in vain for Mike after parting with Charles the night before? Or— not in vain? She certainly looked as if she had had far too little sleep. Suggest that she rest this afternoon? But it seemed a pity—here at Delphi.

"Shall we go up to the stadium this afternoon?" Stella's question chimed in with Marian's thoughts. "It's too crowded to be borne down here." The little Temple of Diana was open free to the public, and the public was making the most of it, complete with screaming children and transistor radios.

"Yes, do let's. And start soon after lunch. Maybe before the crowds?" Up there, with luck, there would be enough privacy so that she could at least make an attempt to find out what was the matter with Stella.

"Let's go on our own." Once again, Stella anticipated Marian's own thinking. "I'm sick of people."

It turned out to be surprisingly easy. The professor said he was going up to the higher slopes to look for bearded vultures, and Mrs. Esmond had dragooned Charles into a taxi drive to Arachova, famous for its hand-made carpets. "And for a Greek victory in their War of Independence." The professor had provided the gloss, and Stella had come in with an odd non sequitur. "You'll watch how you go, up there?"

"I always watch how I go." He had found a sandal-maker to repair the broken strap of his binoculars. "I've still got my surprise weapon." He turned to Marian. "It's odd about this place. Do you feel it haunted by more that the ghost of Apollo? I do. It's on one of the vital passes into southern Greece, you see. If the Greeks hadn't beaten the Turks down the road at Arachova, that bloody December day in 1826, it might have been curtains for them."

"I doubt that," said Stella. "They meant to win."

"And very bloodily they set about it. But I think you're likely right. They did mean to win." He turned back to Marian. "And that wasn't the end of the fighting here by a long way. This was a great Communist hangout when they rebelled after the war. It was pretty rugged up here then. The caves of Parnassus made an ideal hideout for them, with the way open to Yugoslavia if they needed it. That was before Tito split with Moscow, of course."

"Oh," Marian was ashamed of her ignorance. "Did that make a difference?"

"It sure did. It meant their escape route was closed. Well, Albania, of course, but that's something else again. No, I guess Tito's move was the end for Communism in Greece. And a damned good thing too. It was touch-and-go for a while after the war."

"I didn't know," Marian confessed.

"You'd have been in the nursery. But, I tell you, when the Communist guerrillas took to the hills, with those bloodthirsty leaders of theirs, and their classical names, Odysseus and Ares . . . and women too." He stopped for an odd, charged moment, then went on. "They used to come down from their hideouts, shoot it out with the government guards here at Delphi, and, frankly, for a while, no one knew what was going to come of it."

"No," said Stella, "but the peasants knew that what-ever happened they would suffer."

It won her a look of surprised respect. "Right. And that's just why"——he looked quickly round——"the colonels stay in power. No one—absolutely no right-minded Greek —can bear the thought of another civil war."

"It was so bad?" asked Marian.

"It was unspeakable. Well, I must get after my vultures. Don't go too near the edge, you two."

"No, indeed. And you watch out for Communist ghosts up top there."

"I certainly will." What did that strange look mean?

"Have you noticed," asked Stella, as they started up the long, sloping steps of one of the side streets, "that people really are sticking together the way David told them to?"

"We aren't," said Marian.

Stella laughed. "Nor we are. Well I won't attack you, if you don't attack me."

"It's a bargain." But it was, somehow, not quite a comic one.

Climbing up through the last straggle of cottages, Marian gasped with pleasure. "Look! It might be the Alps." The spring flowers had been ravishing everywhere, or so she had thought, but they had been nothing to this brilliant close petit point of purple, white and gold.

"We've got out of the tourist zone," Stella said. *"They* go in at the lower gates. We're in Greece now."

"Yes." A donkey, tethered by the roadside and busy eating unidentifiable flowers, brayed its approval. "And I like it."

"Do you?" One of Stella's strange looks. "I suppose this must be the path."

Sloping gently downwards and along the side of the hill, it led them to a gate where a custodian beamed approval at Stella and let them in for nothing. But Marian, walking beside her, noticed that the twitch was more pronounced than ever in the side of her face.

"There's your peaceful classical stadium." Stella threw back her head and laughed harshly.

"Well," said Marian mildly, "it's what it was built for after all." The long stretch of surprisingly green grass was the scene of a cheerful and violent game of teen-age boys' football. "I imagine it's the only flat place for miles. I told you the Greeks were practical people."

"I wonder," said Stella dourly. Then, "Mrs. F., I must talk to you."

Thank God, thought Marian. "Yes," she agreed. "I've thought that, too."

"You have?" A quick, measuring look. "Somewhere safe." Stella led the way along the lower side of the stadium to a point where the trees fell away below, so that, sitting on what must once have been the lowest tier of the auditorium, they could see round them in every direction. In the centre of the stadium, the boys, busy with their football, took no notice. At the other end, presumably where the path came up from the theatre, a family of Americans were egging each other on to run the length. "It's as private as we'll ever get." Stella sat down on a piece of rock close beside Marian. "I don't know how to tell you, Mrs. F."

"It's trouble? I'm sorry." How strange, how sweetly familiar to be listening once more to the disasters of the young.

"Trouble! Mrs. F., you don't know the half of it. I . . . I'm ashamed."

Marian's heart sank. Worse than she had imagined? But, "Tell me." She kept it level.

"I must. I've been such a fool. I had no idea . . . Mrs. F., you must realise that I had no idea."

"No idea of what?"

"Of what they were planning. I can't go on with it. Only how can I stop? They'll kill us both."

"I beg your pardon?" The phrase sounded absurd, but then, so was this conversation.

"You didn't understand? I thought you didn't. Worrying about my sex life, were you? Oh, dear Mrs. F., I do love you. That's why I can't let it go on. But they *told* me you'd be all right. Of course, I shouldn't have believed them, but back there in England it all seemed different. Glamorous; romantic; the Scarlet Pimpernel. Only now, when I've seen what they'll kill for. . . ." She was silent for a moment, looking down, through a fringe of pine trees, to the far view of the olive-rich valley. "Now I know what they'll do to you."

"Stella, what in the world are you talking about?"

"My job. Your job." She pulled the head off a golden daisy and began systematically tearing out its petals. "Our job."

"I don't understand."

"Dear Mrs. F. Did you never wonder how you happened to get that card from Jobs Unlimited?"

"What do you mean?" Suddenly, horribly, Marian was frightened not just in general, but for herself. She was no longer the middle-aged councillor, waiting to listen to the problems of youth. She was Marian Frenche, alone, on a Greek hillside, and understanding the basic meaning of the word "terror."

"Had you ever heard of Mercury Tours?" Stella went on remorselessly, flaying herself as well as Marian. "No? Nor had I. But I was a sympathiser, naturally, so they were more frank with me."

"A sympathiser? What do you mean?"

Stella threw away the savaged daisy. "Did you ever hear of the Greek children who were carried off by the Communists, when they retreated north in forty-nine and fifty?"

"Yes, vaguely." Stella's look made her ashamed of the admission. "I was at school." It was said in extenuation.

"I was one of them."

"What?" And yet it explained so much. "Your parents?"

"God knows. Maybe they died at Mistra. And you thought I was carrying on about ghosts, didn't you? Well" —Stella was making a painful effort to be rational—"I suppose I was, in a way. You see, I know so little. I had an aunt. She took me out with her, over the mountains into Albania. And then—I don't know—maybe she got bored. Maybe there was a man. . . . Maybe anything. . . . The Martens don't know, so they can't tell me. They thought I was Albanian. . . . Lots of starving children everywhere. . . . He was there on business—it was easier then, of course. She'd gone, too—she acted as his secretary: expenses, I suppose. Childless, they'd always wanted one; they found me. Bought me, I suspect. God knows how they managed to get me out. I hope they think it's worth it now." She picked another daisy. "Mind you, I think they'd be sorry—Mrs. F., what are we going to *do?*"

"Well." It felt colder, up there above the pine trees. "You'll have to explain a bit more, won't you?"

"Yes, of course. I'm a fool. Sorry." It was a painful effort to get it out. "Someone knew who I was—what I was. They approached me a long time ago, soon after the colonels took over. They were forming a secret society, to work for the restoration of democracy in Greece. They wanted—what's the word?—sleepers. People who had no obvious connection with Greece. I was only eighteen. We were all about that. It was such *fun,* Mrs. F. We used to meet in coffee bars . . . discothèques. . . Anywhere with a good deal of background noise. Then someone joined who had a flat—John was older; working. We used to meet there and drink coffee and talk. We were always wanting to do something, protest at the embassy, you know?"

"Yes indeed. But you didn't?"

"No. There was another branch doing that. We were more important. We were secret. We were really going to *do* something. Only, it began to seem like a long time. . . . Some of them stopped coming, joined other groups where there was more happening. I hadn't been myself for quite a while. . . . Well, the Martens sent me off to a ghastly finishing school in Switzerland, so I couldn't. When I got back, John's flat was empty. I thought it was all over. In a way, I think I was relieved." She stopped, looking sightlessly at the far view.

"And then?"

"They got in touch with me. After Christmas. John and another man I hadn't met before. Older. John seemed older, too. They'd had trouble at the flat: a police raid, and of course someone had a pocketful of hash. Don't look so shocked, Mrs. F. I don't." But the twitch in her cheek was more pronounced than ever. "I sometimes wonder if I'd feel better if I did. Anyway, they said they'd had to close down for the time being. And then something big had come up. I was the answer to prayer, they said. Nobody knew a thing about me, you see. I was clean." She used the word with a kind of nervous distaste.

"You don't feel clean now?"

"I don't know what to think. You see, it's such a good plan. So—well—valuable. There's a woman in prison on Aegina—did you know they have one of their top security prisons there?—she was one of the leading democrats before the take-over. . . . A lawyer and a teacher. . . . A friend of Mrs. Vlachou, they said—you know, the newspaper owner who had to get out. I think it was soon after she escaped that this other woman—they won't tell me her name; they say it's too dangerous—anyway, she was arrested about then. For a while it wasn't too bad; she was kept on one of the islands, just detained, but pretty well incommunicado. Imagine what it would be like for someone like her. In the end, she tried to escape and was caught. John thinks maybe the whole escape was rigged by the secret police to trap her."

"He didn't have anything to do with it?"

"No. They can't find out anything about it. Except that she was caught and taken to Aegina to await trial. She never has been tried, you see, not in all this time. And now, it's prison, and it's making her ill. John's not sure whether she's actually been tortured, or whether it's just the threat of it and the solitary confinement that's getting her down, but he says the reports are bad. You see, if they could make her implicate her friends, then they'd try her. Just think of being in prison, all by yourself: no lawyer; no friends; only the prison doctor. Not a bad man, John says, but not a good one. Absolutely alone."

"How old is she?"

"A bit older than you. That's the thing, you see." Stella's hands worked spasmodically. This was the heart of the matter, and she hated it. "She's extraordinarily like you. John said he couldn't believe their luck when he happened to see you, one day, on a bus. Of course he followed you home. He'd only seen photographs of her, but the other man had known her well. The hair's different, he says, and probably by now she looks a good deal older, but that can be coped with by a wig and makeup. Anyway, the whole point is that there should be no one who knows either of you well. That's why you were told to keep me away from people."

"You mean"—Marian was grasping it slowly—"this whole trip is part of a plan?"

"An escape. Yes. I don't know how they are going to get her out of the prison itself—we work in watertight groups, you see; that's not my affair. But obviously the hardest part is getting her off Aegina."

"And that's where I come in?"

"Exactly." Stella was grateful for her quick comprehension. "With your passport and among the tour, she'd be safe as houses. That's why the tour's so oddly planned, with a choice of Aegina or Athens on the last day. Obviously, with only that one day in Athens, most people will opt for the sight-seeing there, but you and I are going to Aegina. I'm to say that I saw Athens on that dreary cruise I did with the Martens. It's true, too."

"Yes." Marian was shivering now. "So we'll be a small party on Aegina. I see that. And there's to be a substitution. How?"

"Mrs. F., I don't know. They only tell me one thing at a time. Safer that way, they say. Well, it's true. But they swore you'd be all right. Just kept for twenty-four hours, till she was safe away, and then released. Of course, it would be a nuisance for you—no passport or anything, but the embassy would soon get you out. That's what they said."

"And do you believe it now?"

For the first time, Stella looked at her squarely. "No. I think they'll kill you. I think they've meant to all along. I think they've made a complete fool of me."

"Which," said Marian, "is not the greatest possible comfort to me." It was surprising how much, all of a sudden, she valued her life. "When did you start to wonder?"

"Well, of course, when the 'accidents' began to happen. Poor Mrs. Hilton. Did you know she told Mike she never forgot a face? But he swore it was only meant to be an accident. It was obvious, he said, that she intended to make friends with you; she had to be got out of the way or she'd be bound to notice the substitution. She was that kind of person, wasn't she?" Stella was asking, incredibly, for comfort.

"Yes. She wouldn't have let it go. I can see that. But—an accident—you mean Mike?"

"No, no. He had nothing to do with it. That's why he was so angry. He was ahead with the torch. It was bungled, he said, or—he frightened me rather—he said, 'Some people like violence.' I think he meant to frighten me. That was at Nauplia, the night it happened to her. I had to talk to him. We had a drink. Miss Gear and Miss Grange saw us. I saw him seeing them see us. Does that sound ridiculous, Mrs. F.?"

"No," said Marian soberly. "I'm afraid it doesn't. Specially not when they made a point of telling me they'd seen you. So that wasn't an accident either?"

"Mike's got friends everywhere." It was not a non sequitur. "When they insisted on coming on to Sparta, he got a friend in the hotel kitchen to put something in their food. But at least they're alive."

"Not like Mrs. Duncan." Marian had not believed she could feel so cold in so hot a sun.

"Another 'accident.' " Stella's voice shook. "Mike told me, the night before, that I was falling down on the job; I wasn't to let you go off by yourself for a moment—that way you'd be safe and no one else would get hurt. Of course, after it happened, I realised he wanted to be sure you and I had alibis. I really fooled you with those hysterics, didn't I?" She was not proud of herself.

"They were faked? Yes, I see." Marian did not like anything she saw. "But you didn't know?"

"About Mrs. Duncan? What do you think I am? Of course I didn't. And of course Mike said that was just meant to be an 'accident,' too. A broken leg or something. She was too bright by a half, he said. Mrs. F., did something happen to you, that afternoon on the Palamede, that you didn't tell me about?"

"Yes, actually." How long ago it seemed. "I nearly got killed by a falling stone. One of your 'friends' after poor Mrs. Duncan, I suppose. She said she thought she'd been followed. And we were wearing the same kind of jacket."

"I thought so. Mike said something, then must have seen I knew nothing about it, and shut up. Mrs. F., you can't hate me worse than I hate myself."

"I don't hate you, Stella." Marian reached out a cold hand and felt Stella's still colder. "But you have to tell me everything now. You must see that."

"Yes. That's why I wanted to come up here. God, it's a relief to talk about it, to tell you. It's been such hell. Ever since the courier wasn't there."

"He was to be one of them?"

"Yes. He was to recognize me by this patchwork bag. David didn't. Well, anyone can see he's no secret agent."

"Thank goodness," said Marian.

"Yes. If only I knew who the others were. . . ."

"You don't?" Marian had been wondering about this.

"No. Just Mike and Andreas. That's the way they work. In separate cells. Safer, Mike says. In case one of them gets caught. He came to see me that afternoon in Athens. They'd telephoned him from London. Apparently the real courier was just hit by a bus—a genuine accident."

"Serve them right," said Marian.

Stella actually laughed. "Oh, Mrs. F., you do do me good." Her face changed, froze again. "I could have killed Mike, back in Olympia, when he told me he'd drugged you, 'So we could talk.'" Her parody of Mike's accent was brilliant. "That's when I knew I'd got to tell you. Of course, I knew he wouldn't really hurt you."

"No," said Marian dryly, "they need me alive, don't they? For the time being."

"Yes." Stella was facing it with her. "That night at Olympia, I knew. I was terrified Mike would see." Her face was grey. "I had to let him make love to me, think me a little fool. Mrs. F., I hate myself."

"Never mind. We all do sometimes. The question is,

what are we going to do. You say you don't know who's arranging the 'accidents'?"

"No. I wish to God I did. Those two Greeks have to be in it, of course, but I don't think they're actually the killers. Mike said something, once, when he wasn't thinking, about 'he.'"

"Not 'they'?"

"No. And, besides, they certainly couldn't have killed Mrs. Hilton because it was only our lot who went down that stair, and I don't really see how they could have attacked the professor and killed poor Mrs. Duncan and got down to the village in the time. I wonder a bit about the professor." She said it reluctantly.

"Nonsense," said Marian. But her mind had been moving on excruciatingly similar lines. "Look what happened yesterday."

"At Itea? Yes, I know, but it was all such a muddle. I don't see how it proves anything." She took Marian's hand in her own icy ones. "Mrs F., what do you think has happened to Andreas?"

"Andreas? But I thought you said he was one of them."

"Yes, but don't you see, he made a terrible mistake yesterday. Trying to kill the professor, he nearly killed you. And then where would they have been?"

"And where would I have been?" said Marian dryly. "But, Stella, you admit it? You take it for granted? That they were trying to kill the professor?"

"I don't take it for granted." Angrily. "But I don't know what else to think. I've not had a chance to talk to Mike about it, and I don't mean to. Not now. The less he thinks I suspect, the better."

"I do so agree. That's why you told him—the professor —to be careful today." Which surely—Marian clung to it—meant that Stella, too, refused to believe that the professor was one of the enemy.

"Yes. I do hope he is. And safe. I did the best I could to freeze him off, but how could I? Not when he'd taken such a fancy to you. Unless—Mrs. F., you don't think he's just pretending?"

"God knows." Marian faced her with it bleakly. "I

certainly don't." Having been fooled so horribly once, how could she ever trust her judgment again?

"That's what I was afraid of. You can read it so clearly either way. If he's not one of them, he's in horrible danger. If he is, he's keeping an eye on us. He easily could be. Which would have made Andreas' mistake yesterday worse still. You can see it's the risk of their cell system. Andreas might actually not have known, not if they were in different cells. But what should we *do*, Mrs. F.? Ought we to warn him?"

"I don't know." Marian was looking over the disastrous history of the tour. "Poor Mrs. Hilton, just because she wanted to be friendly. And Miss Gear . . . and Mrs. Duncan."

"I'm afraid so." Stella was white now, and twitching uncontrollably. "Mrs. F., is it any use saying how sorry I am?"

"Well, not much. What we need to do now is use our brains. You've done nothing to make them think you're going to tell me?"

"No, thank God. That's when I did start to use my head. I wanted to tell you yesterday morning at Olympia, but there was no chance—not after he'd drugged you. And last night there was Charles—But when Mike came back without Andreas, I knew I had to do something. They're dangerous, Mrs. F."

"Yes, I was rather getting that impression." Marian looked anxiously up at the soaring mountain above them, tipped now with the colours of the setting sun. "You shouldn't have let the professor go up there." She would not believe him implicated in the plot; but, if not, there was no doubt that he was in appalling danger.

"How could I stop him?"

"We must go back." Anxiety crawled through her veins. "If we stay here too long, they'll begin to wonder." There was something particularly horrible about this featureless "they." "And what about the Esmonds?" Another grim thought had struck her.

"Oh, they're all right. They were Mike's idea. He says

Charles will notice nothing but me, and his mother's blind as a bat. But what are we going to *do?*"

"I don't know," Marian said. "Think, I suppose. At least we know nothing can happen to the two of us until we get to Aegina. It's the professor I'm worried about. I hope."

"Yes," said Stella. She was crying helplessly now. "Mrs. F., can you forgive me?"

"If he's safe," said Marian.

"And if he's on our side," said Stella.

Chapter 12

THE LIGHT was failing. The boys had stopped playing serious football and were idly kicking the ball towards the upper exit. The guard from there appeared at the top of the stadium and shouted something in Greek.

"It can't be closing time yet," said Marian.

"Perhaps they close earlier up here. Anyway, we ought to be going. I wish someone else had come up so we could all go down together. We don't want Mike getting ideas."

"No indeed." Marian looked towards the end of the stadium where the Americans had been, saw a familiar figure there and felt her heart give a great leap of relief. "There's the professor."

"Thank God," said Stella. "And with luck we'll pick up someone else on the way down." They both waved and moved one way to meet Edvardson as the boys went the other to join the guard and, presumably, leave by the upper gate.

"Well," called Marian as they came within earshot,

"did you find your bearded vulture?" Incredible to manage so nearly normal a tone.

"No." The professor looked shamefaced. "As a matter of deplorable fact, I fell asleep. I've only just come out, and I reckon it's too late for sighting anything. I've left the Esmonds down in the theatre." He gave them his pleasantly conspiratorial grin. "She wouldn't let him leave her there all alone, or he'd be up here practising racing starts on the line." It was there at their feet, surprisingly clear, the stone marker, worn by the feet of athletes long forgotten. And curiously moving, Marian thought; real in a sense that much they had seen was not.

"It's a wonderful place." Her eyes had misted with tears.

"Even without bearded vultures." He turned to lead the way down the steep little path, and Stella, beside Marian, hesitated a moment to put her finger on her lips in warning. She was right, Marian thought. They dared not risk saying anything to him. Besides, they were to spend the next day travelling. He should be safe enough. If he needed safety. It was all horrible, and she turned, almost with relief, to wonder what she and Stella were going to do. But at least they had a whole day to think and plan, and, tonight, the privacy of their rooms in the annexe in which to confer. And, curiously, even through her terror, she was beginning to recognise that Stella's story had given her a most extraordinary psychological boost. She had realised, suddenly, as they walked across the close grass of the stadium to meet the professor, that she had never suffered from delusions at all. When she had thought she was being watched, back there in London, she had been quite right. Stella's friends had doubtless been studying her for the likeness to the unknown woman, whose place of danger she was to take.

Could that be it? She stumbled and caught a pine branch to steady herself. Suppose, as well as getting the unknown woman out of prison, they meant to get her in? What chance would she have then of proving that she was, in fact, Mrs. Marian Frenche? In solitary confinement, visited by guards, and interrogators, and a doctor, whom Stella had described as not a bad man, but not a good one. Suppose they simply decided she had gone mad? Which would suit them very well. Or what if they tortured her for information she could not reveal?

"Are you all right?" She had stopped in her tracks, and the professor turned to hold out a helping hand. It was warm, firm and, somehow, enormously reassuring. The temptation to tell him, to ask his help, his advice, was almost too strong to be resisted. But they were down to the level of the theatre, and Charles Esmond was coming eagerly forward to greet them.

"Was it worth the climb?" he asked the professor.

"Well worth it." Edvardson belatedly let go of Marian's hand.

By agreement, quickly arrived at in Marian's bedroom, Stella and she made sure of sharing a table with the Esmonds that night, though Marian felt, with a pang, that the manoeuvre earned her a quick glance of enquiry from the professor, who was sitting with Cairnthorpe and two hopeful empty places. It was, for Marian, an extraordinary meal. She looked at the other members of the party with painful new eyes. She had realised, more and more, as they came down through the Temple of Apollo, through all those grey bones of history, that there must, inevitably, be other members of the conspiracy in the party besides Mike and Andreas. Not, please God, the professor. But who? But which?

Who of their very ordinary party had seemed, in any way, unusual? She looked about the room. The Esmonds, with whom they were dining were almost painfully normal, but Mike had urged their company on Stella. Were they perhaps involved? Was Charles' devotion to Stella a careful pretence? Had she merely imagined a family likeness between mother and son?

And then there were that curious honeymoon couple, the Adamses. They had always struck her as an ill-assorted pair. Could they be merely professionally linked? She peeled her orange with deft, cold fingers. Perhaps safer not to let her mind wander like this. Besides it kept nagging at her with the worst suggestion of all. Impossible to get away from the professor. Suppose Stella had not told all she knew? Suppose she had had more reason than leapt to the eye for the gesture of silence this afternoon? Because, face it, the professor had had some miraculous escapes. If they were miraculous, and escapes.

She was, suddenly, glad not to be sharing a table with him but, just the same, could not help pausing by him and David as she and Stella left the dining room. "Any news of Andreas?" It was, after all, a reasonable question to ask.

"No." Cairnthorpe looked both anxious and angry. "Mike and I have been on the telephone all afternoon. There's no sign of him in Itea. We've got a relief driver to take us to Athens tomorrow. A local man, but Mike says he's reliable." He gave Marian an engagingly boyish grin. "I vow to Apollo, I'm going to learn Greek before I take on another job like this."

"I think you've done splendidly," said Marian. She and Stella had agreed that they must make not the slightest change in their usual routine, so they sat for a while, over thimblefuls of medium coffee that was almost too sweet to drink, before Marian rose and pleaded fatigue.

"I'm tired, too," said Stella. "I'll come down with you, Mrs. F." And, safe in Marian's room. "So far, so good."

"Yes." Marian looked about her doubtfully. "I suppose they can't have—what's the word—bugged this room?"

It was reassuring to hear Stella laugh. "Come now," she said. "Remember"—but she kept her voice down— "we're not dealing with the secret police, but with their enemies."

"Yes." It was, to an extent, consoling. And it led, inevitably, to another thought. "You don't think." She put it almost apologetically. "You don't think, Stella, that we ought to go to the police?"

"No!" Explosively. And then, more quietly, "You must see, Mrs. F., that I can't? Can't do that to them. There's still that poor woman on Aegina. You do see, don't you?"

"I suppose so. Well then?"

"I've been thinking. Suppose, at the last moment, we say we don't want to go to Aegina? And then keep close to the rest of the party for the last day? After all, we fly out late that night. I don't see what could go wrong."

"Of course. How clever of you. It's the answer. But they'll be terribly angry with you, Stella. Are you sure we oughtn't to go to the police?"

"Only if they try anything," said Stella, and stuck to it, through all Marian's attempts at persuasion.

Left alone at last, Marian lay sleepless for a long time. Should she have given in to Stella on this? Was it not her duty to take some positive action? But then, the thought of that unknown woman, alone in a desolate cell on Aegina, stopped her. They must save themselves, but without risking her. Perhaps, somehow, she could be got away without recourse to the dangerous substitution. Perhaps even now, if the conspirators were to come to her, Marian, openly, and explain the situation, she might agree to help. It was intolerable to think of someone her age—and like her; this made it oddly worse—helpless in the hands of the colonels' men. But on the other side, there was that frightening tale of violence. Would ordinary fighters for freedom, for democracy—would they resort so freely to murder? If the unknown woman on Aegina was to be pitied, what about Mrs. Hilton and Mrs. Duncan, who were beyond pity?

She did not sleep much that night and woke heavy-eyed and wretched with indecision. Stella, calling to go up the hill to breakfast with her, noticed at once. "You look terrible, Mrs. F. As if the Furies were after you." She kept her voice low. "It won't do, not without an explanation. We don't dare let Mike think you've anything on your mind. He frightens me, Mike."

"I thought you were a little in love with him."

"Me?" Stella threw back her head and laughed naturally, an extraordinarily reassuring sound. "In love with Mike. Lord, darling Mrs. F., what an innocent you are. Do you really not know that Mike's one of them?"

"Them?"

"The queers. The homosexuals. Oh, yes, he's tried to keep me happy with his advances, but poor Mike!" She lowered her voice again on the word. "You really haven't seen that it's the professor he's after? Well." Once again that surprisingly full-bodied laugh. "I suppose you wouldn't, would you? But it's true, just the same. I still haven't decided whether he was trying to save you for the cause, at Itea, or the professor for love."

"You can't be serious."

"Oh, can't I? Haven't you seen how he watches the professor while he's saying his piece? He minds horribly when Edvardson gives one of those dismissive grunts of his. Well, even I can see that your professor's quite something. Mr. Rochester to the life." She laughed. "Poor Mike. And not a hope in hell for him. It's lucky for you that they need you alive. Honestly, if looks could kill. . . ." Her voice changed. She had frightened herself as well as Marian. "A pity, really"—she went off quickly at a tangent—"that he got no change out of David."

"Cairnthorpe?"

"Of course. Haven't you noticed how they bristle at each other? I'm sure Mike made a hopeful pass early on —maybe a double-purpose one."

"Double-purpose?"

"Business and pleasure. David adoring him and noticing nothing. Don't you see?"

"Goodness," said Marian inadequately. "But it didn't work?"

"Of course it didn't work!" Angrily. "With David! Mike should have had more sense, but then how would he understand an Englishman? David looks such a boy. That blush of his! But I tell you, Mrs. F., if it comes to real trouble, I'll be glad to have him on our side."

"And he will be?"

"Yes. And now it's high time we got over to breakfast before anyone starts thinking things. And you're looking better, thank goodness. Well enough, at least, to admit to a bad night. What kept you awake, I wonder? Do you think they have nightingales here, like at Olympia?"

"I doubt it," said Marian. "But I could have been worrying because I haven't heard from the children. This was one of the addresses I gave them." And, how extraordinary, she thought, to have worried so little.

"Right," said Stella. "You worry about it at breakfast." And then, "You aren't really worried are you, Mrs. F.? You know what wretches we are about writing."

"I'm learning," said Marian.

She made a point of stopping on the way into the dining room to ask Mike, who was sitting with three of the schoolmistresses, whether there was any chance that mail for their party might have gone astray. "I was expecting to hear from my children here. I'm a bit worried."

"Children?" They seemed to be news to Mike, and Marian had a frightening vision of how capably the organization he belonged to kept its cells separate. No one knew more than they must. "Young children?" Mike was asking. Was he, perhaps, imagining them as orphaned?

"Oh, no, grown up, or so they'd say. Eighteen. Twins. They're in America right now, with their father, but I did hope to have a note from them here. It's stupid to worry, I know. . . ." She let it trail off anxiously, and thought how strange it was to be using her children as they had so often used her.

Mike's handsome jaw dropped. "Twins?" He looked at her as if for the first time. "Mrs. Frenche, they're not—they can't be Sebastian and Viola? Mark Frenche's children?"

"And why not?" she asked tartly. "But, if you don't mind, I prefer not to talk about it."

"And who the hell," asked Stella, safe once more in Marian's room, "is Mark Frenche?"

"My ex-husband," said Marian. "Among other things."

"Well, yes, I'd gathered that, but why does his name have such an effect on our Mike?"

"Well, do you know—" An extraordinary light was dawning on Marian. "I was rather wondering that myself." Had Mark, too, been "one of them"? Did that explain everything? That terrible sense of failure, of frustration. . . . Those nights alone, biting the sheets, while he stayed downstairs, in "planning sessions" with his manager. Odd to look back and see Mark's manager, for the first time, as what he must have been. What fright, she wondered coldly now, what risk to his career had made Mark court and marry her? And those two—her mind jibbed at the word—those two had tried to make her destroy the twins. But she was smiling to herself. What a miracle, face it, the twins had been and, now she could see it, what a surprise to everyone.

But this, though it cast so extraordinary a light over her own past, could hardly explain Mike's horrified amazement at the discovery of who, in fact, she was. It was more than unlikely that he and Mark had ever met, though Mark had visited Greece a few times. But of course there could be a simpler, more frightening explanation of Mike's reaction. The Greek woman, travelling to London as Mrs. Frenche would, presumably, then disappear. But it would not be so easy for the ex-wife of a still-famous man just to vanish. The London cell of the conspirators had fallen down on its work, and Mike must have been seeing trouble ahead.

She had got this far when they were interrupted by one of the ubiquitous little bright-eyed Greek boys, who knocked on the door and made gestures to indicate packing and departure.

"Oh, Lord," said Stella. "I'm only half-packed. See you on the bus, Mrs. F."

She hurried away to her own room, and Marian smiled at the boy as she locked her big case, then felt in her purse for a few of the light little coins among which she had so far failed to discriminate. What, after all, was a lepta or so? "What's Hecuba to him or he to Hecuba?"

The tip seemed to be satisfactory; the boy grinned widely, picked up her case, then put it down again, picked up the pillow from her bed and made passing gestures with it. Of course, that was why his face had seemed so familiar. He had been one of the players up at the stadium the day before.

Impossible to convey her recognition of this, but Marian returned his beaming smile, as he picked up the case once more, and started on her day feeling oddly reassured. It did not last long. Andreas had not appeared, and despite what she now knew, she found she missed his friendly smile and firm hand up into the bus. The fact that Mike seemed overeager to replace him was less than comforting. The new driver, a heavy black-avised man, sat hunched over the wheel, taking notice of no one.

But he was a reassuringly good driver. The bus took the mountain road to Arachova like a master skater doing figures of eight, and Marian forgot the weight of her anxiety in looking back and downwards at the last views of that olive-grey valley where, she felt, she had last known peace of mind.

But then, what use is peace of mind if it is based on ignorance? And, all too appositely, there was Mike, up at the front of the bus, launching into the disastrous story of Oedipus, who killed his father and married his mother. They would reach his fatal meeting of the ways in the course of the morning. "He met his father, ladies and gentlemen, but how should he know him? He thought the other one his father, the man who brought him up and against whom, as he thought, the oracle had warned him. This was merely an arrogant stranger, and in his rage and misery, he killed him, there, where the three roads meet, and loosed a doom on himself and his that was to endure for generations. The fate of the doomed Atrides, ladies and gentlemen, was nothing compared with that of the House of Oedipus. There was death in the blood, and what is there must out. It was his sons, ladies and gentlemen, feuding against each other, who started the disastrous war of the Seven Against Thebes. The Furies may have been after Orestes, but his fate was much easier than that of Eteocles and Polyneices, who slew each other, brothers though they were."

"You'd have thought the Furies would have got after them," said Stella.

"They were dead, remember." Marian chilled at the thought.

"Why don't we stop at Thebes?" This was Mrs. Spencer, reproachfully, on the seat in front of them.

"There's not much left," explained the professor. "They're excavating there now, and I must say I'd kind of like to drop off and take a look, but it's not ready for the general public, by any means. It was destroyed, you know, very thoroughly, by Alexander the Great."

"What a destructive lot they were," said Stella.

"Aren't we?" asked Edvardson. "And at least Alexander spared the house of the poet Pindar."

"Like Milton," said Stella surprisingly.

"What do you mean?" Mrs. Spencer turned round with a sharp question.

"He thought he should be spared by the royalist troops, on account of being a poet," said Stella. "He wrote a sonnet about it, which I'll spare you. But it all seems rather pleasantly old-fashioned these days, doesn't it? I wonder how many poets there were at Hiroshima." And then, "I'm sorry, Professor, I quite forgot."

"That's all right," said Edvardson. "You couldn't feel worse about it than I do."

For some reason Marian had assumed that it would take all day to reach Athens, and it was disconcerting to find that they would get there for a late lunch, with free time in the afternoon for their own exploration. There was no doubt about it, she felt safe now only in the bus. The more she thought about the organisation she and Stella were up against, the more it frightened her. Suppose, for instance, they had told Stella the substitution was to be made on Aegina and in fact planned to kidnap her in Athens? It would, she thought, be the kind of thing they did. But how on earth to guard against it? She considered saying she was ill and locking herself in her hotel bedroom, but one look at the huge modern Hotel Hermes decided her against this. In that great, longcorridored, impersonal building with its connecting balconies outside each window, anything could happen. To shut herself in her room would be at once to awaken suspicion and to stake herself out, the goat awaiting sacrifice.

The bus had stopped. Mike raised a hand to still the usual ensuing hubbub. "Lunch will be ready for you at once, ladies and gentlemen, and then the afternoon is yours. For those of you who plan to come to Aegina tomorrow, I recommend a taxi ride up to the Acropolis. You must not miss the greatest Greek sight of all."

"Badly organised," muttered Mrs. Spencer in front, reminding Marian painfully of Mrs. Hilton. "We should have had longer in Athens."

But Mike had something more to say. "I would be glad, ladies and gentlemen, if you would tell me, as you leave the bus, what your plans are for tomorrow. It is a question of arranging transport on Aegina."

Marian and Stella exchanged glances. They had not bargained for this. "I'll cope." Marian's whisper was covered by the usual confused babble as people reached their accumulated loot down from the crowded luggage racks. A surprising number of people seemed to have got to Arachova the day before and now had bulky parcels of carpets added to the inevitable impedimenta of travel.

Taking their time, Marian and Stella alighted just behind Mrs. Spencer and the professor. "I'm for Aegina, Mike," said Edvardson.

"Me, too," said Mrs. Spencer. "Even if it does mean getting up at seven."

"It will be worth it," Mike told her. "And you two, Mrs. Frenche?"

"Oh, dear," Marian hedged. "I do apologise, Mike; I hadn't realised we'd have to decide so soon. It all depends, doesn't it, on how much one manages to see this afternoon? Would it be terribly tiresome if we let you know this evening? Just the two of us after all can't make that much difference?" She turned to Stella. "What do you think, dear?"

Stella was looking mulish, as she so easily could. "I'd like to go to Aegina."

"Oh, well," Marian dithered, looked back at the impatient queue behind her and smiled apologetically up at Mike. "I expect we'll end up deciding to go."

"Very well, Mrs. Frenche." Mike, who had been entering numbers in a little notebook, made an ostentatious point of writing nothing. He was, Marian thought, very angry. Which was, surely, a good sign? Must it not mean that nothing was planned for today? But then, how could she be sure that even Mike knew everything?

She was letting herself get jumpy, and that would be fatal. She forced a cheerful smile for the professor, who had paused to wait for them. "Silly not to be able to make up one's mind, isn't it?" She was still in part as a fluttering middle-aged fool.

"Not a bit of it," he said gallantly and rather loud. "It *is* a difficult choice. But look, here's a solution for you, if you don't mind skipping lunch."

"What?"

"There." He pointed to a tourist bus that had pulled in behind theirs. "That looks like an afternoon tour to me. Of course in theory you book in advance, but it doesn't look like it's going to be crowded. How about it?"

"Are you going?" Marian and Stella were exchanging quick questioning glances.

"I guess I will. Specially if you two will come along. And you?" He turned politely to Mrs. Spencer, who had hesitated just ahead on the steps of the hotel.

"It's an idea, I must say. But Mike?"

"I'll fix him. He can have our luggage sent up. The hotel won't break their hearts if we don't lunch. And there's bound to be time to get something along the way somewhere."

"Do let's." Stella had made up her mind, and, really, Marian thought, it was an admirable idea. Where could they be safer than among another, innocent tourist crowd?

Unless, of course, the professor was one of the enemy. He had left them, now, to explain their plan to Mike, and

she could not help wondering if the same kind of unspoken exchange was going on between the two of them
as she and Stella so constantly practised.

"A splendid idea." Mrs. Spencer had made up her
mind. "I was feeling really sad at missing so much of
Athens. I'll just make sure that Mike understands I'm
going along."

It was five minutes later, and they were established in
the usual two pairs, but this time with the professor and
Mrs. Spencer behind, as they had originally been in their
own bus. It meant, Marian reminded herself, that everything she and Stella said could be overheard by the other
two, and she hoped that Stella had realised this. No chance
of urging that they stay as closely as possible with the rest
of the party, but Stella, who had been so quick in that
short conversation with Mike, would undoubtedly have
thought of this, too. She was, Marian thought, a re-
doubtable ally. Strange to feel so little anger with her for
having involved them in this danger in the first place.
But then, her danger was at least as great as Marian's
own. She was increasingly sure that Andreas had paid
some horrible penalty for having risked the success of the
gang's plan. What would happen to Stella?

And when had she stopped thinking of their opponents
as an "organisation," with all the comparative respecta-
bility that the name implied, and started recognising them,
frankly, as a gang? And had Stella understood this, she
wondered? There was so much they had not had time
to say to each other.

The bus had been crawling this way and that through
the heavy Athens traffic, picking up passengers here and
there from different hotels. "It's the one-way system,"
Marian heard the professor explaining to Mrs. Spencer.
"But here we are in Constitution Square. Passengers from
the Hotel Grande Bretagne. How elegant." The bus had
stopped outside the expensive-looking frontage and
Marian turned from craning backwards to look at
the big public building at the top of the square. Stella
had squeezed her hand convulsively. Two men were com-

ing out of the hotel to join the bus. Two Greeks. The two Greeks.

"Aren't those the two from Mistra?" The professor, too, had recognised them as they got on the bus and took two empty seats up at the front.

"Yes," said Stella. "I suppose the Athenian one is showing his country cousin round." Her hand, still on Marian's, gave it a warning squeeze.

"It seems odd to choose an English-speaking bus," objected Mrs. Spencer.

Apparently, the Grande Bretagne was the last stop. The guide picked up his microphone. "Ladies and gentlemen, welcome to this GRAT tour of Athens. We are now, as you probably know, in Syntagma, or Constitution Square, so called because of the Parliament Buildings, which were once the royal palace. I beg your pardon—" He stopped to listen to an impassioned outpouring, in Greek, from one of the two men who had just got on. He spoke at last, courteously but firmly, in Greek, then, as the man sat down again, grumbling to himself, changed back to his fluent English. "I apologise, ladies and gentlemen. These two gentlemen have found themselves on the wrong bus, but since they will have missed the right one by now, they will stay with us, and you will, I am sure, bear with me if I—how do you say it?—fill them in, from time to time, in Greek." While this was going on, the bus had got clean out of Constitution Square with its problems of democracy and of royalty, and Marian thought the guide might well be grateful for an interruption that had spared him what must be a difficult bit of his speech these days when Parliament was closed and the king in exile.

He was silent until the bus paused across the road from a handsome triumphal arch. "Hadrian's Arch, ladies and gentlemen, built by one of the Romans who loved Greece. And behind it, the Temple of Zeus, which you should visit if you have the time, but as you can see, our traffic problems, which are like everyone else's, do not make it easy for buses to stop here. We are going on to the stadium and the royal palace."

"This is the way we came in," said Stella.

"Yes." Both of them must be thinking of poor Mrs. Hilton, her grumbles and her espadrilles.

Chapter 13

THAT AFTERNOON'S tour was to remain in Marian's mind merely as a confused jumble of impressions. The kilted Evzones stamping their sabots for the tourists outside the empty royal palace with its dismal boarded windows . . . the huge modern stadium . . . even the Acropolis itself was merely the backdrop to terror. By tacit consent, she and Stella stayed as closely as possible with the professor and Mrs. Spencer and with the rest of the party. But somehow, the two Greeks were always nearby. Did they speak English? Marian found she could not be sure but anyway was careful to talk the merest tourist chatter to Stella and the others.

There was one moment of sudden crisis on the Acropolis, when the four of them had paused to look at the view from the far end, above the museum. She and Stella were trying to decide which was the Pnyx Hill, where the Greeks had held their public meetings, and did not notice that the professor and Mrs. Spencer had moved away to join the rest of the party.

"We must ask Mike." Marian looked up, saw they

were alone, and saw the two Greeks approaching. The parapet was low, the drop beyond vertiginous. She, the double, was safe, but Stella? The Greeks were coming quietly towards them, one from each side of the little alcove where they were standing, closing them in. She raised her voice. "Oh, Professor, could you come here a minute?"

For a moment she was horribly afraid that, deep in conversation with Mrs. Spencer, he had not heard. The next, he was coming back to them with his surprisingly fast, loping stride. One of the Greeks made way for him with a smile. It had undoubtedly all been imagination. "Which is the Pnyx?" she asked, and saw that Stella was cloth-white.

After that, the tour changed from phantasmagoria to nightmare. Waiting for the funicular railway up to the viewpoint on Lykabetos, Marian and Stella stayed well back from the gates. At the top, they hardly looked at the view. Stella provided the excuse. "I'm starving," she announced in a loud voice. "I thought I was going to faint back there on the Acropolis."

The professor and Mrs. Spencer, equally lunchless, joined them at a marble-topped table, for the most expensive sawdust sandwiches Marian had ever eaten. The ouzo was expensive too, but it was worth it. "Tour prices," commented the professor briefly.

"Profiteering," said Mrs. Spencer.

"Profitouring," said Stella, and got a puzzled, inimical look from Mrs. Spencer, who, presumably, did not approve of puns.

It was a relief to find that the next section of the tour was simply a ride through modern Athens. "They will do it," said the professor. "I've had the same thing in Yugoslavia. They're so proud of their modern buildings they want you to see them."

"Hilton and all," said Stella.

"Right."

But it meant a blessed relaxation of tension as they listened to the guide expatiating on the thriving state of Athens and saw, indeed, the proof of this in untidy concrete buildings going up everywhere. "You do have to give it to the colonels," said the professor, as they passed a development of small houses, each with its tiny patch of garden. "They're building houses and roads, hand over fist."

"Soon there won't be a private place in Greece," said Stella.

"The grave's a fine and private place"—the quotation came, unbidden, into Marian's mind. If the professor had not been so quick, up on the Acropolis, would Stella have found her private place by now? At least, blessed thought, this must mean that her suspicions of the professor were entirely unfounded. She had reached the point of starting at shadows and must control herself.

The bus had plunged back into the urban thicket of central Athens and now slowed and stopped. Up front, the guide was announcing that they were to see two Byzantine churches.

"I don't know," Marian said doubtfully. "What do you think, Stella? I'm tired." Much safer, surely, in the bus.

Unless everyone got out, which they showed signs of doing. The professor turned round. "Do come, Mrs. Frenche, the big one's nothing in particular, but I'd like you to see the other."

Everyone else was moving. Marian got up. "Oh, well, in that case . . ." Getting off the bus, she saw the two Greeks going off in the opposite direction. Could they be leaving the tour, or were they perhaps looking for a public telephone? Of course, it might seem odd for them to visit their own churches as tourists.

At all events, it was pleasant to be free of them, at least for a little while, and the professor had been right about the tiny church, where black-garbed old women stopped to kiss the hands of ikons, dark with centuries of just such treatment.

"It's not right to traipse through it like this." Marian emerged into late-afternoon sunshine.

"I know," the professor agreed, "but they've got to live." She had seen him slip something into the church's collection box. "And speaking of living, are you as hungry as I am, you two? How about playing hooky and slipping off to a restaurant I know in the Plaka? It's only a step from here, and I bet now they're going to start the old routine of dumping us back at hotels. *And* we'll be the last, or nearly."

Danger? Safety? Marian and Stella exchanged glances. Mrs. Spencer had got left behind, momentarily, embroiled with a postcard seller. A whole evening free of fear. If one trusted the professor.

"Do let's." said Stella.

"Yes," said Marian.

"Down here." The professor led the way down an alley. Old Athens swallowed them, crowded and alive and smelling of unknown groceries.

"But won't they wait for us?" Marian paused outside a shop that actually sold real espadrilles, thought for a moment of Mrs. Hilton, and shivered.

"Not for long," said the professor comfortably. "They know we're not far from home. People are always doing it. And I'd like you to have one real Greek meal before we go." He looked at his watch. "It's a bit early yet, so we'll go to a café first, shall we?"

"Do let's." Stella had entered into the spirit of this escape.

"Keep close to me," the professor warned, as he guided them through a network of small, incredibly crowded streets. "It might not be just the place for ladies alone." He steered them round a corner past a shop full of extraordinary metal implements.

Ladies alone. Marian almost laughed. If that was only the worst of their troubles. "I thought a woman was supposed to be able to walk right through Athens with a gold bar on her head."

"A woman, perhaps," he said. "A foreign lady?" He left it doubtful. "Ah, here it is." They were in an alley that sloped slightly upwards, and he turned through a wrought-iron gate into a little courtyard, with a vine-covered trellis and small tables. It was half empty at this early hour, the proprietor lounging, hands in pockets, against the trunk of the vine. At sight of Edvardson, his face lit into a smile of extraordinary sweetness.

"Thor!" He came forward with both hands outstretched, took Edvardson in his arms and kissed him on both cheeks. A flood of Greek followed, and Marian was amazed and appalled to hear the professor answer in kind.

"But you don't speak Greek!" They were being settled at the best table. Should she and Stella run for it? Were all her suspicions correct after all?

"Come now, Mrs. F.," said the professor comfortably, pulling out Stella's chair as the owner did Marian's. "You must have realised that was just my laziness."

"Laziness?" She seemed to be sitting down. If there had been a moment for escape, it had passed.

"Well, yes. Just think back. . . . If I'd admitted knowing Greek, at the start there, when poor young Cairnthorpe was having such trouble, I'd have ended up running the tour. And what kind of holiday would that have been? I must admit, I had a kind of a battle with myself when the trouble started. But I was so far in by then, and young Cairnthorpe was coping pretty well, I thought. And then there was your French, Mrs. Frenche."

"Yes." Had they been mad to come? Had the professor his own, sinister reasons for refusing to admit that he understood Greek? She looked across, a quick question, at Stella.

She seemed calm enough. "I must say," she said, "I did think it a bit odd. Someone like you." If she was considering flight, she showed no sign of it.

"Right. Anyone in my position would be bound to learn at least enough to get by with. I'm quite good, in fact. Stavros will tell you." He spoke now, rapidly, in Greek.

It made the proprietor, Stavros, roar with laughter. "You Thor." His English was as good as Mike's. "You were always the joker. So you have left this poor young man to struggle on alone, you who speak like a native. He is a wicked one, this." His smile asked for sympathy from Marian and Stella and got it.

"Nothing of the kind," said Edvardson. "I interpreted for him, in German."

"Pah." It was an extraordinary sound. "We had best drink on that, Thor, my old friend. It is a long time—" He showed signs of reckoning it up.

"A very long time," Edvardson interrupted him. "And a long time, for us, Stavros, without a drink. Except what you get on Lykabetos."

"Oh!" He made a comic face. "Then you are sufferers indeed. But not for long." He was gone, to return with glasses of ouzo and the most elaborate *mezes,* or hors d'oeuvres, that Marian had ever seen.

Starting hungrily on the lumps of cheese that nestled among olives, garlic sausage and improbable cold fried potato, she wondered what she ought to be thinking, what doing. But what was there to do except sit, and eat, and drink, and feel, extraordinarily, safe?

Two ouzos later, she and Stella retired to the surprisingly elegant ladies' and conferred, briefly. "He saved me, up top there," Stella summed it up in a quick whisper. "I don't suppose he knew it, but he did. I'm inclined to trust him. For several reasons." A wicked look for Marian. "Besides, what else can we do?"

It was true. Without the professor, they were lost in this network of alleys that was, he had told them, the old quarter of Athens, the Plaka. With him, they were guided and felt protected. "Besides," said Stella, "I'm hungry."

"Me, too." The *mezes* had merely sharpened Marian's appetite. "I wish we could eat here."

"I like it, too."

But they got an equally enthusiastic welcome at the restaurant, a few corners away, to which Edvardson presently led them. "It doesn't look much of a place," he warned them, and, indeed, here was no vine-covered courtyard, but a small, spare almost basement room, with the best smell of cooking Marian had ever encountered. And here, too, the proprietor hurried forward to kiss Edvardson on both cheeks, to call him "Thor" and to urge him and his guests to the best table.

The food was Elysian. After three ouzos, Marian and Stella were glad to let the professor order for them, to eat the astonishing first course of garlic-rich cream cheese and highly flavoured cod's roe; to sop up the last smears with tough, delicious bread; and to listen with approval as the professor ordered retsina.

"God, I feel better," said Stella.

"Me, too," said Marian. And yet some cautious corner of her mind warned her against telling the professor of the Furies that pursued them. This was a halcyon moment of safety, of happiness. She would take it as such—and take no chances.

The first course was followed by a Platonic ideal of a shepherd's pie, which the professor explained was moussaka made with artichoke hearts. "They use whatever vegetable is in season. And you must try your Greek salad, Mrs. F." He poured retsina for them all as she plunged her fork into the extraordinary mixture of lettuce, herbs, olives, cheese and a few things she never quite identified.

After this came baclava, a confection of pastry, nuts and honey which cried out for more retsina, and strong Turkish coffee. Stella smiled across the professor at Marian and lit one of her rare cigarettes. "To celebrate," she said. "It's been a marvellous meal. I haven't eaten so much for years."

"Or drunk so much." Marian was feeling cheerfully muzzy. "You'll have to steer us home, Professor."

"I wish you'd call me Thor." He poured the last of the second bottle into their glasses.

Drinking, Marian felt a long, cold shiver run down her spine. It was back, for the first time since Stella's confession, that unspeakable feeling of being watched, spied on. And now she knew it for real. She looked round. The restaurant, half-empty when they arrived, was crowded now. But there was no one she recognised. Which meant precisely nothing.

She reached down a hand that would tremble and picked up her purse from the floor. "I must go and powder my nose. And then, Thor, do you think we could possibly get a taxi back to the hotel? I feel as if I'd walked a thousand miles."

"Me, too." Stella picked up her bag to accompany Marian.

"Certainly," said the professor. "I'll ask Andros to send one of the boys out to get us one." He laughed. "That poor Mike will be wondering whether you're coming to Aegina or not."

"Goodness, so he will." Marian looked round her. "Do you know where the ladies' is?"

"No." He caught a passing waiter, and Marian recognised one of the basic words she had learned, *toualetta*.

The man pointed to an anonymous door up two steps at the back of the crowded room, and Marian and Stella threaded their way through the closely packed tables towards it, while the professor moved across the room to where the proprietor was busy at his cash desk.

The door opened upwards into a little yard that smelled deliciously of food and orange blossom. A small light over two doors facing them across the yard showed the usual little figures of a man and a woman. "You go first," said Stella. "It's probably tiny—Oh!" Her breath caught on the last syllable, and Marian, in the act of turning towards her, felt movement behind her, opened her mouth to scream and fell suddenly into blackness.

The light hurt her eyes. She closed them tighter and felt something cold on her forehead. A voice above her said something brief, in Greek. Had she been in an accident? Was this a hospital? Her memory was fuzzy round the edges.

"Drink this." The voice spoke English. "You'll feel better in a minute."

She opened her eyes and saw Mrs. Adams bending over her, glass in hand. Memory sharpened horribly. She pushed the glass away so violently that it spilled. "No!"

"Stupid," said Mrs. Adams. "It's just water. We want you alive, remember."

Remember? How did they know she knew? Stella? She pulled herself up on the hard bed and looked round the little room. No windows. An ill-lighted basement kitchen of a rather primitive kind. A curious, horrible smell of burning, and, in the corner by a surprisingly modern electric stove, a bundle moving a little, sitting up. Stella, gagged, speechless, tears streaming out of her eyes, the arm nearer the glowing hot plate of the stove bare.

"She told us." Mr. Adams—not his name, but what did that matter? "Of course." He was neither glad nor sorry. Everything was going, simply, as he had expected. "It saves time." He kicked Stella aside as if she were a dog and came to stand over Marian. "We've not got a great deal. Those fools gave you too big a dose. I'd have thought the professor knew better."

"The professor?" She flinched, as from a blow. All her suspicions had been right then. She had indeed let herself be blinded by sex or, worse still, the illusion of it. Horrible. She could not face it. She must. She shut her eyes for an anguished moment and received an actual blow, sharp on her face.

"Stupid!" Mrs. Adams was furious. "She's got to look all right."

"So she has. Open your eyes, Mrs. Frenche. It will be where it hurts more, and shows less, next time. Or would you rather watch us do it to dear little Stella there, the double-crossing bitch? Yes—" He was smiling with satisfaction when Marian reopened her eyes. "The professor sent word that was the way to do it, and I bet he was right." He looked at his watch. "Only a few hours till the bus leaves for Aegina. We've got to hurry. So, Mrs. Frenche, you'd better pay attention if you value your life—and Stella's there. The professor says as little bloodshed as possible. I suppose it makes sense." Grudgingly. "So, if you just cooperate with us, Miss Marten will be on the plane back to England tonight, though it's more than she deserves, and you'll be free tomorrow."

The professor. Always the professor. "Call me Thor." The world swayed dizzily round her. Fool, fool, and fool again. And not only her own life lost by her folly, but Stella's.

"She's going to faint," said Mrs. Adams.

"Don't let her."

Something strong and aromatic under her nose. The giddiness passed. What was the use of regretting it? Their situation, hers and Stella's, had to be faced, sooner or later. With an effort, she sat up. It was better to be on a level with her captors. "What do you want me to do?"

"That's better." Adams' voice purred satisfaction. "I thought you were a reasonable woman. Well, you know the story, thanks to our little friend there. There's a lady escaped from solitary confinement on Aegina tonight. Your double, or close enough." He looked at her consideringly as a surgeon might before using the knife. "With a fond farewell from Mike, who's above suspicion, and the rest of us gathering round her, she'll get out all right on our charter plane. That fool Cairnthorpe wouldn't notice if she was twice your age. And we all know what the passport inspection's like on a charter that gets in in the small hours at Gatwick. That's where Miss Marten comes in. I thought the prof. was nuts at first, but he's often right. So long as she doesn't let out a squeak, no one else is going to fret. And if she does"—he turned with sudden ferocity on Stella's huddled figure—"well then, you spend the rest of your life in a cell on Aegina, Mrs. Frenche. What comes out can go in, and don't think otherwise."

Across the horrible little room, with its smell of burned flesh, Stella's eyes met Marian's. What were they saying? What was there to say? To refuse meant more torture. And of Stella. As if to underline the point, Adams moved across the room and turned up the burner under the hot plate. Passing, he aimed another casual kick at Stella's side. "Pity not to be able to mark her," he said. "Believe me, Mrs. Frenche, I'd really enjoy going to work on her."

It carried its own horrible conviction. Perhaps, Marian thought, they really did mean to let Stella go. After all, it was true enough that her cooperation at Gatwick might make the whole difference to their plan. And true, too, that this tour could hardly afford another "accident." "You promise?" she asked.

"Yes. Do what we tell you, and she's safe. Try to

double-cross us and she's a kippered herring. Literally."
A glance at the stove told its own tale.

A quick knocking on the door took him over to it on
silent feet. He opened it a crack, looked out, and said,
"Yes?"

"What the hell are you doing down here?" Mike's voice.
"The old bitch ought to be in her room by now."

"She's ready. Right?" He looked across at Marian.

"Right." That casual, insulting reference to her had
made up her mind. She was not an old bitch, nor was she
dead—yet. She would fight these gangsters to the last
inch, and that meant, for the moment, giving in. Tomorrow, on the bus, on the ferry, on Aegina, surely somewhere there would be a chance for her? And for Stella?
What chance for her? Once again their eyes met, and this
time a message passed between them. Stella's was plain.
This was all her fault, those distended eyes were saying;
Marian must save herself, if she could. Marian gave her a
quick, brisk nod, as if of agreement, and swung her legs
off the bed. "Good-bye for now," she said. "Be good,
Stella. I'll see you in England." Whether she believed them
or not, she must make them think she did. The only
chance for her and Stella was the police, whatever disaster
it meant for the other woman, who had apparently already
made her escape from the prison on Aegina.

"Good." Adams gave her one long, considering look,
seemed satisfied and returned to the door. "Go get the lift,
Mike. We're coming. You and Stella there"—he turned
back to Marian—"were in a taxi accident coming back to
the hotel tonight with the prof. Stella's going to stay in
bed all day, resting up for the flight back. You're a bit
shaken, but you don't want to miss Aegina. Understand?"

"Yes." It was diabolically neat.

"So, you just go with the crowd, do what they do
and say nothing to anyone. Not even the prof. Specially
not the prof. He's got enough on his mind without you
looking daggers at him. 'Call me Thor.'" His laugh
mocked her. "Took you in good and proper, didn't he?
Fine little holiday romance you got yourself, I don't think.
Right?" Mike was at the door. "Then, here we go."

Marian went, without a backward glance. Even looks were too dangerous now. Adams had one of her arms, and his "wife" the other. The door clicked behind them. Stella was locked in there alone. Well, there was a certain temporary safety in that. Marian looked round her. They must be in the basement of the Hotel Hermes. Doubtless that horrible little kitchen belonged to a caretaker's flat. Here was the familiar lift, confirming her guess.

Once inside, Adams spoke. "Mrs. Adams has very kindly spent the night with you. Seeing as how you were a bit shaken up and all. Isn't it convenient the rooms have all got two beds? Now." The lift had stopped at her floor. "One word, one thought out of line, and the girl's for it. You do believe me, don't you?"

"I believe you," said Marian.

It was extraordinarily horrible to find her room looking just the same as ever, the bed neatly turned down for the night. "Better get undressed," said Mrs. Adams. "Rest while you can; you've got a busy day ahead."

Her last? Marian changed obediently into her night-gown and climbed into bed, to lie there shivering, and trying to think, for what seemed little more than ten minutes. The telephone, ringing sharply, startled her into sudden hope. Dared she try anything? No; too soon. She lay there, inert, apparently cowed, and listened to Mrs. Adams take the routine morning call and then ring down to the restaurant to order breakfast for two. "You're not well enough to go down this morning." She replaced the receiver and smiled sweetly at Marian. "Might as well stay in bed till it comes." The suggestion was an order, and Marian obeyed it, saying nothing. She closed her eyes again and tried frenziedly to think. When would her best chance come? The answer was obvious. She remembered the confusion as they got on and off the ferry to Itea. The embarkation at Piraeus was her best chance, and going ashore at Aegina the second best. But it must be Piraeus if possible. There would be more and superior police there. The vital telephone call that would save Stella would be much easier than across from an island. She knew that when she made her bid for freedom, she would be risking Stella's life, as well as her own, and she knew that she had Stella's free permission to do so. In the meantime, she would be every inch the subdued prisoner, in the hope that Mrs. Adams would begin to take obedience for granted.

Breakfast came, and she ate coffee and rolls in silence. Mrs. Adams did likewise, merely remarking, "We'll save the friendly bit till we're on the bus. My 'husband's' not coming today, so I'll be able to sit with you. Lucky us. And if it's any comfort to you, you bore me to tears."

"Thanks," said Marian dryly, got a sharp look and regretted it.

The coffee revived her a little, but in her state of fatigue it was easy enough to be passive, frightening to think that her chance might come and she be simply too muddled with exhaustion to recognise and take it.

"Time to get dressed," said Mrs. Adams. "You won't do anything stupid if I let you in the bathroom alone, will you?"

"No." It was too easy to sound hopeless. "Why should I?" But what about when it was Mrs. Adams' turn? Would it be worth a quick dive for the telephone?

Mrs. Adams was looking at her consideringly. "I don't rightly know what to think about you. But just in case you were thinking of trying anything silly, we've got a friend on the switchboard. We've got a lot of friends," she added, and it rang, horribly, true. "Oh." She turned at the bathroom door. "They've moved the girl of course. Don't kid yourself she's in the hotel anymore. No one's going to find her without our help."

It was a blow, and one she must not let show. "But she's all right?" Marian asked, as if that was all she cared about.

"Of course. We stick to our bargains. And besides, we need her in shape for the plane tonight."

Later, dressed and ready, she looked Marian over critically. "That bruise is beginning to show on your face," she said angrily. "Damn fool of a man. He knew you mustn't be marked, either of you. If anyone should mention it, you got it in the taxi accident. Hit the front panel, did you?"

"I should think so." Marian's hand went up to the throbbing place below her cheekbone. "What kind of accident was it?"

This won her a quick, suspicious glance, and she wished it unsaid. "Not stupid, are you? Well, maybe it's a good thing. So long as you've got some sense. Your taxi ran into a parked car on a blind corner. Nothing serious, but it shook Miss Marten up."

"I see. I just thought, if anyone asked. . . ." She let it trail off hopelessly.

"Any other questions?" Mrs. Adams picked up her bag. "Because from now on I'm the ministering angel, and you're my grateful protégée. Right?"

"Right."

"Oh, and by the way," casually. "They picked Andreas up out of Itea harbour last night. Funny thing, he must have got in a fight. His throat was cut."

"Oh," said Marian.

Chapter 14

THE REST of the Aegina party were already assembled in the hotel lobby, depressingly few of them. The schoolmistresses were gathered round Mike, all talking at once, and Marian remembered, with a new sinking of the heart, that he was in entire charge of their party for today. David Cairnthorpe was taking the Athens tour, so there was no hope of help from him. No hope from anyone. She found herself looking round for the professor, saw no sign of him, knew she should be relieved and could not, somehow, manage it.

"You poor thing, how are you?" Meg and Pam had detached themselves from the little crowd round Mike at sight of her. "What with poor Andreas and your accident, I really do feel as if the Furies were after us. Have you heard about him?"

"Yes." All she could stand.

"Some dockside quarrel, Mike says. But how are you, and Miss Marten?"

"I'm fine, but she's not too good, I'm afraid." Marian

was amazed how normal her voice sounded. "She's spending the day in bed."

"What a shame to miss Aegina," said Pam.

"The professor can't come either," put in Meg. "He's had to go down to the police station about your accident. Really, what bad luck!"

"Isn't it?" Marian's feelings were beyond analysis.

"To the police station?" asked Mrs. Adams. "Why?"

"I don't know," said Meg. "Mike told us."

And here was Mike, coming forward to enquire solicitously how Marian felt. Was she really sure she was up to the long day on Aegina? "You wouldn't rather spend it quietly with Miss Marten?"

"No, thanks." Again she was proud of her tone. "She says she's just going to sleep all day. And I'm fine, thank you, really. They don't need me at the police station, too?" It was, surely, a natural question to ask.

"Of course not." Something sharp in Mike's tone made her wonder if, however natural, the question had been wise. "Who wants a woman's word when they can have a man's?" And then, as if aware of some failure of his usual suavity. "And naturally they know how badly you'd been shaken, Mrs. Frenche. They didn't want to disturb you."

"Kind," she said mechanically, and moved forward with apparent docility as they all began to file out towards the waiting bus.

It was half empty. Most of the older members of the party had opted for the less exhausting city tour, but the schoolmistresses were all there, and Charles Esmond leaned eagerly forward in his aisle seat to ask Marian how poor Miss Marten felt.

"Not too bad. She'll be fine by tonight, I hope." How passionately she hoped it.

Mrs. Spencer was sitting behind the Esmonds. "All on your own today?" She smiled at Marian. "Won't you join me? I've lost my partner, too. The poor professor has had to go down and give evidence or something."

"Thanks." Marian hesitated for an endless moment, horribly tempted. Mrs. Adams could hardly stop her sitting down beside Mrs. Spencer, and surely, once there, she would be able to pass a note, do something. It seemed so simple. Dangerously simple? She had hesitated for only an instant. Now, "How nice of you," she said, "but Mrs. Adams is very kindly looking after me. I was a bit shaken up too." She made it rueful. "I don't know what I'd have done without her."

"Nothing like a good first-aid course." Mrs. Adams was jolly about it. "But that bruise of yours is beginning to show again. You ought always to put your head in your arms when you see an accident coming."

"Yes," said Marian, "but I didn't see it coming."

"You go first." Mrs. Adams gestured her into the window seat. "I wish I had some witch hazel. Your friends at home are going to think you got yourself beaten up in Greece."

Marian sat down silently. The unspeakable woman was enjoying every moment of this. It was horrible, and yet somehow, she felt, it might provide some clue of hope, some chance. . . . Play up to it? Let her enjoy herself? But, carefully, she warned herself. Oh, so carefully. There had, surely, under the assumed jolliness, been an increase in tension in Mrs. Adams since they came downstairs. Well, natural enough, you might say. But just the same Marian's sharpened perceptions told her that something, somewhere, had not gone quite as Mike and Mrs. Adams expected.

The professor's absence? Could that be the trouble? She had assumed that the story of his having gone to police headquarters had been merely a link in their endless chain of lies, but suppose it was true? Suppose some small stitch of the elaborate conspiracy had unravelled and the professor had been pulled in? Surely that opened up all kinds of possibilities of hope?

It was so horrible to be thinking like this that Marian had suddenly to bite back tears. What was it that Adams had said last night? A fine little holiday romance she had got herself indeed. All the stories of all the middle-aged female fools she had ever heard crowded to mock her. He had played her so skilfully, so gently. . . . Even when she

discovered that he could speak Greek, she had not let
herself be warned. They had gone, she and Stella, to that
fatal restaurant like lambs to the slaughter. How he must
have laughed, internally, when, belatedly cautious, she
asked for a taxi back to the hotel. He who knew that his
friends were already waiting for them in that sinister,
orange-scented backyard.

What would have happened if they had not gone to
the ladies'? Presumably an attack in the street or a "lift"
in a friend's car. There must have been a car, after all, to
get them back to the hotel. It had doubtless been used
again to take Stella to wherever she was now being held.
And there was a horrible new problem that must be faced.
If Stella was really now hidden somewhere else, the
chances of the police getting there before the gang killed
her were slight. But—the thought had been nibbling
round the edges of Marian's mind ever since Mrs. Adams
had made her casual announcement—suppose this was
another of their web of lies?

After all, the basement of the Hotel Hermes was much
the most convenient place to keep Stella, granted that
she must leave with the party in the small hours of the
night and give her protection to the false Mrs. Frenche.
And this part of the plan carried conviction. Stella would
get back to England, Marian thought, and through cus-
toms, and that was about as far as she would ever get.
Dead girls tell no tales. A gang that had demonstrated
such a genius for "accidents" in the course of the tour
would have no trouble in disposing of Stella somewhere
between Gatwick and London.

"Are you all right?" Mrs. Adams' voice was convincingly anxious.

Had she been silent too long? But what in the world
could she be expected to say? "Yes, thanks. A bit sleepy."
She breathed a sigh of relief when Mike stood up, took the
familiar microphone, and began to give them instructions
for boarding the ferry at Piraeus.

It sounded unpleasantly well organised to Marian. They
were arriving early, it seemed, because the island boats
got so crowded. They would be the first on board, and

Mike advised them to make sure of seats in the cabin. "You can always watch each other's seats and take turns on deck afterwards."

"Cabin for you," said Mrs. Adams briskly. "You don't want to risk pneumonia up on deck. Besides, another coffee will do you good."

The ferry was there, waiting. The bus pulled up on the wharf quite close to it. They debouched in the usual untidy crocodile, were handed individual tickets by Mike and proceeded on board like good children on their way to Sunday church. One wild look round had shown Marian no sign of a policeman. The chance was gone before it had come. She was on board, following Mrs. Adams down to the cabin, hearing Mrs. Spencer ask if by any miracle they played bridge.

"I do, just a teeny bit," said Mrs. Adams. "How about you Mrs. Frenche?"

Better to play cards than to keep up this horrible pretence of conversation. "Not very well," she admitted.

"Splendid." Mrs. Adams settled them at a table with high brown leather seats. "You deal." She handed a pack of cards to Mrs. Spencer. "And I'll see if I can find us that coffee. A pity we haven't a fourth." She looked round the cabin. "Mrs. Esmond doesn't, I know. It looks as if we'll just have to make it cutthroat." The word, in the light of Andreas' fate, was horrible.

As Mrs. Spencer dealt the first hand and the inevitable discussion of bidding conventions broke out, a tall woman with heavily dyed red hair stopped by their table. "You let me make a fourth? I play well." Without waiting for an invitation, she pulled a chair up to the table, snapped her fingers at the waiter who was bringing their coffee and ordered another one in quick French. "So. You and I will be partners"—she was facing Marian—"or do we, how do you call it—" She made gestures as of one cutting cards.

"Might as well stay as we are." Mrs. Adams was grudging, but short of actual rudeness there was not much she could do. The three of them listened patiently to a

confused disquisition half French half English on what
seemed a most unusual bidding system.

"I'm afraid I'm not very good," said Marian again, lost
in the abstruse meanings of five no trumps.

"Not to worry—Is that how you say it? With me,
Marcelle, you cannot lose. Just do your best, and leave all
to me."

She had extraordinary bridge conventions and equally
extraordinary luck. After the first game, which she had
bade to three no-trumps against a timid one heart from
Marian and made with a trick over, she said, cheerfully
shuffling, "We play for money? Yes? It is much more
interesting that way. Not much money, just a little to add
a touch of drama. In drachmae, if you like? Perhaps ten
a hundred? That way, no one is bankrupt and all are
happy. We do not count this last game, of course. That
was just—what do you say—a trial canter?"

Mrs. Spencer and Mrs. Adams were exchanging glances.
Marian, after all, was still a dark horse, having being
dummy in the first game. At last, "I don't see why not,"
said Mrs. Adams. "If you don't mind?" to Marian.

It was all mad. What did it matter if she lost ten drachmae, or a hundred, or a thousand even? The chances
were about ninety to one that she would be dead tomorrow. What was that phrase? "To move wild laughter in
the throat of death." She would have liked to laugh,
wildly, hysterically. She had next to nothing to leave the
twins anyway, nor did they need it. Might as well play
this last game for any stakes they chose.

"Suits me," she said casually. "It does make it more
interesting."

Her partner played an extraordinary, incomprehensible
game and won consistently. "I tell you, I have the luck."
She smiled benevolently round the table after bidding and
making a little slam in spades. She talked consistently as
she played, and this was making her opponents angrier
and angrier.

"I like to concentrate on my cards," said Mrs. Adams
pointedly.

"Oh, so do I," agreed Marcelle, stubbing out a half-smoked cigarette in the ashtray under Mrs. Adams' nose. "Always I concentrate, madly, like this." She wrinkled her brow, showing layers of casually applied makeup. "And always I talk, and I win. You are lucky, is it not, madame?" She smiled her warm smile at Marian, who suddenly found herself wondering if she was quite so old as she looked. "By my count"—she had a piece of paper by her, with indecipherable squiggles on it that passed for the score—"we are five of your pounds the richer already. "What will you do with it?"

"I don't know. Lose it, I expect."

"That's no way to think. Never think of defeat, madame; think always of victory. It is a maxim of some general's. I do not clearly recollect which. Perhaps our Napoleon, perhaps your Wellington."

"Only one of them won," said Mrs. Spencer disagreeably.

"Madame, you are so right. So of course it must have been your Wellington who said it. Unless, by any chance, it was that odious Bismarck." She dealt with swift, clean movements as she talked, gave one glance at her quickly organised hand and bade three diamonds.

"Four spades." On Marcelle's left, Mrs. Adams showed signs of fury.

Marian took one gloomy look at her hand with its one face card. "No bid."

"Five hearts," said Mrs. Spencer, and got a viperish look from her partner.

"Double," said Marcelle sweetly. "You are brave, mesdames. I order you a drink to celebrate." She had a genius for catching waiters' eyes, and four ouzos arrived in time to ease the crisis when Mrs. Spencer went down five.

"Doubled," said Marcelle amiably, "I drink to you, partner." And then, as the inevitable postmortem broke out between the other two ladies. "If you will excuse me a moment, I must go to the *toilette*. You wish to come, madame?" Once more that heartwarming smile.

But Mrs. Adams' hand was firm on her knee. "I don't believe so," said Marian.

"You are lucky," said Marcelle. "Coffee and ouzo go through me like lightning. A little moment, and I will return and give you your revenge. Unless you wish to change partners?"

"No, thanks." Mrs. Adams was so definite that Mrs. Spencer had no chance to speak.

Returning five minutes or so later, Marcelle reported that they were well out from Athens. "There are islands everywhere? We go to see. Yes?"

"Do let's. It's so hot in here." Marian put up an instinctive hand to her bruised cheek. "If you feel like it?" She turned deferentially to Mrs. Adams and hated herself for doing so.

"I don't see why not. So long as you don't catch cold. Madame here was in an accident last night," she explained to Marcelle. "She is not well today."

"She is well enough to play a good game of bridge," said Marcelle. "But a puff of air will do us all good. Come then!" She put a loud mock fur coat round her shoulders and led the way out of the crowded saloon and up the steep double stairs to the main deck. Following, Mrs. Adams and Mrs. Spencer were still hotly disputing the responsibility for the disaster of the last game. For just one moment, Marcelle and Marian were alone at the rail, looking forward to the long mole of Aegina harbour, with its blue domed chapel. Marcelle's hand closed over Marian's, hard, on the rail. "Do nothing," she said. "You are not alone. Wait." And then, "Yes, that is Aegina. It is the Chapel of Saint Nicholas. Not in the least interesting. You have seen it, madame?" She turned to ask Mrs. Adams as the two other women joined them.

"No. And I don't intend to." Mrs. Adams had not quite regained her temper. "We're nearer in than I thought. Might as well stay up on deck. If you feel up to it. She turned to Marian with her sickening pretence of concern.

"Oh, perfectly." The fresh air combined with the message she had just received was helping to wake her out of the trance of despair into which she had let herself sink after the fiasco at Piraeus. She had, apparently, allies. Impossible to imagine how she had acquired them, and no chance of asking Marcelle any more, but the knowledge changed everything. It meant hope, not just for herself, but for Stella. If they knew of her plight, they must surely know of Stella's, might even have done something about it already.

"Do nothing," Marcelle had said. "Wait." It was lucky, after all, that she had achieved nothing at Piraeus. She might have wrecked everything, even have killed Stella by precipitate action. But—waiting is the hardest thing of all. She shivered a little in the heavy, all-concealing cardigan Mrs. Adams had chosen from among her clothes and made her wear.

"You are going to the temple?" Marcelle was making polite conversation with Mrs. Adams.

"Yes. I imagine that is our bus waiting on the quay."

"Very likely. Me, I am not fond of buses. They make me sick. I have a friend with a velo—what do you say?— a motor something? He will take me, fast, fast, and I will be in Aghia Marina long before you. We do not go to the temple, he and I, only to lunch and shop for the carpets they make there or say they make there. So perhaps we had better settle now, had we not, in case by any chance we do not meet again."

"Oh, yes, of course." If Mrs. Adams had hoped that the seven pounds odd that she and her partner now owed were to be forgotten, she concealed her disappointment manfully. "Do you mind it in sterling?"

"Far from it," said Marcelle, cheerfully pulling out her purse. "I love money of all kinds, do not you, madame?"

Marian was remembering something Marcelle had said earlier in the game: "Never think of defeat; think always of victory." Well, they had won themselves seven pounds each. She accepted the money Mrs. Spencer was handing her and made herself smile at Mrs. Adams. "We'll have to have a drink on this at lunch."

Would she be alive at lunchtime? When would it happen? And did Marcelle really know? Her hands gripped hard on the rail.

"You are feeling worse?" Mrs. Adams missed nothing. "You would like to go below again?"

"Oh, no, it's nothing. Just a bit sleepy still." She ought to tell Marcelle she had understood and would obey her message. "I think I'll try and get some sleep in the bus," she said. "After all there's nothing to do until we get to the temple."

"Very wise," said Mrs. Adams.

"You are lucky," said Marcelle. "Me, I will be clinging tight, tight to my boyfriend's rear end, but you will be wise to rest while you may, madame. It is a long day you make for one who has been in an accident."

"Oh, it was nothing," said Marian vaguely. She had just seen a policeman directing traffic at the harbour side. Would Marcelle cover her if she were to try and make a break for it? But Marcelle had said, "Do nothing."

Besides, she was now shaking hands warmly all round. "I shall say *au revoir,* and thank you for a very pleasant game. I see my boyfriend there, by the policeman." She laughed. "That policeman. He directs the traffic so beautifully, and if he saw a crime committed, I promise you, he would look the other way. There! Jacques has seen me." She waved vigorously. "He does not like to be kept waiting, that one. Well"—she conceded it cheerfully—"he is a little younger than I am, in fact."

He looked it. He had stopped talking to the policeman now and was pushing his heavy motorbike towards the landing stage, and Marian, taking the warning about the policeman, thought that this unknown Jacques looked like a much more promising ally. She must hope he *was* an ally and try not to let her eyes follow the retreating back of Marcelle, who was now pushing her way briskly through the crowd, conspicuous in the bright fake fur.

"Well!" said Mrs. Adams.

"Cheating, of course," said Mrs. Spencer.

"Oh, dear," said Marian. "I am so sorry; I had no idea. You really must let me give you your money back."

"No, no, not at all," said Mrs. Spencer. "It will be a lesson to me not to play with strangers."

"And to me." Mrs. Adams sounded even angrier than Mrs. Spencer. "Did you see how she did it?"

"Can't say I did. Some French trick, no doubt. Of

course one could see that you knew nothing about it." Her tone of patronage irked Marian suddenly, and then she thought how absurd it was to let a trifle annoy her, now, when her life was at stake.

People were filing ashore, and they followed rather behind the main crowd. "No hurry," said Mrs. Adams comfortably. "Mike will wait."

The motorbike went off with a roar of exhaust as they were crossing the dock to their bus, and Marian could not help a new pang of despair. Did Marcelle know that nothing would happen before they got to Aghia Marina? It was easy to say, "Do nothing," but extraordinarily hard to do it.

In fact, to her own amazement, she actually did fall asleep in the bus, after it had made its precarious way out of the narrow, hilly streets of the little town, and woke with a start to find her head resting cosily on Mrs. Adams' shoulder. "There," said the latter in motherly tones, "haven't you had a splendid sleep. I expect you feel all the better for it."

"I feel like hell," said Marian.

"Never mind." Mrs. Spencer turned round from her seat in front. "You missed a very dull talk from young Mike. I don't think his mind's on his job today. If the professor was here, I'm sure he'd have corrected him on a point or two. Why, even I know that the Temple of Aphaea here is older than the Parthenon."

"Is it really?" It was hard to feel that it mattered.

"Yes, fifty years or so, I believe. I expect it's one of the reasons the Athenians disliked Aegina so much. What with that and their being such a progressive lot here. Real money, you know, before anyone else. Well"—brightly— "here we are."

The bus had been climbing through pine groves for some time and now pulled into a car park that already had its complement of tourist buses.

"It's going to be crowded, I'm afraid," said Mrs. Adams gloomily.

"Looks like it," agreed Mrs. Spencer. "Well, it always

is. So near Athens. One would need to come in midwinter to have it to oneself."

Marian pulled on her heavy cardigan. If the temple was crowded, it could not be going to happen here. She did not let herself specify what exactly she meant by "it." What was the use? She would find out soon enough. But climbing down from the bus, she could not help a quick look round the car park, or a pang of disappointment at sight of several cars, one of them a small red one that might be unpleasantly familiar, but no motorbike.

The temple was as crowded as the one at Sounion had been, and thinking this, Marian felt as if she were looking back on some remote, almost archaeological past. She remembered escaping from the crowds there and sitting peacefully, dazed with sleep as she was today, among gold and yellow flowers, brooding about the twins. That was the day when Mrs. Hilton had sealed her own doom by insisting on sitting with her on the bus going back. The professor had not been there, but the Adamses had, and doubtless reported Mrs. Hilton to him as a possible hazard. Was she really thinking of the professor as the leader of this gang? It was horrible, but granted his part in it, she could imagine him as nothing else.

The harassed custodian of the site was shouting at a party of German boys who were clambering on the rare upper row of pillars. "Disgusting," said Mrs. Adams, "they ought to be kept under better control." She looked at her watch. "It's about time we were going."

"Going?" They were in the midst of a group of older Germans, who were busily discussing their guidebook.

"Yes. Don't you remember, you wanted to walk down? I still think it's a bit much for you, but since you insist, I'll have a word with Mike, and we'd better get started. If we leave now, we ought to get to the café in Aghia Marina at about the same time as the others. So long as you're sure you're up to the walk." This was a little louder, for the benefit of Mrs. Spencer, who had climbed over a fallen pillar to join them. "Mrs. Frenche wants to walk down to the village," she explained. "It was an idea of

Miss Marten's actually." The name rang a warning bell
in Marian's head as was undoubtedly intended.

What had Marcelle said? "Do nothing." Well, surely,
that meant go along with what was suggested. Besides, for
Stella's sake, she must. "Of course, I'm up to it." She
sounded quite convincingly cross. "This place is too
crowded to be borne. But let's just have one more look
at the view."

If it was her last, of any view, it was worth it.

Chapter 15

"HI, THERE!" Marian and Mrs. Adams had cut through the car park and started down a narrow path through the pine woods, when the shout from behind made them stop and turn. Mrs. Spencer was hurrying after them. "Wait for me!" she called. "I want to walk down, too."

Marian, who had already been encouraged by the fact that the sinister little red car was no longer in the park, felt a wild leap of hope. Surely Mrs. Spencer's presence must be some kind of protection? Mrs. Adams was certainly greeting her with a signal lack of enthusiasm. "It's a very rough path. Are you sure your shoes are up to it?"

"Yes, don't you think you'd be better in the bus?" Remembering the gang's ruthlessness, Marian felt it the least she could do to try and protect Mrs. Spencer.

"Nonsense." Mrs. Spencer fell into line behind Marian on the narrow path.

It was surprisingly quiet among the trees, and dark with the sinister darkness only pine woods have. Ahead Mrs. Adams set a brisk pace that left no time for conversation. Stumbling, sometimes, with fatigue, Marian was aware of Mrs. Spencer coming steadily along behind her. The path came out into the open suddenly to cross a bend in the road that zigzagged its way up the hill. They paused for a moment, to let a minibus pass, then crossed and plunged into a still deeper, more silent stand of pines. No birds sang here, and even the noise of cars from the road seemed muted. Only the sharp smell of the pine trees served as a reminder of living.

"Here." Mrs. Adams stopped at a fork of the path. "This is our way." Suddenly, she and Mrs. Spencer had an arm of each of Marian's as they turned into a surprisingly broader path, wide enough, surely, for a small car.

"How far?" asked Mrs. Spencer.

"Ten minutes. But we'll have to hurry. There's a lot to do." And then, as Marian caught her breath. "Quiet now. Not that anyone could hear you. It's a geological fault, if that means anything to you."

Marian was silent. She was digesting her own extraordinary stupidity. Mrs. Spencer was one of them. If she had applied to her, back on the bus, it would have meant disaster.

Well, and what was this? Marcelle, down in the village of Aghia Marina, seemed worlds away, and Stella, back in Athens. . . . Poor Stella. She was young.

"Here we are," said Mrs. Adams with satisfaction. The track had turned a corner and emerged into a clearing where stood a typical little one-storey Greek summer home, all white concrete and geraniums in petrol tins.

A young man was sitting on a kitchen chair outside the front door, cleaning a gun. "Good." He pushed the door open, and they filed in to the large, main room of the house. Marian had recognised him as one of the two Greeks of the red car, which was doubtless parked out of sight behind the house somewhere. The other one awaited them inside. "You're late," he said.

"I know." Mrs. Adams turned on Marian. "No time to lose. Your clothes. All of them. In there." She pushed her into a tiny slip of a bedroom, threw a black bundle after her and, mercifully, closed the door.

The room was windowless and furnished only with a pallet bed and another kitchen chair. Marian sat down on the chair. What now? Every instinct told her not to co-operate. She had friends, after all. Marcelle and the young man on the motorbike must be somewhere. Time, now, had to be on her side. If anything was. . . .

What had Marcelle said? "Don't think of defeat. . . . Think of victory." Time. . . . She got up from the chair, threw herself on the hard bed, which smelled, and pretended sleep. Was there a hole in the door? Were they watching? Apparently not. A few minutes passed with nothing but the sound of rapid Greek from the main room. It was, she supposed, not surprising that Mrs. Adams and Mrs. Spencer both spoke it fluently. She could hear their voices now, and another woman's, loud, harsh, angry. Her double? She would know soon enough.

The talk in the other room came to a crescendo, then stopped on one grating monosyllable from the strange voice. Marian made herself lie relaxed on the bed, as if she had fallen there in complete exhaustion. She heard the door swing open, and a furious exclamation. In a moment, Mrs. Adams and Mrs. Spencer were standing over her. You said she'd cooperate. Mrs. Spencer's voice vibrated with fury.

"She will." Mrs. Adams' blow caught Marian exactly on last night's bruise. The pain was exquisite. She pulled her upright on the bed. "We've not much time. What we do to you here they do to that girl in Athens. It's been hard enough to keep Adams off her as it is."

"If you mark her," said Marian. "How will she explain it?"

"The motor accident, cretin. No one's seen her since, have they? Now, off with those clothes, or do we get the men in to strip you? I expect they'd enjoy it. A little." As she talked, she had pulled off the enveloping cardigan, was now busy with the buttons of Marian's blouse.

"Bra and girdle?" asked Mrs. Spencer, as one might have said, medium or rare.

"No need. Marks and Spencer's, and she's got on her own size." The word "she" carried a curious aura of respect, and for the first time Marian found herself actively wondering about this double of hers. Would she see her?

"There." Mrs. Adams pulled off her skirt. "Grateful to me now I made you wear your Marks and Spencer pants? Here!" She threw her the black bundle. "Quick. She wants to see you."

It was the kind of shapeless black garment worn by elderly Greek women, and like the bed, it smelled, but Marian put it on gratefully, noticing, as she did so, that Mrs. Spencer had already vanished with her own clothes and bag.

"Right," said Mrs. Adams, as the heavy, dirt-engrained folds fell around her. "Now, just once I will warn you. She is not one to cross. One word out of tune, and you are dead, and Stella, too. Possibly even I. . . . So, understand me, there will be no word out of tune."

"I understand," Marian said.

"Good. Then come, and let her see you. Though how she will make herself so meek and sweet, God knows." This was spoken in a quick undertone, and Marian was suddenly aware of waves of fear emanating from Mrs. Adams. If *she* was afraid. . . .

Best not finish that sentence. She followed, meekly ("meek and sweet?"), as Mrs. Adams led the way into the main room, then stopped, amazed.

She faced herself across the room. "Good," said the other woman, in Marian's voice. "Very good. She knows herself. Speak to me, Mrs. Frenche. The tape recording is not always perfect. I may have some accent wrong. You will tell me . . . show me."

It was extraordinary. Her own voice? No, not quite. But once she had spoken to this consummate mimic, it would be. So: silence. She folded her lips in a mutinous gesture remembered from the twins and stood there, silent, still, aware of the smell of her garment; beyond humiliation.

"So?" said her double. "We must make you speak? In Athens, Miss Marten will not even have the comfort of crying out. She is gagged, of course. Nikos, the telephone, that our guest may know we mean what we say."

But—gagged, thought Marian, as the Greek called Nikos picked up a telephone in the corner of the room. Then, surely, still in the Hermes? Perhaps, even, rescued already? But he had made the connection, spoken swiftly in Greek and nodded across the room to the nameless woman, who was so nearly Marian. Why not quite? The wig was too tidy, for one thing. Doubtless it had been made back in London, when Marian was looking for jobs, keeping herself, always, scrupulously tidy. Besides, her hair had grown on this trip. . . . But that would be no problem.

Her double was exchanging look for look as the unintelligible conversation continued. Now she smiled, and Marian could have laughed with relief. There is something extraordinarily disconcerting about seeing one's self. But the smile had split their personalities once and for all. Her mirror had never shown her a smile capable of that cruelty. No wonder, Marian thought, freed from a burden of superstition she had not knowingly borne, no wonder this woman's own people were afraid of her.

"Who are you?" She regretted the question the moment it was spoken.

"Good." A gesture stilled the young man at the telephone. " 'Who are you?' " The imitation was horribly perfect, the faint, false intonation wiped out, as by the reverse feed of a tape recorder. "I am Medusa." Again that terrifying smile. "And"—satisfied—"you have never heard of me."

"I have, Medusa." At the professor's voice, every head in the room swung round. "I have waited a long time to meet you again." He was standing in the doorway, holding the gun the Greek outside had been cleaning. "If any of you move, I shoot her." His gesture showed that he meant the woman called Medusa. Behind him, men were coming quietly into the room disarming first the second Greek, then Mrs. Adams and Mrs. Spencer.

"Good," said Edvardson. "Line up against the wall there, facing outwards. All but her. I want to talk to her for a moment."

The woman called Medusa spat something at him in Greek, and he shook his head. "We will keep it in English, if you please. My friends all understand it, and so, I think, do yours. I wonder how many of them know just what they were doing." He turned first to Marian, who had been surveying his friends with astonishment. One was the proprietor of the café the three of them had visited, another the restaurant owner, another, surely, the stand-in bus driver who had brought them from Delphi. The bus driver confirmed this by winking at her cheerfully.

"I don't understand," she said.

"Why should you? And we've no time for explanations. But what I must know is what Stella told you. Trust me, Marian."

Absurd? But she did. Completely. And tears of the most exquisite relief and happiness were running down her face to prove it. "Yes," she said. "I trust you." And, saying it, knew how much more she was saying. The air between them seemed to vibrate with unspoken messages. No time for them now. Marian turned to gaze at her double, the woman called Medusa. "She's a liberal sympathiser." Her voice totally failed to carry conviction. "Stella thought she was a friend of Madame Vlachou." Impossible, now, to believe it. "She's escaped from the prison here on the island. She was to take my place on the plane home."

"And you hers in prison? Or just be found convincingly dead, I suppose, thus ending the search. And the rest of you?" His gaze swung along the row of staring, angry, puzzled faces. "Is that your story, too? A gallant bid for freedom by a tortured woman? She doesn't look too bad, does she, for someone who's been in solitary confinement for years? In fact, they only caught her six months ago, when she made the mistake of coming back to Athens."

"Coming back?" This startled Mrs. Adams into speech.

"Children, the lot of you." There was conviction and contempt in Edvardson's tone. "Just gullible children. You did not begin to think, like Miss Marten, that it was a very violent plan for a political escape? That there might be some political detainees not quite so entitled to support? Even the name 'Medusa' gave you no clue?"

"She's too young. She explained all that." It was the Greek by the door.

"You're too young, or you'd have recognised her for the lying Jezebel she is. Medusa"—he turned and spoke to Marian as if only she mattered—"was the name of a leading Communist in the rebellion after the war. You remember, I told you about Odysseus and Ares, the guerrilla fighters, back at Delphi? Well, she was one of them. The worst of the lot, in some ways. There's no time to tell you the things she did, and I wouldn't if I could, but she had reason enough to know about Stella as one of the Greek children who were carried off. I rather think she was her aunt. But we won't tell Stella that, I think."

"Stella?" Marian was taking it in slowly.

"Safe. She's had a change of guards, that's all. And now, we must get going. You"—he would not even use Medusa's name—"into that room and out of those clothes, if you want a chance to live."

"What do you mean to do with me?" Her eyes challenged him across the room.

"It's a problem." Marian was aware of tension between them, thick as dried blood. Then, visibly, he came to a decision.

"It's a problem," he repeated ruefully. "We don't kill, my friends and I, so easily as you do. And I cannot bring myself to hand even you back to the colonels' police. But I would no more take your word than I would a viper's. So my friends here are going to take the lot of you out into the wildest part of the island, tie you up and leave you. If you've not got loose by tomorrow, someone will come. If you try anything, I'll hear of it and tell the police. But, frankly, I'd like to keep the police out of this."

You could see her weighing chances. "Very well." She opened the door of the little room Marian had used. "Give me my clothes."

Ten minutes later, the exchange had been made once more. In her own clothes, and without the wig, Medusa did indeed look much older, and one of her own Greek followers spat at sight of her. "It's true," he said. "You *are*

Medusa. *Kyrie*"—to Edvardson—"you must be the mad American. The one they talk about. I am your man."

"Oh, no, you're not," said Edvardson cheerfully. "You're for the bushes with the rest of them. You can sort it out among yourselves later." He looked at his watch. "No time to be lost. We're going to be late as it is. Stavros"—to the café proprietor—"you're in charge of the island party."

"I shall enjoy that," said Stavros.

"Now, you two." Edvardson turned to Mrs. Adams and Mrs. Spencer, who had stood rigidly side by side throughout all this. "Which is it to be?"

"Oh, God, take me home," wailed Mrs. Adams. "I had no idea. . . . He made me do it." In her despair, she had aged incredibly. She's older than I am, thought Marian amazed.

"Do you know, I'm inclined to believe you," said the professor. "Though you seem to have taken to violence pretty naturally. But you could be useful to us, and will be, if you want to get home. If you behave, we'll get you out. But you're something else again." To Mrs. Spencer. "You joined the party in Athens—it was the first thing that made me wonder—and you are going to leave it here. I'll explain to Mike." He smiled. "Isn't it a fortunate thing that your gang operates to such an extent in separate cells? Our friend Mike still believes I'm one of you. Right, off with you, Stavros, and tie them up tight."

"Believe me, I will."

"But not to kill."

"Since you say so." His voice was regretful, but resigned.

"Now." Left alone with Marian, Mrs. Adams and the bus driver, Edvardson took another anxious look at his watch. "The substitution continues. You are Medusa, Marian, and you, Mrs. Adams, are in charge of her. If you want to get home alive, you won't put a foot wrong. Loukas here"—he smiled at the bus driver—"is going to hitch a ride back with us across the island. He'll be sitting right behind you two, and I'll be in front. So, no idiocies." He turned to Marian. "Can you do it?"

Pretend to be pretending to be herself. "I don't see why not. Her wig was wrong, did you notice?"

"Yes. And so would they have, and cut it. They're professionals."

"You'd hardly think so," said Marian. It was incredible to have the tables so entirely turned.

"Ungrateful." He was laughing at her. "Did it seem too easy? Well, console yourself, my love, I was a professional too in my day. Loukas here would tell you if there was time."

Loukas grinned broadly. "Those were the days," he said. "Shoot first, questions afterwards; none of this tying up in woods. You're getting soft, madman."

"I'm getting slow," said Edvardson. "And we can't risk it." He looked quickly round the hut. "Off we go. Side by side, you two, and don't forget to look cowed, Marian."

"No." After what he had just called her, it was impossible to meet his eye.

Mike was waiting anxiously in the little main street of Aghia Marina, where the path branched off up the hill. "There you are at last." He was carefully casual. "I was beginning to think you'd lost yourselves." He saw the professor. "You found them then?"

"Told you I would. And a good thing. A bit of trouble. Nothing serious. Come on, let's eat." Edvardson led the way round to the harbour side of a little café and settled the four of them at a table. In some curious, unspoken way the initiative seemed to have passed from Mike to him. And he had settled them, Marian noticed, at a table close to four of the schoolmistresses, so that the double pretence must be kept up throughout the meal, and Mike had no chance to ask the questions with which he was obviously bristling.

She was glad of it. Too much had happened too fast, and it was easiest to be a rather tired Mrs. Frenche, eating a late lunch, or, in Mike's eyes, Medusa, giving a brilliant imitation of that tired Mrs. Frenche.

By the time they had finished charcoal-grilled fish and the inevitable choice of huge apples or still huger oranges, the bus had pulled up behind the café. The schoolmistresses had been for a walk along the shore and came back saying they wished they had brought bathing costumes; Marcelle and her boyfriend had parked their motorbike behind the bus, and Marian realised for the first time that he had been one of Stavros' group up on the hill. Presumably this meant that Medusa and her friends were safely immobilised somewhere.

Marcelle waved cheerfully. "No bridge going back," she called to Marian. "My friend comes too."

Aware, suddenly, of Mike's eye upon her, Marian looked puzzled for a moment, then shrugged and said, "Too bad."

"Nothing of the kind," said Mrs. Adams briskly. "She cheated something shocking coming over." Something had slipped a little about Mrs. Adams' accent since the confrontation on the hillside, and Marian wondered if Mike's English was precise enough for him to notice but, hopefully, doubted it.

When the bus emerged from the intricate network of streets onto the quay at Aegina town, Marian saw the professor stiffen in front of her. As the bus turned, she saw what he had, a loose line of police strung out all along the quay and a control point at the end of the mole where the ferry docked.

"Looks like trouble of some sort." Edvardson sounded casual. "They've got a prison here on Aegina." He turned to explain to Marian and Mrs. Adams. It looks like they've had an escape. No problem of ours, of course."

"I do hope not." Pam leaned across the aisle. "We don't want to miss our plane."

"No fear of that," said Edvardson comfortably. "We can all vouch for each other after all. It will just mean a bit of a holdup while we do so. Incidentally, it might save time if no one mentions that I came across on the other ferry. Would you like to pass the word down your side? And I never did see that Orphean warbler," he finished ruefully.

The bus had stopped on the quay, and one of the smartly dressed police had walked over to enter as the door was opened.

"Ladies and gentlemen." His English was extremely good. "You will forgive me if I ask you to remain in this bus. We have a small problem here on Aegina today, and everyone must be checked before they take the ferry. It will be easier for us all if you stay here, and let us examine your papers as you sit in comfort."

The back of Mike's neck was rigid. "Naturally," he said, "we will cooperate with you in every way, Captain, but I can tell you now that these are the group I brought over from Athens this morning. Oh"—he remembered Loukas —"with the exception of this man, who asked for a lift back from Aghia Marina."

"And him I know," said the police captain. "Off with you, Loukas. You're not what I want—today. But if the rest of the ladies and gentlemen would have their papers ready, we can make this very quick and easy."

Mike rose and picked up the microphone. "You have all heard what the police captain says? I do hope you have your passports with you and will make them available for his inspection. Here are my papers." He handed over a neat wallet which received only the most cursory examination.

The same was true of the bus driver, but then he was, of course, a local man, addressed by the police captain as Alex, before he moved down the aisle to examine the papers of the four schoolmistresses who sat across the front of the bus. They were all in their late twenties, and their papers got merely the briefest examination and a laughing comment on one of the likenesses, before the policeman moved back to four rather older members of the party. Here, he was much more thorough, producing, Marian saw with a qualm of pure terror, a small photograph from his own wallet and comparing it both with the women themselves and with their passport photographs. Beside her, Mrs. Adams had seen too and was beginning to shake.

The policeman had given Charles Esmond's passport the briefest glance and was now working steadily through every page of his mother's. A middle-aged woman. There could be no doubt that this was what he was looking for; the question was, how good was the photograph? And how strong were Mrs. Adams' nerves? "I told you the walk down would be too much for you," Marian turned on her angrily. "Are you feeling worse again?"

"Better give her some of this." Edvardson leaned over the back of the seat and handed Marian a silver-topped flask. "It's only brandy." He had seen Mrs. Adams' quick start of terror. "Do you good." The policeman had reached him now, having disposed summarily of the rest of the younger schoolmistresses. He took his passport to give it a quick look reserved for those of men, then took another look. "Professor Edvardson!" He held out a friendly hand. "I remember you from when I was only a cadet. Welcome back to Greece!" And then, with a sudden change of tone. "You here on business?"

Edvardson laughed. "Not your kind. Nor mine, come to that. I'm looking for birds this time."

"By God, I remember." For a moment, the man had forgotten his immediate problem. "That's why they called you the madman. You found owls on the Acropolis when we found hand grenades."

"I found grenades, too," said the professor mildly. "You have some trouble on the island today?"

"Yes. An escape. A middle-aged woman. Or a devil. You'll remember her, madman. Medusa, they called her. A Communist devil." He was looking beyond Edvardson now, at the next two women to be examined, Marian and Mrs. Adams, and suddenly his face stiffened. "Yes: Medusa. Your passport, madame, if you please."

"Here." Marian had it ready and handed it over with a hand that, proudly, did not shake.

"That's interesting." The professor was half turned to watch what was going on. "You see the likeness, too. I can tell you, when this lady got her hair wet, back at Olympia, it gave me a real shock for a moment. But Medusa must be much older by now, surely?"

"In reality, yes," said the policeman. "In disguise, who can say?" And, to Marian, "I think I must ask you to come to headquarters with me, just as a matter of form. And your friend, perhaps? She is not well?" Mrs. Adams was now shaking all over.

"Neither well nor a friend," said Edvardson. "She insisted on walking down from the temple to Aghia Marina with us and has been suffering ever since. That's why my fiancée is sitting with her, instead of with me, where she belongs."

"Your fiancée!" The policeman slapped his thigh. "The madman married at last!" He sobered for a moment. "You have told her of the other one? What Medusa did to her?"

"Not yet. We only met on this tour, but you will understand, I am sure, that I can vouch for her absolutely."

"It's not everyone whose word I'd take, but yours, in these circumstances, yes." He handed Marian back her passport. "Madame, I congratulate you. You are to marry a very brave man."

"And I thought he was just a bird watcher." For some reason, this broke the tension. The police captain gave a bark of laughter and a quick look at Mrs. Adams' passport, recommended more brandy, went quickly through the papers of a miscellaneous group of young women at the back of the bus and left them, with a final, friendly clap on the professor's shoulder and a quick phrase in Greek.

"What did he say?" Marian could not resist the question, seeing the effect it had had on the professor.

"He wished me many handsome sons."

"What no daughters? asked Marian.

The ferry had pulled in to the mole while the inquisition had been in process, and now two junior policemen appeared to shepherd them on board. The professor took Marian's arm firmly, then offered the other one to Mrs. Adams. "I do hope you are feeling better."

"Much, thank you." She was looking from one of them to the other, in an obvious mixture of suspicion and amazement.

Settled in the same brown leather cabin, or its twin, Marian saw that Mike, too, was eyeing them with considerable interest. She stretched out her ringless left hand to the professor. "Isn't it time you did something about it?" she asked.

She had not expected him to lift and kiss it nor imagined what this would do to her. "High time," he said.

"Shall we go to the museum this evening and steal you a gold ring from the grave of Agamemnon?"

"Nothing of the kind." She was Medusa, playing at being Mrs. Frenche. "Diamonds or nothing for me."

"Then"—regretfully—"I'm afraid it will have to be nothing until we get home."

If we get home, her mind supplied the gloss. But at least Mike had taken his cue and was busy circulating the news of this surprising "engagement" among their party. People came up in ones and twos to congratulate them, while Mrs. Adams, plied with ouzo by the professor in apparent celebration, was rapidly getting beyond rational thought. It made Marian anxious, but a quick look at Edvardson decided her to leave all to him. In fact, inevitably, she fell asleep, waking, this time, with her head on his shoulder. "And very nice, too," he said, "but we're coming in to Piraeus."

There was another passport check here, but a much less thorough one, and they were soon in their bus, where Loukas awaited them, looking, Marian thought, as if he had been there, peacefully, all day. Where was Medusa now, she wondered, and what had the policeman meant when he asked if she had been told about "the other one"?

She would probably never know. Playing up to Edvardson, in their pretended engagement, how had she let herself imagine for an instant that it was real? Lunacy, of course. She had let his consummate acting fool her, just as it had the others. Well, face it, she had wanted to believe him, to be fooled, to be happy. Please God he had not noticed. When they got back to London—if they got back to London—she must release him as lightly, as easily as possible.

The ride back to Athens passed swiftly, her senses blurred by exhaustion and misery. They were at the hotel, which she had never expected to see again. There was something she had forgotten to ask the professor. Something vital he had not told her.

"I hope Stella's feeling better," she said loudly as she stood up to collect her cardigan from the rack.

Edvardson was standing, too, feeling at the back of the

shelf for his binoculars. "I expect she will be," he said. And, then, very low, "Medusa."

So she must keep up the pretence, even with Stella. Well, she could see that it was safer so. "Mike." She paused by him as she left the bus. "I'm worn out. Would you be a darling and have me some supper sent up? I think I'll sleep till it's plane time."

"A very good idea." He approved. "Indeed I'll look after it for you, Mrs. Frenche. And I don't believe I'd disturb Miss Marten if I were you. The doctor was going to give her something to make her sleep."

I'll bet he was, thought Marian. She turned to Edvardson, who was hovering beside her. "You won't think I'm too unsociable if I catch up on some of last night's sleep?" She ought to use some endearment, but could not.

"No, indeed," said Edvardson. "How could I, when it was my fault you lost it?" And then, aware of the unexpected double meaning, gave her a grin so wicked that there was nothing for it but to make tracks for the lift, hearing, as she went, his instruction that she quit worrying, leave everything to him and get her some sleep.

Perfect, she thought, both for her and for Mike. She resisted the temptation to knock on Stella's door, opened her own, told herself to do some packing before she slept, fell on her bed and was asleep.

She was being shaken awake. An instinctive gesture got the shaker in the face. Mrs. Adams? Medusa?

"Come now," said the professor. "Just because you've got a bruised face. I've done your packing," he went on, as she pulled herself muzzily up from the depths of sleep, "and here's your ring. That was a good thought of yours." He was fitting it on her engagement finger, and the diamond winked at her mockingly. "There's bound to be another checkup on the plane. Isn't it lucky my credit's good in Athens?"

"It's not real?" She looked at it with something like horror.

"Well, for Pete's sake—" For a moment he loomed over her, close enough to take her breath away, then, at a knock on the door, broke into that familiar, irresistible grin. "Foiled again." He turned away to hand out her two suitcases.

"Stella?" She was remembering it all.

"Gone down with Mike. He's seeing us off at the airport. Nice of him? Over and above the line of duty, that's for sure. Come on, love, time to go. And make that hair of yours just as untidy as you can."

"That," said Marian crossly, "is no problem."

In the bus, inevitably, she had to sit beside Stella and thought she felt her instinctive recoil. Of course, Stella thought her Medusa and must continue to think so until they were safely on the plane. What a blessing that this was a night flight. In the dimmed light of the bus, the chance of Stella's recognising her must be slight. But she could not, herself, resist one quick, anxious glance at her silent companion. After all, it would be logical to be summing her up. In fact, Stella looked better than she had feared, but was keeping her head sullenly turned in the other direction and had, so far, said nothing.

She kept it up all the way out to the airport, while, behind them, the professor explained to the Esmonds that Mrs. Spencer had suddenly decided to have another week on Aegina. Mr. Adams was missing, too, but nobody mentioned him, and Marian could only wonder how Mike and the professor had explained his disappearance. His wife (if she was his wife) was sitting by herself, staring stonily out into the darkness. It was a quiet, tense ride, and Marian, silent like everyone else, could not help wondering whether disaster awaited them at the end of it.

But the airport looked reassuringly normal. No strung-out lines of guards here to alarm the tourists. It was incredible to remember back to lighthearted talk—it seemed aeons ago—about the importance of the tourist trade to Greece. And yet could even the tourist trade be more important than the escape of a known Communist agent like Medusa, and one with a career at which Thor Edvardson had only, horribly, hinted? For the first time, Marian found herself questioning his judgment, back there on Aegina. Surely Medusa should have been handed over to the authorities? It seemed, now that she had her wits again, an extraordinary decision for Edvardson to have made.

They were out of the bus now, with a last friendly beam and shake of the hand from Loukas, the driver who had helped to save her yesterday. Was she safe now? They straggled, in the usual ragged groups, into the air terminal. She and Stella walked side by side, totally silent as they had been since they first met. Mike had gone on ahead, but Cairnthorpe kept at the back of the party, and Edvardson close behind Marian. At the top of the stairs, entering the final departure lounge, she could not check a start. There were police behind the officials at the desks. Another bus had pulled in just ahead of them, and the party from it were making a slow, stop-go progress through the checkpoints.

She saw Mike speaking to one of the policemen. Then he came back to where they had joined the loosely formed queue. "Just a formality," he said. "Nothing to worry about."

Nothing to worry about! Marian's hand seemed to have frozen onto her passport. Beside her, she felt Stella rigid. The line moved forward slowly, erratically. Once again, it was middle-aged women who were being stopped and cross-questioned. Hopeless. Turn and run for it? Impossible, undignified and absurd.

Edvardson must have read her thoughts. He took her arm. "Chin up, love," he said. "It's the last hurdle."

It got him a look of quick amazement from Stella on the other side. And yet why should she be surprised? She must be convinced by now that he was the head of the gang. They were getting horribly near the control point. The other coach party was through, milling down the steps into the final lounge, and Marian saw Mrs. Esmond and Charles present their passports. Charles was waved through, and his mother let pass after a hard look at her passport by one of the policemen. Miss Gear and Miss Grange, who had joined them on the bus, got the same treatment. Hopeless. Would they arrest Stella, too, as an accomplice? And Edvardson?

His arm was firm under hers. "Look!"

Ahead of them, Mrs. Adams had reached the check-point. Her passport was handed back to the policeman, who took one look at it and snapped his fingers. Two others appeared on either side of her. There was a little scuffle as she resisted for a moment. Marian saw Mike move forward, then, apparently, think better of it. He did nothing as she was led away, screaming horribly now in a torrent of language Marian had never heard before.

Belatedly, Mike made some kind of protest but got a short answer. The queue was moving forward again, very quiet now. Instinctively, Marian let Stella go first. With luck, no connection need be seen between them. Stella was through and looking back; could it be anxiously?

Marian handed up her passport with a cold hand that did not shake. "I trust you have enjoyed your visit, Mrs. Frenche," said the passport officer, glancing at it. "We think highly of your husband's work, here in Greece."

"Her ex-husband." Edvardson was close behind her. It was incredible. They were through. Turning to look back, she saw the look of relief on Mike's face wiped clean off. Two policemen had appeared beside him. The last thing Marian saw, as she started down the stairs to the lounge, was his defeated back as they led him away.

"And that's that," said Thor Edvardson as he settled her and Stella on one of the stiff brown plastic seats. "And calls for a drink."

"You mean, we're through?" Marian still could not believe it.

"As near as dammit. It looks to me as if Stavros bungled. Whether accidentally or otherwise I guess we'll never know. I don't know that I blame him either way. But clearly they've got Medusa, and someone's talked."

"Adams perhaps," said Stella. "He was mad enough for anything." Suddenly, her arms were round Marian, and she was sobbing on her shoulder. "Oh, Mrs. F., I'm so happy; I'm so ashamed. . . . Will you ever forgive me?"

"You knew?" The question hardly needed answering as Marian planted a firm kiss on the white cheek.

"All the time. But David said we must keep it up till

the last minute because of Mike. In case he had accomplices we didn't know about."

"David?"

"Yes. He and the professor rescued me, yesterday morning." Marian felt the shudder that ran through her. "A good thing they did. That Adams was getting madder every minute. He kept kind of circling round me as if he didn't know where to begin. Or when. But here's the professor. He'll tell you."

"Medicine. And your last ouzo." Edvardson handed them round. He had heard Stella's last words and looked at her gravely. "Yes," he said. "I'm glad I wasted no time. I think the strain of that fake honeymoon must have been too much for him. That's why he killed when he was told only to create accidents. And that's why"—apologetically, to Marian—"I thought Stella must come first."

"Just so," she said dryly. "Besides, you wanted me as bait to catch Medusa, didn't you?"

"You're no fool. Will you forgive me in the end? For that terrible day?"

"I expect so. But what I can't understand is why, when you'd got her, you let her go."

He looked from her to Stella, then back. "Well, you see." He plunged into it. "She was my wife."

"Your—" Marian's eyes went down to that huge diamond.

"My ex-wife. I married her when I was first sent here. God, what a young fool. . . . After all the briefings we'd had, I let her make a monkey of me. I wasn't even suspicious when she insisted we keep our marriage secret. Mind you, it was lucky for me she did. She left me soon enough, when she found I didn't talk secrets, even to my wife." He looked somberly back at the past. "You heard what that policeman said. Later there was a girl. Medusa had her killed. I divorced Medusa, of course, in her real name, when I got back to the States. Frankly, I hoped she was dead. And then I saw the likeness between you, that day at Olympia, and knew she must be alive, must be behind all the crazy disasters of the tour. Then I had to find her. I think I meant to kill her. With my bare hands.

Something romantic and absurd like that. But when it came to the point, of course, I couldn't."

"I see." She did. It would take years to think about. And she would have lonely years to do it. But it reminded her of an easier subject. "Talking about exes"—she made her voice light—"how do you think the people here knew about mine?"

"I expect Mike told them, don't you? As an added protection for what he thought was Medusa."

"Of course." She remembered that odd little conversation when Mike learned who she was. "Well, it came in useful," she said fairly.

"It sure did. Just like that gang's absurd cell system. Ah, there you are, David—" Edvardson pushed over the extra ouzo he had brought. "I was just going to tell Marian about our great rescue operation."

David blushed and laughed and sat down on the other side of Stella. "Poor Adams," he said. "He was the most surprised man I ever saw. He was so sure you were the boss. Of course he let us in—" This was to Marian.

"And then?"

"David knocked him out," said Stella. "Bang. Like that." Could she and David really be holding hands?

"It was a pleasure," said David grimly, and put a firm arm around her. "Thank God you wasted no time, Professor."

"I knew there was none to spare. God, I was in a rage with myself. After all the precautions I'd taken, to walk you into a trap like that! In the old days"—he turned to Marian—"that restaurant was a safe house. How was I to know they'd put a gate into the yard? And there I was thinking I had you snug for the evening." He smiled grimly. "I was just waiting till I'd got you safe back to the hotel to have it out with you. I couldn't be sure, you see" —he was still talking mainly to Marian—"how much you knew."

"Or which side I was on?"

"I guess I felt pretty sure about that. Now Stella here was something else again. I wasn't completely sure about her till I saw what Adams had done to her."

"Thanks," said Stella, looking down at her bandaged arm.

"What I still don't understand," said Marian, "is how you got on to it in the first place."

"Don't forget my sordid past, love. You don't forget the habits of my kind of business in a week, or a month, or a year. And it stood out a mile that there was something fishy about that tour. I'd taken lots of them, you see. It was a way of seeing Greece without getting mixed up with my old friends and maybe compromising them. There's nothing like a tour for protective colouring. But this one was something else again. One accident, yes. Two, odd. Anything more. . . . No, ma'am. So then I did start getting in touch. Lucky I did, too. Mind you, it cost me plenty to get that football match organised at Delphi when the crazy pair of you went off to the stadium."

"Well, we had to talk," said Stella.

"A pity you didn't choose to talk to me." He looked from one embarrassed face to the other. "Don't tell me; I know. You thought I was one of them."

Marian, scarlet, was speechless. Stella spoke up for them both. "You must admit that it seemed pretty odd, your not admitting to speaking Greek, when things got so serious."

"Fair enough." His smile forgave them. "But you'd be surprised the things you learn when people think you can't understand them. "That's how I found out about their cell system. And admit, Stella, that saved you. We'd never have been able to break into that underground fortress of theirs at the hotel."

"No." Her face was grey with recollection. "I still don't understand how you worked it."

He smiled at them benevolently. "Easy as rolling off a log. As soon as I realized that none of them knew who the boss was, I decided to take a hand. They just got messages, you see, in hotel pigeonholes. So easy. And so easy to fake. I'm an old bird at this game, remember. And they were nothing but a bunch of young amateurs. Lucky for us they were. All we needed was for one of them to remember me as the crazy American from that

Christmas of 1944 when we shot it out with the Communists in Athens, and I'd have been sunk. But that was the whole point, don't you see? They'd been picked, the Greeks, that is, just because they were too young to remember. Anyone who really knew about Medusa wouldn't have been fooled by that story of her being a 'liberal sympathiser'—not for a moment. Well, you saw what happened when they did recognise her."

"What will happen to her?"

"I hope she's dead this time," he said.

Marian was looking down at her new ring—the ring she would give back so soon. But for the moment, she still had a part to play. "I can see how you managed to fool them into thinking you were the boss, but who *was* really?"

"Mrs. Spencer, of course. I hope they caught her along with Medusa. I figured that out pretty fast, because I knew she hadn't been on the flight out. I don't forget faces."

"Like poor Mrs. Hilton."

"Yes." As they looked soberly back over the disasters of the trip, the loudspeaker crackled into life. "There's our flight at last. Time to go home, love."

The false endearment was more than she could bear. "Don't." David and Stella, so shining with happiness themselves, were looking at her strangely. "I can't. . . ." She looked down at the flashing, mocking diamond. Medusa. Thor's wife. Her own double.

Around them, people were standing up, collecting the accumulated loot of their holiday. She sat there, silent now, turning the ring with cold fingers. All illusion. Get it over with. End it now, tactfully, gracefully. And mourn him for the rest of her life.

"Time to go." David was on his feet, pulling Stella up with a brisk, loving hand.

"Not quite." The professor watched them move away across the lounge, then reached down to put his own hand over Marian's icy ones. "Nonsense," he said. "And you know it."

"Do I?" Her wide eyes, looking up at him, were pitiful.

"Yes." He pulled her, almost roughly, to her feet. Standing, she was nearly his height. Beside them, the

Esmonds, laden with packages, paused for a moment. "Shall I prove it to you, here and now?" asked Thor Edvardson, looming over her.

"No!" She looked around the crowded lounge. This was no place for their first kiss. "Are you always going to read my mind?" she asked, falling into step beside him.

"If you'll let me," he said.